A Warm Welcome to Christmas 2025

It gives me great pleasure to welcome you to this year's edition of "The Magic Of Christmas".

As the festive season fast approaches, we aim to fill your heart with seasonal cheer with this wonderful bookazine.

It has everything you need to get you in the mood for the celebrations and times of reflection ahead.

Of course, it wouldn't be the "Friend" without some new stories to relax with and there are nine brand new tales to envelop you in a warm hug of Christmas spirit.

There's puzzles galore too. In other words, everything you need for some well-deserved me-time at this frequently hectic time of year.

Your magazine is packed with ideas for how you can make your Christmas the best ever. A whole range of show-stopping cookery ideas, from the simple to the spectacular, are sure to give you, if you'll excuse the pun, food for thought.

Meanwhile our craft section is packed with ideas for decorations and gifts. I am sure you will be inspired by our collection of projects.

And, of course, Christmas is about more than material things, and there is no-one better to talk you through the true story of the season than our good friend, David McLaughlan.

With fascinating real life, natural marvels and pop culture fun, there really is something for everyone in these pages.

All that is left for me to say is I hope you all have a truly magical Christmas and a very happy new year.

Stuart

Stuart Johnstone, Editor.

4

What's INSIDE

The Magic of Christmas

Poetry
7 Christmas Domestic by Karen Stokes
144 Stocking Time by Maggie Ingall

This Christmas We're Loving
8 Our pick of festive news, products and fun

Heartwarming Tradition
14 David McLaughlan guides us through the Christmas story

Top Tips
26 50 simple ways to make Christmas a breeze

Entertainment
32 Our essential guide to the finest festive pop culture moments. Is your favourite there?

Puzzles
40 7 pages of brainteasers
47 Solutions
136 7 more pages of puzzle fun
143 Solutions

Colouring
48 Relax with colouring

Real Life
52 Behind the scenes at Christmas at Kings College, Cambridge
56 Luminous Landscapes – Laura Coventry explores the most wonderful displays of festive lights
62 O come, all ye carol singers! How the singing tradition has remained for centuries

Food For All
68 Easiest Ever Christmas Dinner – Marvellous dishes without the fuss

72 Alternative Roasts – If you don't feel like turkey
74 Make a delicious, gingerbread house – A fun project for all the family
78 Festive Christmas Pancakes – Tasty snacks with a festive twist
82 Delicious Desserts – Spoil yourself with these decadent delights

Nature
86 Polly Pullar on the natural wonders of winter

86

18

96

MADE easy

13

99

78

Travel

86 A Place Called Christmas – there's lots of them!

Nostalgia

92 Fun, Festivities and Fireworks – Angela Finlayson recalls Christmas in the 1970s

The 12 Crafts of Christmas

96 Treats For All – Dainty cones to store your gifts

98 Pick a Poinsetta – Make this lovely crochet version of the seasonal blooms

99 Puddings and Berries – A simple wreath made from pompoms

100 Stunning Snowflakes – Add a seasonal twist to your clothes with these festive buttons

102 Oh, Christmas Tree – Scandi-inspired festive baubles

103 A Festive Friend – A cute little gingerbread man decoration

104 Angel On High – Crochet an angel as a symbol of friendship and love

106 Table Topper – The perfect touch for your festive table

108 Gnome Sweet Gnome – Create a tree with a difference!

110 In The Bag – Lovely re-usable gift bags

112 Santa Baby – The star of the show!

Fiction

114 That Festive Feeling by Gabrielle Mullarkey

116 Rise To The Challenge by Rebecca Holmes

119 Room At The Inn by Alison Carter

122 Say It With Flowers by Becca Robin

125 A New Chapter by Fiona Thomson

126 Kindred Spirits by Alison Wassell

129 Just Desserts by Graeme Edwards

132 Becoming Mrs Claus by Marian Myers

134 The More The Merrier by Eirin Thompson

116

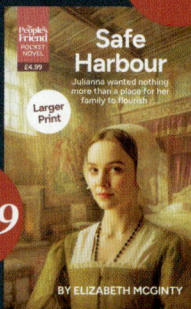

Published in the UK by DC Thomson & Co Ltd, Dundee, Glasgow and London. © DC Thomson & Co Ltd, 2025. Registered Office: DC Thomson & Co Ltd, Courier Buildings, 2 Albert Square, Dundee, Scotland, DD1 9QJ. Distributed by Frontline Ltd, Stuart House, St John's St, Peterborough, Cambridgeshire PE1 5DD. Tel: +44 (0) 1733 555161. Website: www.frontlinedistribution.co.uk. Export distribution (excluding AU and NZ) Seymour Distribution Ltd, 2 East Poultry Avenue, London EC1A 9PT. Tel: +44(0)20 7429 4000. Fax: +44(0)20 7429 4001. Website: www.seymour.co.uk. EU Representative Office: DC Thomson & Co Ltd, c/o Findmypast Ireland, Irishtown, Athlone, Co. Westmeath, N37 XP52. For advertising queries, contact lee.rimmer@canopymedia.co.uk or call 0204 5532900. For subscription queries, contact shop@dcthomson.co.uk or 0800 318846/01382 575580 (UK) +44 1382 575580 (International), www.dcthomsonshop.co.uk/pfd. Editorial communications to "The People's Friend", 2 Albert Square, Dundee DD1 1DD. While every reasonable care will be taken, neither D.C. Thomson & Co., Ltd., nor its agents will accept liability for loss or damage to any materials submitted to this publication. The People's Friend is a member of IPSO (the Independent Press Standards Organisation), which regulates the UK's newspaper, magazine, and digital news industry. We abide by the Editors' Code of Practice and are committed to upholding the highest standards of journalism. If you think that we have not met those standards and want to make a complaint, please contact readerseditor@dcthomson.co.uk or Readers Editor, The People's Friend, DC Thomson & Co Ltd, Courier Buildings, 2 Albert Square, Dundee, Scotland, DD1 9QJ. If we are unable to resolve your complaint, or if you would like more information about IPSO or the Editors' Code, contact IPSO on 0300 123 2220 or visit www.ipso.co.uk.

ipso. Regulated   DC THOMSON

CHRISTMAS DOMESTIC

You're skating on thin ice my dear
My poorly wife warns me
You'll never keep that angel
Atop the Christmas tree

It's leaning to one side my dear
The tree can't take the weight
The crib just looks all wonky
It'll never stand up straight

Rudolph looks far from festive
He seems to nurse a glare
The angels look quite grumpy, dear
They don't like hanging there

I hold my breath and count
To Lords a Leaping ten
I simply don't have time
To dress this tree again

I've hymns and holy readings
A sermon to prepare
Jesus isn't in his crib
He's in the crypt somewhere

My wife her arm in plaster
Usually such a dear
Is testing me quite sorely
At this holy time of year

I humbly re-arrange the tree
For I know there'll be no rest
The Christmas spirit now restored
We Vicars know what's best!

By Karen Stokes

This Christmas We're LOVING

Meaty Morsels

Did you know that Christmas puddings in the Middle Ages comprised of a shin of beef stewed with dried fruit? Once the Victorians got their hands on it, the recipe became much sweeter. . . and boozier with added brandy! They also upgraded the tradition of including a dried pea or bean into the cake, choosing to replace legumes with silver coins or charms to signify good luck.

Figgy's award-winning pudding is a modern, light, and fruity version which starts from just £12.95. Order at figgys. co.uk before December 17 for Christmas delivery – if it doesn't sell out first!

Feed the Birds

Even if you're not hosting family at home this year, you can open up your garden for guests. This build your own bird feeder is a great gift for a loved one . . . or for yourself!

The handy kit includes a step-by-step guide to construct the wooden house, which can be attached to a tree or to a window.

Plus, 100% of the sale of this product goes to Macmillan Cancer Support, which is a gift within itself.

Gift in a Tin: Build Your Own Bird Feeder, £14.50, shop.macmillan.org.uk

Drawing Laughs

Board games are a must at Christmas . . . but sometimes something a little more light-hearted is required. Enter 'Telestrations'! Best described as if 'Pictionary' met 'telephone', this game has a huge potential for hilarity and is a great pick for the whole family. **£24.99, John Lewis**

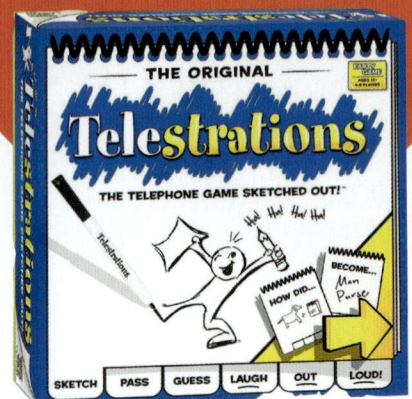

Magic After Dark

One sure-fire way to get into the festive spirit is to take a trip to Blenheim Palace this December. This year, the Illuminated Trail is set to be more spectacular than ever before! If you're in the mood for daytime activities, why not follow the yellow brick road in the Palace of Oz to spot some famous faces from L. Frank Baum's classic? The Christmas Market is a must-see, packed with tasty festive treats and gorgeous gifts for everyone to enjoy. Book tickets at tickets. blenheimpalace.com

Festive Four-Legged Friends

Let Santa Claws visit your furry friend this Christmas! Why not treat your pet to a festive box which includes a selection of toys, an edible Christmas card, all-natural Christmas treats and a pet portrait experience worth £100? **Visit postmanpooch.co.uk for more info.**

A Crafty Christmas

Why not put a personal touch to your Christmas gifting this year? Adding embroidery to clothes, stockings, and other textiles is a great way to create memorable pieces to keep for years to come. This book features stunning imagery from the Cornish coastline alongside 20 step-by-step hand embroidery projects. **Buy for £18 from October 23, tgjonesonline.co.uk**

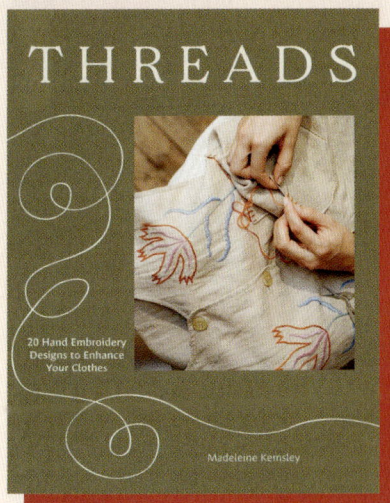

THREADS

20 Hand Embroidery Designs to Enhance Your Clothes

Madeleine Kemsley

Donate a Gift

Giving to charity at Christmas is a really kind and heartfelt thing to do, and something you'll remember doing for a long time to come. Many families and individuals go without presents, lovely food or celebrations on Christmas Day, so donating your unwanted clothes, books, household items and toys could make someone else incredibly happy. The Salvation Army has a special Christmas Present Appeal where you can donate your goods to someone who needs and deserves it.

Visit www.salvationarmy.org.uk/christmas-present-appeal to find out more.

Volunteer Your Time

Similarly, volunteering your time and energy at Christmas to a greater cause is a selfless thing to do if you're looking for a hobby or festive job to take part in. There will be many food and homeless shelters in your area which are always looking for extra help at Christmas, or you can search for groups on Facebook and around your community for local charities who could use a helping hand.

Visit www.crisis.org.uk/crisis-at-christmas to see how you could lend your kindness and energy this Christmas.

Make a Gingerbread House

It's traditional to make a gingerbread house at Christmas – at least, it certainly is in our books! It may not turn out perfect every time, but the fun in making a gingerbread house is the decoration time. Get your piping bags at the ready! If you feel like taking on the ultimate festive baking challenge this year, don't forget your chocolate buttons and icing sugar for the adorable finishing touches!

Find a brilliant and easy recipe on p74.

Christmas Pantomimes

If jamming to Christmas music yourself isn't your bag, it could be a sweet family outing to go to a Christmas pantomime and watch other talented locals or touring companies perform for you.

Consider "Snow White – Christmas Pantomime" on Christmas Eve in Blackburn, or "Cinderella" on December 5 in Newcastle. There's also "Sleeping Beauty" at the York Theatre Royal on December 2 or, if you're after a classic, "A Christmas Carol" in Windsor on November 4.

Catch a longer list of shows on your local theatre's website.

Christmas Karaoke

Having a family sing-along during Christmas is one of the most magical and wholesome experiences you can have to round off the year! And it's a chance to get your groove on, too. What's your go-to festive karaoke song? Ours has to be "Last Christmas" or the dreamy "Have Yourself a Merry Little Christmas". Whatever yours may be, get YouTube up on the TV and find some karaoke backing tracks to sing along to. But if you really want to make the game fun, why not buy a karaoke machine as an early Christmas present? You can get some for over £100 if you feel like splashing the cash, or you can spend £30-£50 on one.

Try the RockJam SingCube 10Watt Bluetooth Karaoke Machine – Two Mics from Argos, RRP £45.

Wreath-making

Having a Christmas wreath is almost a rite of passage for feeling festive. But instead of buying one, which is the boring way of doing it, why not make one in a crafty DIY session? There are plenty of ways to do this and an abundance of DIY guides online, but all you really need is a wire frame, pliers, gardening gloves and a variation of fir branches and flower heads. You can choose more decorations if you fancy (we recommend cinnamon sticks and acorns for a Christmassy feel), or you can make it as simple as possible for yourself.

For easy-to-follow instructions, visit education.teamflower.org/learn/design/ssl/how-to-make-a-wreath-its-easier-than-you-think.

Making DIY Baubles

Christmas tree baubles are some of the most common household decorations during the festive period. But instead of wasting money and buying loads of them or being boring and using the same ones every year, it could be a fun-filled activity to make your own! There are plenty of easy ways to do this and accessible material to make them from. Choose coloured card or wool, or any other scraps you have lying around, to tie up tightly, then spread the material out to make them up into a bauble shape. Then use scissors and snip round the edges to make them perfect. Alternatively, use pinecones and dried citrus to make natural, rustic baubles!

Learn more here: www. bakerross.co.uk/craft-ideas/ category/kids/activity/baubles.

Non-Traditional Christmas Dinner Parties

Have a Christmas dinner party with your family and close friends but give it a twist! This year, try making non-traditional Christmas dinners that you're likely never to have tried before. Options include honey glazed ham, butternut squash lasagna, salmon en croute, nut roast, mushroom Wellington, stuffed pork tenderloin and beetroot and red onion tarte tatin. You can even take it in turns and each cook a different dish every week in December!

Cosy Candles

What's your favourite Christmas scent? Ours has to be peppermint or gingerbread

Whatever yours is, have a look for some candles that smell just like it for a comforting, cosy home this holiday. Yankee Candles are always a good bet for these.

Visit www.yankeecandle. co.uk and search for their Christmas collection.

Hire Reindeer

Have you got a special Christmas party lined up, or a winter wedding, or a festive show you're part of? You may not have thought it possible, but you can actually hire a reindeer out for the day! It's also a really sweet way to visit a loved one in hospital or care this Christmas. Having a live reindeer come to see you is surely a magical way to spend the holidays! Remember not to use flash photography round them and be sure to treat the animals with respect and care. You'll be brief on how it all works if you decide to book one, though.

Find out all the details here: reindeerforhire.co.uk.

Movie Marathon

Need some underrated Christmas movie suggestions? Here are our favourites:
- "Arthur Christmas"
- "Nativity!"
- "Klaus"
- "Last Christmas"
- "Noelle"
- "Gremlins"

Christmas Colours

Deck your house and wardrobe out in red, green and gold to feel the maximum amount of joy! Did you know that green is the colour symbolising eternal life and evergreens? Not a bad one to keep wearing throughout the year! Gold, unsurprisingly, symbolises the sun and light, but also the gifts of the three Wise Men if you're thinking of biblical times. Red is religiously associated with the blood of Christ, but commercially it's associated with Santa Claus and holly berries.

the Greatest Story ever told...

is a surprisingly simple one.

Words: David McLaughlan. Images: stock.adobe.com, Alamy.

It begins in the streets of Judea, a small outpost of an empire that would eventually be transformed by it. The words were spoken by awe-struck witnesses to enraptured crowds. Thirty or forty years after the events occurred, scribes began recording and translating them. Copies of these early "biblos" were sent wherever Christians had planted churches.

The books (papyri or scrolls) became revered, because they contained both the meaning of life and the secret to the afterlife.

Gospels and epistles (the letters of the Apostle Paul) were gathered and studied by those who never met the main characters in the story. Some were decreed problematic and excluded, but the messages closest to the core message and the original sources were kept, and preserved.

Of course, all things pass. Paper decomposes. But countless copies were made. In days when most of the population went unschooled, a scribe might have made a career of copying this most revered of books. Everyone, it seemed, wanted to know what was in it.

The Codex Sinaiticus is thought to be the oldest surviving Bibles, and it is more than sixteen centuries old.

In the fifteenth century, automation of a sort came to the world of book production. When Johannes Gutenberg perfected his printing process, the first book he made was the Bible. Since then, well . . . it isn't possible to give an accurate number for how many Bibles have been printed, but educated guesses place the number at between five and seven billion!

When radio arrived, one of its pioneers also wanted to share the great story. On (appropriately) Christmas Eve 1906, Canadian inventor Reginald Fessenden broadcast the first ever radio program. Ships at sea heard a rendition of "O Holy Night" and a reading from the Bible where the angels told the shepherds that a saviour had been born.

Holywood, searching for storylines for its silent movies and early "talkies" knew where to turn. 1897 saw the filming of "The Horitz Passion Play" – a Bohemian tradition transplanted to the silver screen. A series of big-budget biblical epics followed – "The Robe", "Ben-Hur", "King of Kings", and, of course, "The Greatest Story Ever Told".

Television took up the baton with Franco Zeffirelli's multi-award-winning mini-series "Jesus of Nazareth" airing on the BBC in 1977.

When humanity slipped the embrace of Mother Earth and ventured into the coldness of space, they took this defining story with them. During their ninth orbit of the moon, astronauts Lovell, Anders, and Borman read from the Book of Genesis while the world listened.

The heart of the greatest story ever told is the birth of Jesus. So much gilt and glory has been added to it that we tend to forget how simple it really is. A child was born to save us all. And His message was love.

And because the Christmas Story is a message – a beautiful, hopeful, letter of love – to each of us, let's take a look at it.

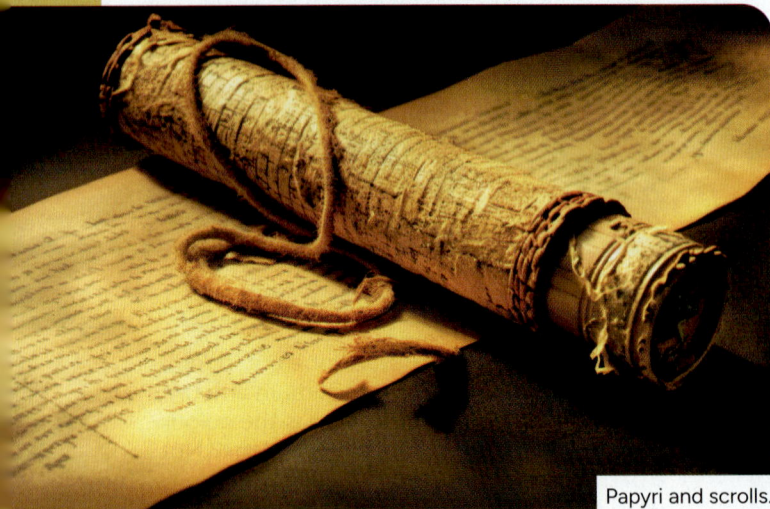

Papyri and scrolls.

The Brightest Star

ANYONE can follow a star. If it was a short walk, you would only ever travel in a straight line in one direction, with no final destination. If you walked for long enough you might see the star you are following turn around the Pole Star — which might confuse your journey a little. Or your star might disappear below the horizon.

In none of those journeys, would the star indicate anything on the earth. And, despite what Hank Marvin sang in "Paint Your Wagon", there is no such thing as a "wandering star". Stars are near-permanent fixtures in the night sky. They rarely just appear. But the Star of Bethlehem appears to have done all three of these things! It was visible "from the East", from a different country. King Herod asks exactly when it appeared, and it leads the Magi from Jerusalem to a particular house in Bethlehem — where it stops!

So, was it a star, or was it something else? We might be happy to believe it was simply a guiding light, sent from above for a particular purpose. But, in keeping with its contradictory nature, the Magi had been looking for a sign, where they had been told to expect it, in the stars!

The scribes in Herod's court were also expecting a star. The Book of Numbers contains what is known as the "Star Prophecy." It says, "I see him, but not now. I behold him, but not near. A star will come out of Jacob; a sceptre will rise out of Israel." It's a vague prediction, but for people whose power and privilege depended on service to foreign masters, any hint of a Jewish Messiah was bound to sit uncomfortably in their minds.

The Star of Bethlehem has intrigued scholars and astronomers ever since the Apostle Matthew laid down the only reference to it in his Gospel. Some have speculated it was a star that went nova, others conjectured that an alignment of the planets might have produced a bright and unexpected light in the daytime sky. Comets have been suggested, and Halley's Comet would have been visible in the sky in the year 7 AD.

Perhaps unsurprisingly, the church and the faithful don't concern themselves too much with such details. It happened. It revealed the Christ-child to the world in what has become known as "the Epiphany", and if it is beyond our understanding then... aren't most of God's works?

John Chrysotom, a Church Father was firmly on the side of a God-wrought miracle. How else, he asked, "did the star point out a spot so confined, just the space of a manger and shed, unless it left that height and came down, and stood over the very head of the young child?"

So, did the Star shine over Bethlehem to proclaim Jesus to the world? A case could be made for it, and a case could be made against it. But a light has shone out, regardless, ever since that wonderful night!

Mary And Joseph

Mary and Joseph on their journey.

THERE were great powers in the world at the time, of the Christmas Story, earthly powers based on domination and, all too often, death. When God decided it was time to come to earth, He, most emphatically, avoided those. Instead, He came to a young woman, barely more than a girl, who, in a patriarchal society would have seemed insignificant. But, by her very nature, she had the power, to give life, to nurture a child, and love that child to its fulfilment.

The Almighty obviously thought more of those abilities – that power – than he did of any number of armoured legions.

People speculate that Mary, as a child, had been dedicated to the temple. This might be seen as an attempt to make her appear more holy, more worthy. Extra holiness wasn't really needed, though. Her ordinariness is the point. But she did have connections to the temple, so it is possible. Her older cousin, Elizabeth, was a descendant of Aaron, the brother of Moses. And Elizabeth's husband, Zechariah, was a priest of the temple.

Her relative lack of importance is shown by her marriage to Joseph. In a time when marriages were often arranged for the good of society, she, just old enough to be engaged, was partnered with Joseph, an older man and perhaps a widower. The arrangement was likely less for love and more so a working man would have someone to raise his children.

Joseph, by every account a good man, was a "tekton". We traditionally think of him as a carpenter, but the word "tekton" gives us "technician" and "architect". We can assume he was a builder, and one of good repute.

The engagement period seems to have lasted a while, and into that happy time, with complete disregard to human priorities, came an angel followed by the Holy Spirit.

Mary's character is shown by her response to the news that she is to bear the Son of God. The Book of Leviticus says the punishment for adultery was death. Mary wasn't yet married, but the consequences of an unexpected pregnancy would surely be severe.

Something in that angelic visitation must surely have convinced and comforted her. Her dignified response was to ask "How will this be?" When the angel explained, she replied, "I am the Lord's servant. May it be to me as you have said." Or, as we might say . . . "Amen."

Telling Joseph about her new and wonderful pregnancy might not have been too straightforward, for "at that time Mary got ready and hurried to" her cousin Elizabeth's house for a while. But a second angelic visitation convinced Joseph that Mary's child would "save his people from their sins". Well . . . what else could he do?

The simple piety of these ordinary people earned them a reward no other celebrity couple could hope to achieve; to be honoured in Heaven and to have their likenesses gazed at by adoring children, generation after generation, in Nativity scenes all around the world.

The angel Gabriel appearing to Zechariah to announce the birth of John the Baptist.

Elizabeth And Zechariah

IT'S a nice idea. A man and woman meet. They fall in love and get married. Somewhere along the line a baby or two arrive. They live happily ever after.

But life is often less (and more) than ideal.

Joseph's proposed wife was young, healthy, would be a good home-maker and look after his children while he worked to earn their keep. All good stuff. Then she came to him with a strange story about God making her pregnant! He could never have imagined that when he was planning for the future!

Elizabeth and Zechariah had been married a long time. They were good people, respected in their community. No doubt they had worked hard for their community and the temple. But no child came to their little family. The implied promise of the family ideal went unfulfilled and Elizabeth age out of her child-bearing years.

But, even before the angel visited Mary, one appeared to Zechariah, her cousin Elizabeth's husband.

Imagine the scene. Zechariah is at work in the temple. His task is to burn the incense while the faithful wait outside. And, just as he is performing this solemn duty, he is startled to find a "man" standing beside him. With their traditional disregard for earthly priorities, the angel tells Zechariah his prayer are been answered and Elizabeth will bear him a son.

Zechariah's response to this news was much like Mary's when she asked, "How will this be since I am a virgin?" He asked, "How can I be sure of this? Since I am an old man and my wife is well on in years." But the angel – Gabriel – was less patient with Zechariah, taking away his doubting voice until the child would be born.

Explaining his day at work to his wife must have been difficult, but she would soon come to know the truth of it when she found, against all expectations, that she was carrying a child.

Into that awe-struck and confused situation walked Elizabeth's young cousin, Mary. We don't know why she went to Elizabeth. We don't know what Joseph had to say about it all. Perhaps this was before his own angelic visitation when he "had it in mind to divorce her quietly" to avoid her "public disgrace." Whatever the reason, Mary knew she would be welcome at Elizabeth's house.

And, as joyous as the initial meeting of the two women might have been, it was overshadowed by the greeting the unborn babies gave each other. Later in the story, John the Baptist (as Elizabeth's so would grow to be) wondered if Jesus was truly "the One", but, in the womb, he had no doubt. Elizabeth told Mary that, as soon as she heard her voice, "the babe leaped in my womb for joy".

As happy as they were at their great good fortune, neither Mary or Elizabeth was in any doubt that world-changing forces were being birthed – through them.

And Zechariah? This was his work and faith coming to life!

A pregnant Mary welcomes a pregnant Elizabeth.

Annunciation to the Blessed Virgin Mary by the Archangel Gabriel.

Angel Or Star!

WHEN the Christmas tree is almost decorated, what do you top it off with? A star? An angel? A fairy?

Either of the first two are fine. Both appear in the Christmas Story. Fairies – beautiful additions to the tree as they may be – are nowhere in the Bible. But, is there much difference? Well . . . yes!

The angels described in the Book of Revelation would give anyone nightmares. But, elsewhere in the Bible they appear (usually) as men, serious sober heralds of God. Their job is to present the words of God to humanity – and very occasionally to destroy something. These are not pretty, whimsical, fairies.

In Exodus, God sends an angel to lead the chosen people to the place He had prepared for them. And he adds the warning, "provoke him not, for he will not forgive your transgressions".

When Zechariah – not too unreasonably – questioned the angel's assertion that his (older) wife would have a baby, the angel leaves him unable to speak until after his son is born.

Jesus softens the angels' image somewhat when he tells us they hold the images of children before the face of God, giving rise to the notion of guardian angels.

The angel Zechariah annoys, stands on his dignity, announcing that, "I am Gabriel. I stand in the presence of God . . ." But, to be fair, he had begun with a phrase, angels seem accustomed to using, "Be not afraid!" So, they are aware of the impact their appearance has on people.

Six months later, Gabriel appears again, this time to Mary with the news that her first-born will change the world. We know that Gabriel had been presenting the words of God to humanity for at least six hundred years because of his conversations with Daniel. This time however, he was declaring the Word of God would walk the earth in human form. It must have been quite a moment, moving him to be gentler with Mary than he had been with Zechariah.

He explains to Mary that she is highly favoured by God, that she shouldn't be afraid, and that she wouldn't be in this alone. Her cousin Elizabeth would help. When Mary agrees, Gabriel simply leaves.

And angel – perhaps Gabriel – make a considerably bigger deal of the birth in the Book of Luke. He appears with the glory of the Lord shining around him and terrifies the poor shepherds. He delivers the traditional "Be not afraid" greeting, tells them of the birth of Jesus, then lights the night sky with a heavenly choir, all singing praises to God.

That choir has inspired carol-writers and hymn-writers ever since.

So . . . a fairy certainly adds a little something to a Christmas tree. But, if you want to be accurate, if you want to be true to the faith . . . have a star on your tree or an angel. Both were in the heavens at the birth. Each could be imagined as the light, or the glory, of God. Let them shine down on your manger.

The birth of Jesus depicted in a cave.

In The Stable

THE Book of Matthew, which gives us the best account of Jesus' early years, completely skips his birth! It goes from angelic announcements to "when Jesus was born in Bethlehem". A surprising omission, given all the other details provided. It is from the Gospel of Luke that we get the image of the baby in a manger "because there was no room for them at the inn".

Perhaps surprisingly, given the importance the church would later place on such matters, the couple were still only "pledged to be married". The King James Bible describes Mary as Joseph's "espoused wife". It also uses the lovely term "swaddling clothes".

Actually, mothers have always swaddled their babies. It might be that the blanket they are wrapped tightly in was the only clothing available, or a baby might be finely dressed and wrapped in a shawl passed down through the generations. The point is that they are wrapped tightly, giving the comforting impression that they are still in the womb.

Baby Jesus, no less than any other child ever born, found his first comforts in the closeness of His mother and the tightness of His swaddling clothes. Nothing else would have mattered.

Which was just as well, as nothing else about His birth was ideal. Scholars debate the reason for the journey. Luke says it was a census. Whatever the reason, Joseph took Mary to the town his family came from, a distance of ninety-some miles to the hilltop village of Bethlehem. It wouldn't have been a comfortable journey at the best of times, less so for a pregnant woman.

When they arrived, despite Joseph's family connections, they find themselves dependant on the local inn-keeper. But he has no rooms left. Families in those days often shared their homes with livestock, but it must still have been a disappointment to travel all that way and be offered a stable for comfort. Still, a manger, a trough or cradle for the animal's feed, would have made an very practical crib for a new-born baby.

Perhaps, in those nights in the stable, Mary wondered about God's promise for her son. Or perhaps she understood that to save "the least of these" Jesus would need to begin His earthly journey from the lowest station possible.

Other, apocryphal, gospels have His birth be even in even humbler circumstances. Some suggest that Mary and Joseph didn't make it to Bethlehem in time and she gave birth in a cave or by the roadside. These accounts often include fantastical elements like time standing still, strange midwives, and animals kneeling down in worship.

Stable or cave, it really doesn't matter (except to Christmas card manufacturers, who often use both images). What matters is that no one in history could claim a more lowly beginning. And no one would ever rise to such glory. But the mission and the message that was to come would show there was a path, and a home, for each of us, no matter where our journey began.

The Wise Men

The Magi travelling.

IF you can't be Mary or Joseph or the angel in the Nativity play, then you probably want to be a Wise Man. They saunter on the stage, wow the audience, and saunter off again (maybe waving to their mum or their gran on the way). And they have the best costumes!

Which is not unlike their appearance in the actual Christmas story, to be fair!

The church has a non-committal attitude to the Wise Men. They cannot be denied. The Gospel of Luke doesn't mention them at all. The Gospel of Matthew most emphatically does. They were often thought to be astrologers and the Old Testament was very much against those. They weren't Christian, and they didn't seem to be converted by their experience, but they paid the infant Jesus more honour and respect than he would receive in the rest of His time on earth

So, in their robes and turbans of scarlet, purple, and gold (or whatever curtains might be available) they steal the show every year. But, who were they?

Well, they weren't kings – that we know of. But they financed a caravan that travelled a long way, they gave kingly gifts, and they seem to have been received by Herod as near-equals. The King James Bible describes them as "wise men". The New International Version describes them as "Magi".

We get the word "magician" from Magi, but in a world where working for a living was a priority for most anything to do with science seemed like magic. And the only people who could "waste" time studying science and the stars were generally princes, earthly or temporal. That is, churchmen, or royalty of some sort. So the terms "Magi", "Wise Men" and "Kings" become interchangeable in the story.

How many of them were there? Every Nativity will show you there were three Wise Men. The song declares "We Three Kings of Orient Are". But there could have been any number of noblemen in that visit. We assume there were three because they gave three noteworthy gifts.

Where did they come from? The Orient? Most versions of the Bible tell us they came from . . . the east! And that's it! A case might be made for them being Persian because they knew about the prophesy of the Messiah. They may have read of Daniel and his time in captivity in Babylon. But . . . no one really knows!

But the importance of the trip is shown by the fact that they see the star rise when Jesus is born, and only find Him as a child. An infant, not a baby. Some suggest, the pilgrimage of the Magi took two years.

For all we don't know about the Magi, they show us how it ought to be done (providing we don't trip on our bathrobes). They waited for Him. They searched for Him. They worshipped Him. Then they, humbly, left the stage. But no doubt they kept telling the story of the time they met the Son of God.

Three Magi before Herod.

The Shepherds

THE Gospel writers Matthew and Luke would have known each other. Both are believed to have been at Gethsemane with Jesus before He was arrested, although Luke would have been a boy. The younger man would have known of the older man's Gospel, and may have been influenced by it. But there are significant differences.

In Matthew Jesus is announced to the world (the Epiphany) through the Magi. In Luke, the Magi are nowhere to be seen, instead some local shepherds share the miracle. And they arrive on the scene almost immediately, unlike the Magi who may have taken two years to get there.

We might wonder at these differences, but we will never get an answer in this life. Instead, we could look at the significance. This birth was important to princes and to ordinary working people, just as it would later be significant to a King, and a Governor, and the blind, the lame, the poor. This was an event for the world – and everyone in it!

The shepherds watching the flocks at night may not have owned the sheep. They might have been hired-hands. Perhaps older men, or young boys. No one works the night-shift if they have a choice. They were of significance to no one except their sheep – and God!

Imagine the setting. The sheep were out in the fields. Perhaps the shepherds watched from a vantage point, perhaps they guarded gates. They may have been alert, dozing, bored . . . It's a wonder none of them had a heart-attack when the night sky lit up and an angel appeared.

No sooner had the first angel proclaimed his message of the Nativity than the sky filled up with angels singing praises to God.

Finding the night sky becoming the night sky again, the shepherds

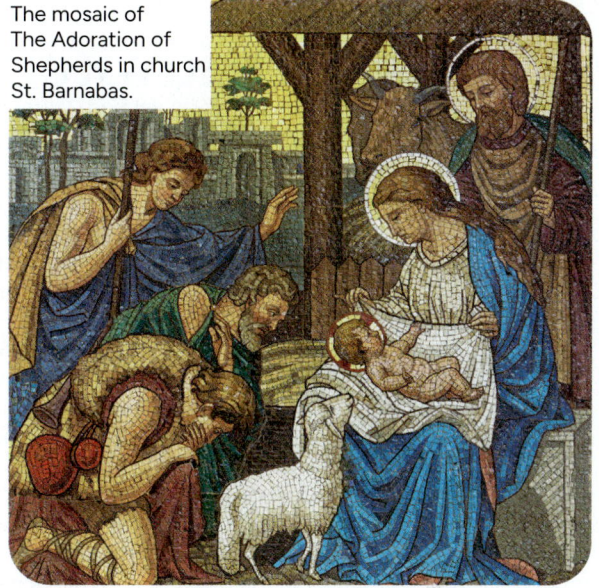
The mosaic of The Adoration of Shepherds in church St. Barnabas.

looked at each other and said something like, "Well . . . let's see what that was all about!"

They ran into Bethlehem and – somehow – found the stable where Mary and Joseph were. And there was the baby the angels had told them about, the Messiah, the Lord in the manger.

Like most new mums, Mary must have been exhausted. But when a bunch of men burst into your "home" talking excitedly about angels, you pay attention. Then they ran out again – to tell the whole town. In the silence that followed the shepherds' departure, Mary thought about all they'd said. Of course, she'd heard it before, but the confirmation must have been comforting.

Then like cats, or exited children, unable to decide whether to come in or go out, the shepherds came back in a much more sedate mode. They'd been startled, they'd seen their prayers answered, then gone out to spread the word, and now they were back – to worship.

We have to hope they left a lad or two looking after the sheep while all this went on. Or the baby who would one day be known as both the Great Shepherd and the Lamb of God would have been less than pleased.

...gel of the ...rd visited the ...epherds and ...ormed them ...Jesus' birth.

Mary's Midwife

THERE is no doubting the Bible is a patriarchal book. It was a patriarchal time!

Women are mentioned in Jesus' story, as followers and helpers. But, a more enlightened reading of the texts suggests that these "helpers" were actually mainstays of his mission.

Mary, of course, is there all the way through the story of Jesus. We know of her joy at His birth, her grief at his death. We know she encouraged His first public miracle at the wedding in Cana. We can be sure she did so much more, was an incalculable help to her son. But this "soft power" was exactly the sort of thing men in those days were condition to ignore, or take for granted. A Gospel told from the point of view of a female follower would, inevitably, present a very different picture.

Salome and the midwife Geloma, bathing the infant Jesus.

While a new appreciation of the women in Jesus' life is happening, there is one woman who must surely have played a part but is completely missing from every account. The midwife!

The Bible tells us next to nothing about Jesus' birth. It sets the scene, it talks of angels and glory, and shepherds, and kings . . . But, of the birth itself, we are simply told it happened.

Artwork and Christmas cards over the centuries have depicted the manger scene in various ways, but, inevitably, Mary will be the only woman in the scene. Which is extremely unlikely.

Women in every society, at every level, have traditionally given birth with a midwife in attendance. If they were lucky, the other woman would know a thing or two about the process. If they were less blessed, it might simply be a "sister" who had made this journey herself. The mother-to-be would be very unfortunate indeed, if she gave birth alone.

Mary was not in that situation. Arriving in Bethlehem, there was no room at the inn and they were billeted in the stable, which was unfortunate. But, Joseph was a tradesman, he wouldn't have been poor, and he was in the town his family came from. As patriarchal as those times were, he would not have attended his own wife's labour. And, given that this was Mary's first child, it was more important than ever that she be attended by someone who knew what was going on.

There are mentions of an un-named midwife, who announced to a woman called Salome that she had seen something she had never seen before – a virgin birth! This part of the story can be found in "apocrypha", writings not adopted into the Bible, and accepted to different degrees by different churches.

So, why is she even mentioned. Well, because the greatest story ever told isn't just a male story. And because the anonymous midwife, in a way, represents the best of us, the best of Christianity, the ones who quietly do God's will, then go on their way, uncelebrated, and with no reward other than having brought more good – or more God – into this world.

Midwife Salome attending Mary and the baby Jesus.

The Gifts

FRANKINCENSE, gold, and myrrh. If you say those words, people the world over will know what you are talking about. More famous gifts have never been given.

The value of these gifts reflects the honour and respect the Magi offered the Holy Child, but we sometimes forget the effort that must have gone into transporting valuable items from another country, through Roman occupied land, and in and out of the court of a greedy King Herod. The caravan of the Magi must have been a formidable thing.

So, why those gifts?

Frankincense is a tree-resin, prepared and burned as incense. But it had a special significance for the Jews, as an important part of the offerings to made to God in the Tabernacle, the home of the Ark of the Covenant. If the Magi knew this, it shows a rare sensitivity and understanding of a faith that, most likely, was not their own. It also shows they knew they were in the presence of the divine.

The gold was the least interesting of the gifts, and the most difficult to transport. Gold was a gift given to royalty. But, if you were giving it, you couldn't skimp. Imagine telling a king you only respected them enough to give them a tiny bit of gold. But, even a purse-full would have made them a target for bandits.

Myrrh, was one of the spices Moses was instructed (by God) to use in the purifying of the Tabernacle. It was used as perfume, as an incense, as a pain reliever, and the Ancient Egyptians had used it in the mummification process.

At the time, it was an expensive, multi-use, gift. It has been suggested that the "gall" Jesus was given to drink on the cross contained myrrh (to dull His pain). Others suggest, the gift was given in prediction of the crucifixion and would be used for embalming Jesus' body. A very sombre gift to give a child.

The idea of gifts as offerings to Christ continued for centuries. Just as most of the offerings given at the Tabernacle were food, so the gifts given to the church and clergy were similarly useful in midwinter.

After all, there were no gift-shops back then. Gradually, the gift-giving spread beyond the clergy, perhaps as a form of charity. Of the gifts given in the song "The Twelve Days of Christmas", seven of them were food and drink related.

It wasn't really until the industrialisation of the Victorian era that gifts as we might recognise them came to be produced.

Much as we all like to get something nice at Christmas, it isn't our birthday. But . . . what gift could we give the one whose hands are supposed to have spread the stars in the skies?

For that, we need to go to the Victorian poet Christina Rossetti. In her poem "In The Bleak Midwinter", she says, "If I were a wise man, I would do my part. Yet, what can I give Him . . . Give my heart."

The three kings of the nativity in a UNESCO listed mosaic from 1,600 years old.

Herod's Evil

ANY world that needed a Jesus was bound to have a Herod. Otherwise, what would be the point? In this case, there was more than one Herod!

Herod the Great may or may not have been an evil man. Certainly, he lived in what might be called evil times, where power was taken and held at the point of a sword. History records him carrying out great building works, some for the common good but many for his family's reputation and protection. The remains of his rebuilding of the temple can still be see in Jerusalem at the Wailing Wall.

But he also built for the pagan aspects of society. That, and the way his family behaved earned him the enmity of the Pharisees and the Sadducees, two major Jewish sects who rarely agreed on anything.

He is the King Herod associated with the Massacre of the Innocents. The Book of Matthew tells us that when Herod heard about the birth of the predicted Messiah he had every boy-child, two-years-old and younger in the Bethlehem area, killed.

The evil of such an act might seem reinforce the idea that humanity needed saving from itself. Historians doubt it occurred – but they wouldn't have to search far for worse examples of how we treat each other. Some suggest the real Massacre of the Innocents was when Herod had some of his own children killed.

And Herod was far from the worst in the world at that time. It's not difficult to imagine a Heavenly Father thinking humanity might need to be reminded of its . . . well, humanity.

Heron the Great died, in his 70s, around the time Jesus was born. His cause of death is not understood by modern medicine, but has come to be known as Herod's Evil, which

The Massacre of the Innocents.

might say something about how he was remembered.

Herod Antipas, who had both John the Baptist and Jesus executed, was way down his father's list of ideal successors. He and two of his brothers (one called Herod) eventually sailed to Rome seeking the emperor's backing. The land was divided between them, but they held it for the emperor.

Antipas ruled in the style of his father. Both men have historical credits to their name, good deeds done. But each indulged their human failings with all the power at their disposal.

If the Christmas Story reminds us of nothing else, it should remind us that we are all prey to those failings and that when we find the "power" to kneel in humility, we take those worst aspects of us down into the straw as well, we show them that creation and love are the greatest things the world has ever known.

We forget. Oh, how quickly in this busy world, do we forget? How often in the hustle and bustle of modern life do we find ourselves chasing the wrong things? Christmas is our yearly reminder. If only we could take Charles Dickens' advice and keep it in our heart all year round.

Jesus brought before Herod Antipas.

Christmas Ever After

HOW did Christmas come to be?

You might think that Jesus was born, we started celebrating, and we haven't stopped. But it wasn't that straightforward. The fact that it survives as a tradition all this time later just adds to the wonder!

For the first thirty years, Jesus lived an ordinary life. No one outside of his family would have thought of celebrating his birthday. By that age, he would have been earning a living for a while. When he started preaching, those who knew his family asked, "Isn't this the carpenter? Isn't this Mary's son?"

After the crucifixion, he would have been remembered as a rabble-rouser by some, and as a good man who didn't know when to quit by others. His followers went into hiding, some left the country. Some carried on spreading the word, others established house-churches wherever it might have been safe to do so. But, at this time, it was the message that was important, not the birth.

A "date" for Jesus' birth appears relatively early. Not in any census or birth certificate, but in the writing of Hyppolitus, a Roman theologian, in 204 AD. He says the event occurred eight days before January.

The early church tended to focus more on Epiphany, than on the actual birth. The thinking was that the visit by the Magi represented the time Jesus was really presented to the world.

With a date established and accepted, the Christ Mass, entered the church calendar of Holy Day. It would have been celebrated solemnly, with prayer and reverence.

The Twelve Days of Christmas – between Christmas and Epiphany – gradually introduced the party element. People can only be pious for so long. The offerings that were supposed to be made on each of the days, became more extravagant, the hospitality offered more lavish. For many around the world Epiphany, Twelfth Day, is still the major celebration. But Christmas Day has become established around the world as a major event for people of faith, people of no faith, even people of other faiths!

Sometimes, of course, we go too far, become too secular. For times like that, we have the Midnight Service. We know that Jesus birth occurred "while shepherds watched their flocks at night" and many churches celebrate this with a midnight mass. These tend to be simple, solemn affairs. And, as we step out of the church afterwards, the (hopefully) crisp and clear night sky can be a fine reminder of our humble place in the Grand Scheme.

When it comes to celebrating Christmas, we can't ask, "What would Jesus do?" He never celebrated it. Christmas appears nowhere in the Bible. But it is the perfect time to consider what He would do every other day of the year, consider how far we have strayed, and get ourselves back on that path.

And the best way to celebrate Christmas, even after all this time? Invite Him to your party, celebrate – in love and happiness – when Love came down to earth.

1 *Keep stress to a minimum by starting early and spreading the tasklist and – importantly – the cost. It doesn't mean that you are starting Christmas far before time, just that you'll be able to enjoy it more when it happens!*

2 Use up unwanted slices of bread to make a breadcrumb batch and freeze until needed for bread sauce or stuffing.

3 Christmas can be a lot to manage on top of the usual demands of life, especially if it all tends to fall on your shoulders. Teamwork is the answer. When you have planned out all the "to dos" of the forthcoming months, assign some tasks to other family members.

Fifty Festive Hacks

Claire Saul gifts you with some great ideas to save you time, money and stress this Christmas.

4 *If there aren't any willing cooks in your house, or if you'd simply rather let someone else have the stress of Christmas dinner this year, consider eating out on Christmas Eve. Prices soar after the 24th but up to that date, venues will be offering their Christmas party prices.*

5 Plump for own brands for your festive food table. These are less expensive and consistently perform well in taste tests.

But you can always add your own touch of pizzazz. Add cranberries and chestnuts to sausage meat for stuffing with some zing, sprinkle edible glitter on basic cupcakes . . .

6 If job sharing is not an option, make sure you factor in some regular time for yourself to keep stress at bay. Enjoy coffee catch ups, have a quiet afternoon with a book – whatever works for you!

7 Rather than spending money on a physical gift for someone, opt for an experience you can enjoy together. Buy a ticket to an event or activity such as a panto – after all, they are for the young and the young-at-heart, too!

8 Investigate what events your local council have planned and plan some shopping or a social get-together around it. Living advent calendar activities, community carols around the town centre Christmas tree or a Christmas light switch on make a great focus point for the culmination of an afternoon out.

9 *Alleviate any stress with a walk. It will help to lower your cortisol levels and reduce brain fog. Even a quick 10 minutes around the block can be invigorating.*

10 Provide glass charms to help family and guests identify their drinking vessel. They also make lovely gifts.

11 Hang decorative items in front of a wall mirror or place on a mirror tile to double the visual effect.

12 Instead of sending a Christmas card, arrange an online chat to impart your season's greetings. You'll save on the cost of the card and postage and have a more sociable and detailed catch up in the process.

13 Ask all your party guests to nominate five music choices to create a personalised playlist for your gathering that will keep everyone entertained.

14 *If space is an issue, or if you lose sight of your Christmas tree once you are in the area where you tend to sit in the evening, buy a potted mini fir tree. It is relatively inexpensive, easily decorated with one small set of lights and it can last for years. Keep it in the garden January to November, where it can then be watered along with your other plants.*

15 Avoid money-wasting tat in stockings. Packets of seeds, books, organic soap . . . there are many alternatives that won't be discarded within weeks and sit in landfill for years

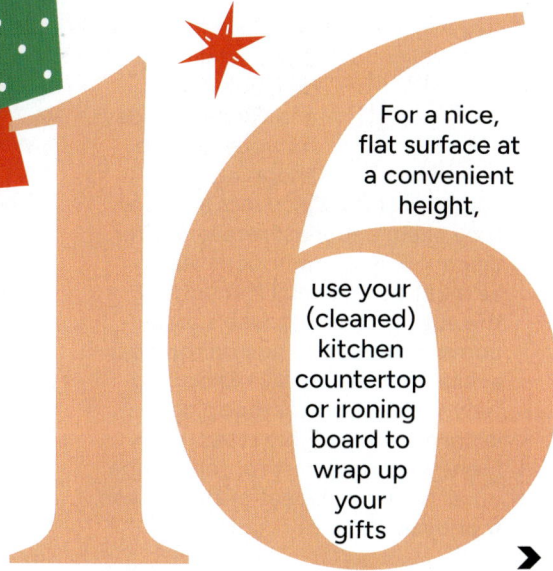

16 For a nice, flat surface at a convenient height, use your (cleaned) kitchen countertop or ironing board to wrap up your gifts

17

Make a "to do" list and allocate the different tasks into each week between your starting date and December 24. It will be a long list but the tasks will be smaller, more manageable and less stress-inducing. Enjoy the sense of achievement as you tick them off.

18

Christmas gifts arrive in a ridiculous amount of packaging, much of which is not recyclable.

Save the £££s, and the planet, by purchasing the individual elements and gifting them in a recyclable gift bag instead.

19

Break away from traditional paper wrapping (or at least, try a different one). Furoshiki is a traditional Japanese wrapping technique using fabric and it is a creative and responsible way to re-use unwanted scraps of material. It's also ideal for wrapping awkward shapes. Learn all about it at www.furoshiki wrapcompany.co.uk.

20

Create a house-based Christmas treasure hunt to entertain young guests. The 'treasure' could be individual prizes such baubles for the tree or sweets, or elements that combine for a final activity, such as those to make a gingerbread house, or pieces of a puzzle.

21

Don't solely rely on Black Friday and Cyber Monday for your bargain shopping – sometimes the discounts aren't all they seem and most retailers offer discounts and promotions such as multi-buy savings throughout the autumn months. Use a price comparison site to ensure the best available price. Google Shopping (www.google.co.uk/shopping) is consistently highly rated. Use MoneySavingExpert for top advice on all financial aspect of the season. moneysavingexpert.com

22

While busy hosting a Christmas party, help yourself by creating a drinks station, offering bottles, glasses, ice, slices of lemon, olives and anything else to help the event go with a swing. Advise your guests to help themselves to their choice of tipple and all refills.

23

A paper tablecloth offers an inexpensive way to wrap a large item . . . or use it to wrap multiple smaller gifts.

24

25

Collect some glass jars of different sizes and shapes. Grouped together and filled with different items such as mini baubles, fir cones and LED lights – they will make an interesting display for a shelf, sill or table.

26

If you need to present a gift to a group of people, make a tray bake, such as tiffin or brownies, divide it up and wrap each portion with cellophane. Hand them over in a large gift bag or presentation box.

27

Most Christmas crackers are expensive, non-recyclable and filled with plastic tat. Invest in some reusable crackers, such as the personalised fabric ones from Lottie Lane (lottielane.co.uk), which will last for years. Fill them with chocolate treats, mini bars of soap, a lottery ticket, trial sized cosmetics and the like . . .

28

. . . these would also serve as special gift wrapping for a small gift.

Wrap Christmas lights, tinsel and anything else with a tendency to tangle, around a plastic coat hanger to store it away.

31

Christmas jumpers are always fun but often expensive. Give yours a makeover instead, by stitching on some Christmas motifs, sparkles, beads or tinkly bells.

29

For an instant touch of Christmas magic at home, thread some fairy lights over the mantlepiece, spice up some existing pot pourri with some festive room scenter and play some seasonal music. You're good to go.

30

Deconstruct an unwanted wooden pallet to make a 'Santa Stop Here' sign or an arty 'tree' for the garden.

32

An unwanted china cup and saucer, caddy or jar are all innovative packaging options for edible gifts, or those with multiple components.

33

34

Think beyond the front door when considering your wreath display. These are easy to move around, to be enjoyed to the best effect. Put one on a guest bedroom door or hang over the mantlepiece. If yours is looking a little worn, give it a makeover. Spray it a different colour, add bows or crystal embellishments, fairy lights . . .

35

Costume jewellery can provide some fun options for partywear. If you are allergic to plated earrings, replace the hooks with real gold or silver hooks, purchased from your local jeweller.

36

Completely stuck for a gift idea? Flowers are always a joy to receive and unlike edibles or a desperation buy, a plant will continue to deliver your Christmas wishes for many months ahead.

37

Pages of carol or seasonal pop song lyrics can be used in several ways; use them to wrap smaller presents or to cover a small box that you are using to contain a gift item. Cover or paste onto thicker card to make into gift tags or place settings. Cut into triangles to create bunting, or into strips to make paper chains. If you can't find any pages, print out your own. You may choose to use coloured paper or to add some embellishments, such as festive graphics.

38

Combining orders for items such as wines and spirits with someone else may open the door to a multi-buy discount, the provision of glassware or some other retailer incentive.

39

Secret Santas work well for groups of friends or work colleagues, and they can do the same for a family group. Decide who is buying for who and the spend level and off you go.

40

Trim ribbon loops from the shoulders and waistbands of your clothes and reuse them as ties for your gift tags or to breathe new life into hanging decor.

41

Instead of buying a chocolate-based advent calendar for a child, fill a reusable one with individual pieces from a LEGO set, construction toy or basic puzzle that they can build through the days leading up to Christmas. Don't forget to add the instructions, too.

42

The loops of hanging decorations can easily become tangled up during storage. Avoid this by threading the loop through a large safety pin. Take the organisation to genius level by grouping like colours together.

43

Modern advent calendars are often gift related. Try something different this year and resolve to give something each day, instead. This could be a physical item, such as taking a mince pie to a neighbour or a sprig of holly with berries from your garden to a friend for their décor, or more an act of kindness, such as helping a fellow shopper to unload their trolley at the supermarket till, or even paying a compliment to brighten up someone's day.

44

Opt for an experience rather than a physical gift and creatively present any tickets or vouchers. Deliver cinema vouchers in a small bucket of popcorn, for example, or tickets for a gardening festival pinned to some gardening gloves.

45

Go retro with plain or brown paper wrap. Use a printing block such as this one by Cambridge Imprint (cambridgeimprint.co.uk) for an arty twist or team it with string or twine, with some scavenged foliage or cinnamon sticks tucked into it.

47

Repurpose packaging infill such as shredded paper and used tissue paper to disguise the contents of a gift bag. You can also decorate the bags using bows you have saved from last year's crackers.

46

Tuck away a gift you can reach in a crisis. Items such as festive jams or chutneys, a tin of shortbread or a bottle of fizz are all ideal as emergency gifts. Put a blank gift tag and a pen next to it so you can personalise it in a hurry.

48

Amalgamate your online orders with those of a neighbour or a nearby friend, or people who you'll see well before Christmas. Share delivery charges – you may avoid them altogether due to the combined spend level.

49

Get the best mileage from your purchases by choosing items that not only work throughout the Christmas season, but year-round, too. Avoid paper, ribbon, tableware etc with 'Season's Greetings' or Santa Claus motifs, for example, and choose colours and designs which can be redeployed repeatedly, such as this retro wrap from Storigraphic (**storigraphic.com**).

50

Tickets and vouchers are your go-to, for gifts you need in a hurry. Purchase a voucher for an experience, lesson or treat, which can be emailed to the recipient within minutes or downloaded and printed at home.

20 *Memorable* MOVIE, TV & MUSIC MOMENTS

Relive some most magical memories of Christmas as we delve into the beloved films, television shows and songs that make this time of year special to us all.

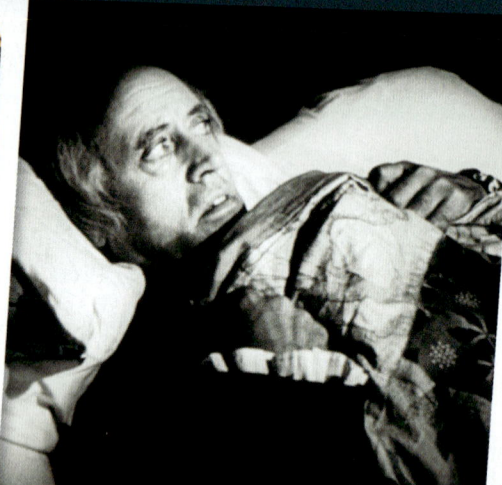

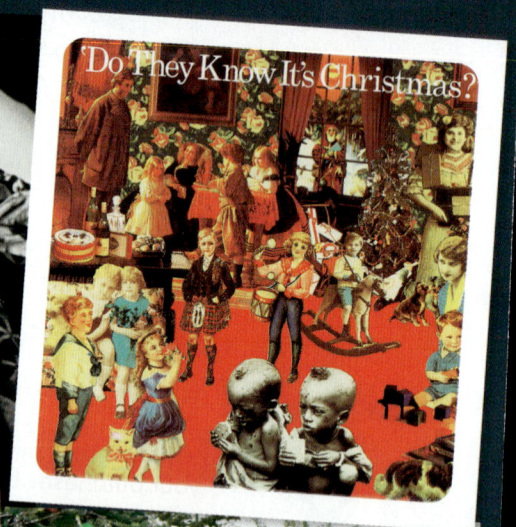

Film

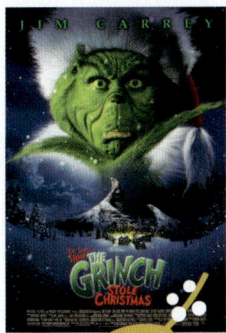

How The Grinch Stole Christmas

There are now several adaptations of "How The Grinch Stole Christmas", but the most iconic is undoubtedly the 2000 film starring Jim Carrey as the grumpy yet lovable protagonist. While it's based on a Dr Seuss book and complete with his trademark nonsense, Christmas in Whoville certainly isn't just for kids.

This classic has us laughing out loud every year.

Home Alone

Featuring a screaming Macaulay Culkin, the famous poster advertising "Home Alone" is one you can't forget in a hurry.

When eight-year-old Kevin McAllister is left home alone over Christmas, he's forced to fend for himself — and fight off home invaders!

This film is filled with outrageous mischief. Always a fun-filled watch, this is perfect for all the family. "Home Alone" was so successful it turned into a six-film franchise.

Elf

Buddy the Elf grew up in the North Pole, but when he ventures to New York in search of his biological family, he is faced with a rude awakening.

New York is a far cry from the whimsy of the North Pole, and Buddy is forced to acclimatise. This comedy starring Will Ferrell is as popular as ever over 20 years after its release and brings the Christmas spirit every year.

Christmas With The Kranks

Featuring an all-star cast, including Tim Allen and Jamie Lee Curtis, "Christmas With The Kranks" sees the Krank family face condemnation from their local community when they decide to opt out of Christmas in favour of a winter cruise.

Based on John Grisham's "Skipping Christmas", this light-hearted watch is perfect to pop on while decorating your Christmas tree.

A Christmas Carol

Based on the much-loved Dickens novel, "A Christmas Carol" is an annual must-watch. Another story with several iterations, personally we're fans of the 1951 version, starring Alastair Sim as Ebenezer Scrooge.

Featuring the famous ghosts of Christmas past, Christmas present and Christmas yet to come, the film's timeless message of the power of redemption never gets old.

Miracle On 34th Street

Another classic, the 1994 film starring Matilda actress Mara Wilson sees Richard Attenborough play a man employed as Santa Claus in an American department store claiming to be the real thing. The trial which ensues to get to the bottom of the matter is both entertaining and uplifting.

This heartwarming John Hughes film is one of our favourites.

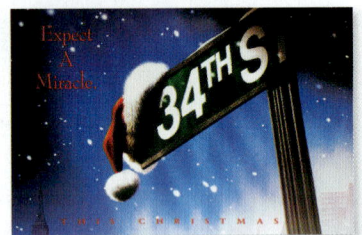

The Nutcracker

Based on the well-known Tchaikovsky ballet, "The Nutcracker" sees a young girl receive a Nutcracker doll for Christmas and proceed to dream about them going on an adventure together.

Featuring mice battling toy soldiers and the enchanting "land of sweets", this film inspired by the ballet sees the magic of Christmas personified on the big screen.

TV

The Final Episode of "Gavin & Stacey"

Will they? Won't they? They were the questions on everyone's lips as we tuned into "Gavin & Stacey: The Finale" on Christmas Day 2024.

We all wondered if Smithy and Nessa would tie the knot after the 2019 proposal, and there were a few twists in the last-ever episode of the hit show.

The 2024 episode was watched by 12.8 million people making it "the UK's most-watched TV programme shown on Christmas Day in 23 years"! Afterwards, in a spin-off documentary, James Corden (who plays Smithy) and Ruth Jones (Nessa) – who co-wrote the hit show – shared their feelings with cast members about recording the last one.

Only Fools & Horses – Batman & Robin

Often referred to as "the greatest moment in British comedy history", we had to include this in our collection of Christmas TV moments. It's that hilarious scene of Batman and Robin, aka Del Boy and Rodney, that make the "Heroes & Villains" episode of "Only Fools & Horses" such a hit with UK audiences.

The pair are on their way to a fancy dress party when chaos ensues in the first part of a three-part Christmas Special from 1996. BBC Comedy Greats has posted the clip on its YouTube channel, attracting almost two million views and more than 850 comments. Fan comments include: "It doesn't get any better than this" and "You can see it coming from a mile away, but it still kills me every time!" Another says: "If this isn't the greatest moment in British comedy history it's very close".

EastEnders 1986 Christmas Day Episode

It's usually a battle against the soaps at Christmas as the TV giants ("EastEnders", "Coronation Street" and "Emmerdale") try to attract the most viewers. Each year, EastEnders usually wins with its dramatic storylines all coming to a climax on December 25. In 1986, this was particularly true as "Dirty Den" Watts (Leslie Grantham) served long-suffering wife Angie (Anita Dobson) with divorce papers.

The Christmas episode broadcast that year was "the most-watched soap opera episode of all time", with over 30 million viewers.

INDEPENDENT TRADING Co.

JLG 755G

NEW YORK • PARIS • PECKHAM

The Snowman First Broadcast

Watching "The Snowman" on Christmas Eve or Christmas Day has become a family tradition across the UK for more than four decades since it was first broadcast in 1982.

The following year, the film was nominated for an Oscar for Best Animated Short Film.

Regarded as "the film that changed Christmas" (which was the title of a 2024 documentary on Channel 4 about the film), "The Snowman" is based on the Raymond Briggs' book of the same name. It tells the story of a boy who builds and befriends a snowman, and together they go on a wonderful adventure to visit Father Christmas.

Morecambe & Wise

Would you believe that more viewers tuned in to watch the comedy duo Morecambe and Wise one Christmas than the combined number who watched King Charles's first Christmas message and the "Gavin & Stacey" finale?

Regarded as the "best-loved double-act that Britain has produced" Eric and Ernie were hugely popular at the height of their career. Their Christmas show was eagerly awaited each year. In 1977, the show pulled in its biggest audience ever – with a staggering 28 million viewers!

The pair continued to entertain audiences as a duo until 1984, when Morecambe passed away, devastating fans.

King Charles's First King's Speech Following the Queen's Death

Each year, it's the broadcast of The King's Christmas Message that tops the polls for the most-watched programme on television.

King Charles III gave his first ever Christmas Day speech as a Monarch on December 25, 2022, although his Coronation was not until May 6, 2023.

In it, His Majesty reflected on Queen Elizabeth II's passing, and her faith in people, as he thanked those who give their time to help others. Around 8.1 million people tuned in.

The following year, his speech was also the most watched, despite attracting an audience of around 600,000 viewers less than the inaugural speech.

Around 7.48 million people watched the 2023 broadcast when it was televised across six channels. Last year, as the King reflected on his and the Princess of Wales' cancer diagnoses, less than seven million watched on.

The Monarch's Christmas Message was first broadcast, on radio, by King George V in 1932.

Music

Do They Know It's Christmas? – Band Aid

When Bob Geldof tuned into a BBC news report about the devastating effects of famine in Ethiopia, the Boomtown Rats frontman was so shocked he vowed to do something.

He and Midge Ure from Ultravox wrote charity song "Do They Know It's Christmas?" and called up every star they knew to meet in London one Sunday morning to record the song. The resulting single went to number one in the charts and raised eight million pounds for Ethiopia within a year, surpassing all expectations. It's still played on repeat each year and is considered an iconic Christmas song.

White Christmas – Bing Crosby

Since its release "White Christmas" has been covered by many artists, but no version is as famous as the original, sung by Bing Crosby and released in 1942. It was written by Irving Berlin for a musical that eventually became "Holiday Inn", and it won the Best Original Song at the Oscars in 1943. In 1954, it was the title track of another Bing Crosby film, "White Christmas", which has since become an enduring festive favourite.

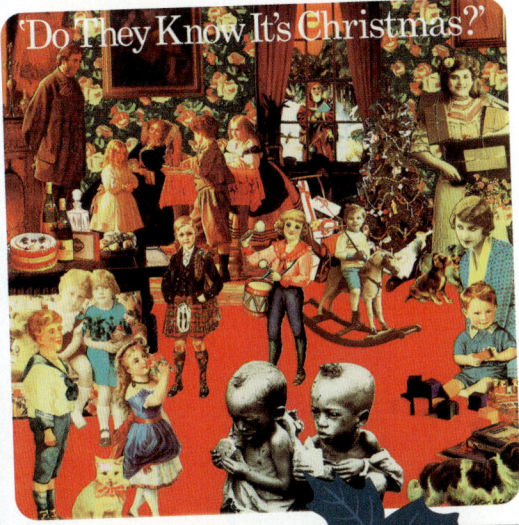

Stay Another Day – East 17

It's not so much the tune that makes this stand out as a classic (strictly speaking it isn't festive at all, as it was written by singer Tony Mortimer about a family tragedy), but the accompanying video is Christmas with bells on. The angelic-looking London quartet – known for not being in the least angelic – are kitted out in white, fluffy parkas, seen floating around in the ether and fully embracing the Christmas spirit.

There's even dodgy fake snow superimposed on the video. What's not to love?

Merry Xmas Everybody – Slade

Noddy Holder recently revealed he wakes his wife up every Christmas morning by bellowing the lyric "It's Christmas!" at her. And why not?

This tune is one of the most well-known festive songs. Originally released in 1973, it went to number one in the charts, beating another classic, Wizzard's "I Wish It Could Be Christmas Everyday", to the top spot. Quite remarkably, it has re-entered the charts every December since 2007.

It's no surprise that Noddy refers to the song as his pension scheme.

Walking In The Air – The Snowman

The haunting voice of a fourteen-year-old Aled Jones is not, contrary to popular belief, the one you hear when you watch the animated film based on Raymond Briggs's 1978 children's book. That was recorded by Peter Auty, a choirboy from St Paul's Cathedral, while Aled Jones's version was released later, in 1985, for a Toys R Us advertising campaign.

This, however, is the one that gets played year after year, and which is embedded in our festive memories. Beautiful.

Fairytale Of New York – The Pogues with Kirsty MacColl

This high-octane, rumbustious and somewhat bitter tune from the Pogues and Kirsty MacColl is a universal favourite that took almost two years for Shane MacGowan and Jem Finer to write.

While it is universally loved and regarded by many as the one of the best Christmas songs of all time, it has never made it to number one in the UK charts. That said, "Fairytale Of New York" has re-entered the Top 20 every December since 2005 and shows no sign of losing its appeal.

All I Want For Christmas Is You – Mariah Carey

This tune often tops the polls as the greatest Christmas song ever written. There's no doubt its appeal has snowballed after gaining only modest traction when it was first released in 1994.

Since then, it has become one of the most played Christmas songs ever. In contrast to the Pogues "Fairytale Of New York", it took Mariah and fellow songwriter Walter Afanasieff only 15 minutes to compose what many believe is the perfect pop song . . . that just so happens to be about Christmas!

PUZZLE FUN *for all*

Grab yourself a festive drink and relax with our super crop of brainteasers. There's hours of fun on the eight pages ahead, but if that's not enough, there are eight more pages from p136!

Crossword

ACROSS

1 General acceptance or use (8)

5 Liquid starter (4)

9 Keep away from (something) (5)

10 Chinese vegetable dish cooked in hot oil (4-3)

11 Old musical instrument (4)

12 Society for avid readers (4,4)

14 Imaginary, make-believe (6)

15 Mind as opposed to body (6)

18 Genial (8)

20 Newborn child (4)

23 Thin stiff fabric of silk, cotton or nylon (7)

24 Revolving blade (5)

25 Lug, carry (4)

26 Red suit of cards (8)

DOWN

1 Move on hands and knees (5)

2 Farmyard cock (7)

3 Swirl round (4)

4 Space, universe (6)

6 Butcher's scraps (5)

7 Owed (7)

8 Greet without touching (3-4)

13 Pouring down (7)

14 On the level (7)

16 Punish (7)

17 Acid neutraliser (6)

19 Oblong block of moulded gold (5)

21 Sailors' tales (5)

22 Cheerless, severe (4)

Mini Jigsaw

Fit the pieces into the grid to make six festive words. We've given you two letters to start off.

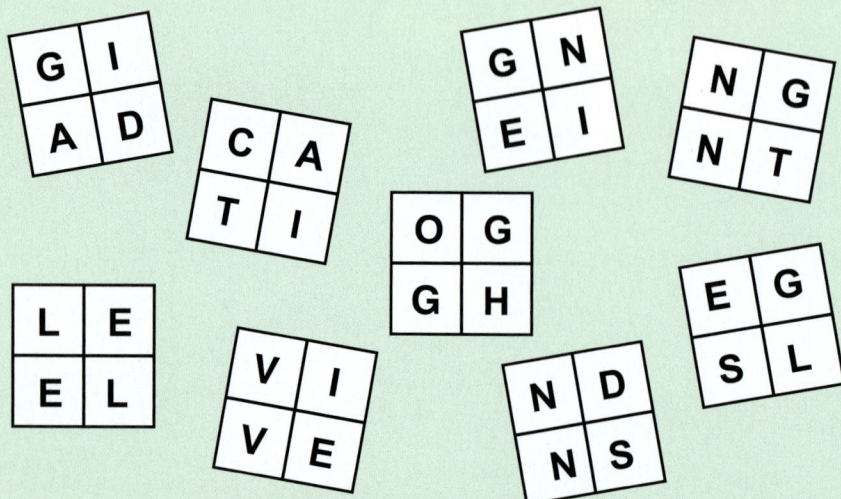

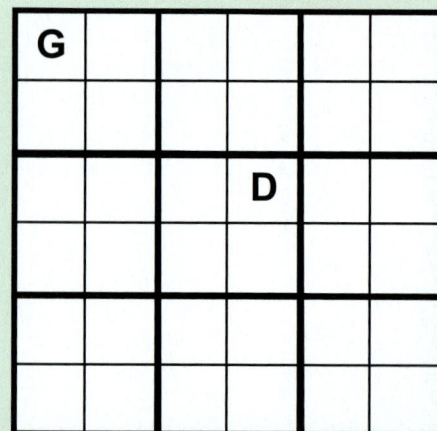

Wordsearch

Find all these words associated with the movie Love Actually in the grid. Words can run forwards, backwards or diagonally.

ACTUALLY
AIRPORT
AMERICA
CHRISTMAS
COLIN
COMEDY
COUPLES
DANIEL
DAVID
DRUMS
ENSEMBLE
HARRY
JOANNA
JULIET
JUMP
KAREN
KARL
LOBSTER
LOVE
MARK
MARRIAGE
NATALIE
PETER
ROMANCE
SARAH

G	A	I	R	P	O	R	T	G	B	E	H	S	T	C
N	E	R	A	K	J	E	G	D	L	N	M	E	S	O
O	T	I	H	O	N	L	C	B	R	A	S	V	O	L
D	T	I	A	B	E	E	M	N	R	U	G	O	N	I
S	S	N	O	I	T	E	I	R	A	E	M	L	P	N
H	N	E	N	N	S	Y	I	U	S	M	E	S	P	D
A	S	A	L	N	M	A	R	K	A	O	O	M	P	I
A	D	N	E	P	G	T	S	E	M	N	U	R	E	T
C	S	E	A	E	U	A	O	I	T	J	L	T	T	E
T	G	B	E	T	R	O	M	C	S	D	N	R	E	I
U	Y	H	S	A	A	U	C	E	I	D	I	O	R	L
A	R	T	H	E	P	L	V	L	R	N	I	R	E	U
L	R	A	K	I	S	O	I	T	H	I	Y	V	E	J
L	A	C	O	M	E	D	Y	E	C	C	C	D	A	L
Y	H	R	G	N	R	E	T	S	B	O	L	A	I	D

Answers on p47

Take Two

Each word in a clue can be preceded by the same two letters to make three new words. The three pairs of letters will then spell out a Biblical figure.

| | BLESS, COSE, KEY |

| | CEDE, CURE, RUM |

| | ISH, RASE, ONES |

Codeword

Complete the codeword as usual and transfer the encoded letters into the bottom grid to discover a festive song.

The codeword grid (top) contains numbers 1–26 with the following given letters: **H U G** (16-9-21), and **U** at 22, **G** at 21, **H** at 16.

A B C D E F ~~G~~ ~~H~~ I J K L M N O P Q R S T ~~U~~ V W X Y Z

1	2	3	4	5	6	7	8	9 U	10	11	12	13
14	15	16 H	17	18	19	20	21 G	22	23	24	25	26

| 11 | 14 | 6 | 16 H | 17 | 25 | 22 | 1 | 14 | 23 | 24 | 6 | ' 3 |

| 4 | 16 H | 2 | 24 | 3 | 6 | 18 | 12 | 3 | ? |

Sudoku

Fill the grids with the numbers 1 to 4 so that each row, column and 2x2 block contains the numbers 1 to 4.

Grid 1

3	4	1	2
2	3	4	1

Grid 2

3	4	1	2
4	1	2	3

Grid 3

3			2
	2	3	
	3	1	
1			3

Riddle

The first eight lines each stand for a letter. Put them together to solve the riddle!

Answers on p47

My first is in BADGE and also in BROOCH,

My second's not in MENTOR but is found in COACH.

My third is in EDGE but never in BORDER,

My fourth is in DISCIPLINE but not in ORDER.

My fifth is in RECEIPT and also in BILL,

My sixth's not in TABLET but is found in PILL.

My seventh's in OBJECTS but not in STUFF,

My last is in STRONG but never in TOUGH.

My whole is an instrument that needs lots of puff!

Home Front

Four people have decorated the front door of their houses, for Christmas. From the information given, work out who lives at which house.

Janet

'I like to put a 'Santa Stop' sign by the door, for my children.'

James

'My house has a red door.'

Beth

'I love my glowing icicle lights.'

Craig

'I don't have a wreath on my door.'

Kriss Kross

Fit the words about Santa Claus into the grid. There's only one correct solution.

4 letters
LIST
SACK

5 letters
COCOA
MUSIC
TOOLS

6 letters
GROTTO
RIBBON

7 letters
COOKIES
HELPERS
LETTERS

8 letters
ASSEMBLE
REINDEER

9 letters
ENCHANTED
ORNAMENTS

Logical

Try solving this little logical problem in your head before putting pen to paper.

Each year, three friends flee the winter and spend time in the warmer climes of Europe.

From the information given, work out who goes where and for how long.

Beryl, who doesn't escape to Nice, spends two weeks less in the sun than Pearl spends in Majorca.

At 9 weeks, Olive escapes for the shortest time, but not to Lisbon.

The person going to Majorca isn't the person escaping for 11 weeks.

PYRAMID

Each answer contains the letters of the previous answer, plus one extra.

1 Personal pronoun (1)

2 State of being verb (2)

3 Honorific title used with the forename only (3)

4 Increase in salary (4)

5 Wharves (5)

6 Religious officer (6)

7 Muscle principally responsible for the straightening of the arm (7)

8 Baked pastry covering (8)

9 Another name for the school subject of Religious Education (9)

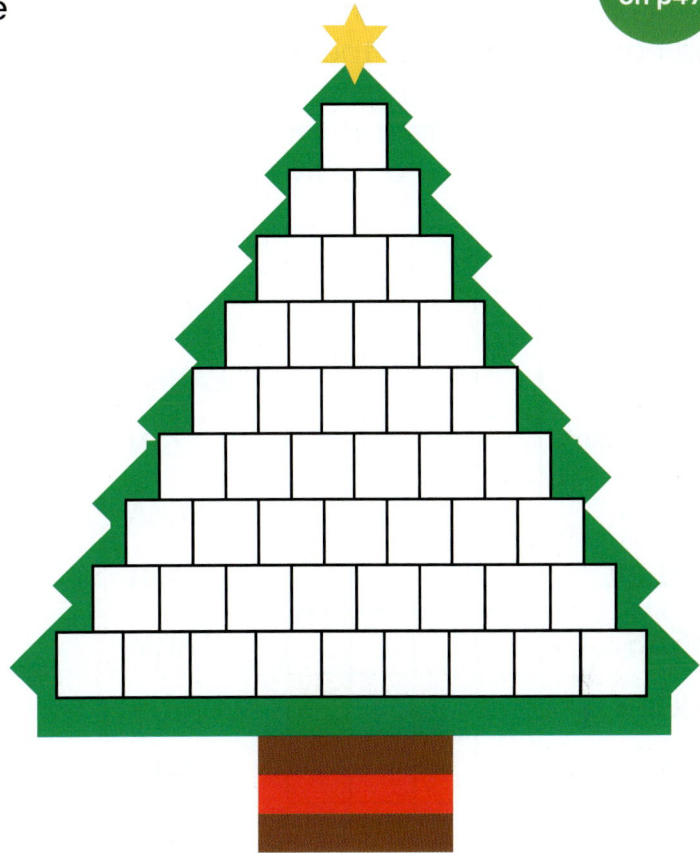

Answers on p47

Wordsearch

In the grid you should be able to find 16 words that can follow or precede 'gold' or 'golden' to make a new word or phrase.

BRACELET
BULLION
COMPASS
CREST
HIND
MEDAL
NUMBER
PLATED
RULE
SHARE
SMITH
STAR
SYRUP
WONDER
WORK
YEARS

K	I	M	I	B	H	I	N	D
P	Y	E	A	R	S	L	E	R
U	O	D	E	A	I	T	B	E
R	N	A	O	C	S	U	T	B
Y	S	L	E	E	L	U	R	M
S	I	M	R	L	R	E	N	U
O	T	C	I	E	S	A	E	N
K	R	O	W	T	D	T	H	C
A	N	I	N	E	H	N	A	S
P	L	A	T	E	D	O	O	R
S	S	A	P	M	O	C	L	W

Missing Link

Fit ten words into the grid so each one connects up with the words on either side eg - wishing - well - done. Read down the letters in the shaded squares to spell out a festive plant.

STICKY						MEASURE
LOST						FOOD
EXHAUST						CLEANER
SHOCKING						GIN
SUGAR						OPERA
BARLEY						BAR
PRESS						FARM
SINGLE						LIQUOR
DESK						SUM
HIGH						HOG

Ladder

Change one letter at a time (but not the position of any letter) to make a new word – and move from the word at the bottom of the box to the word at the top using the exact number of rungs provided.

C O A L

S L E D

Hide and Seek

How quickly can you identify the squares in which each of the numbered shapes appears?

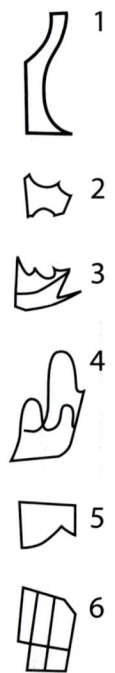

SOLUTIONS

Crossword

C	U	R	R	E	N	C	Y		S	O	U	P
R		O		D		O		A		F		A
A	V	O	I	D		S	T	I	R	F	R	Y
W		S		Y		M		R		A		A
L	U	T	E		B	O	O	K	C	L	U	B
		E		R		S		I				L
U	N	R	E	A	L		P	S	Y	C	H	E
P				I		A		S		H		
F	R	I	E	N	D	L	Y		B	A	B	Y
R		N		I		K		G		S		A
O	R	G	A	N	Z	A		R	O	T	O	R
N		O		G		L		I		E		N
T	O	T	E		D	I	A	M	O	N	D	S

Mini Jigsaw

GIVING
ADVENT
CANDLE
TINSEL
EGGNOG
SLEIGH

Wordsearch

G	A	I	R	P	O	R	T	G	B	E	H	S	T	C
N	E	R	A	K	J	E	G	D	L	N	M	E	S	O
O	T	I	H	O	N	L	C	B	R	A	S	V	O	L
D	T	I	A	B	E	E	M	N	R	U	G	O	N	I
S	S	N	O	I	T	E	I	R	A	E	M	L	P	N
H	N	E	N	N	S	Y	I	U	S	M	E	S	P	D
A	S	A	L	N	M	A	R	K	A	O	O	M	P	I
A	D	N	E	P	G	T	S	E	M	N	U	R	E	T
C	S	E	A	E	U	A	O	I	T	J	L	T	T	E
T	G	B	E	T	R	O	M	C	S	D	N	R	E	I
U	Y	H	S	A	A	U	C	E	I	D	I	O	R	L
A	R	T	H	E	P	L	V	L	R	N	I	R	E	U
L	R	A	K	I	S	O	I	T	H	I	Y	V	E	J
L	A	C	O	M	E	D	Y	E	C	C	C	D	A	L
Y	H	R	G	N	R	E	T	S	B	O	L	A	I	D

Take Two

JO/SE/PH

The added letters spell: JOSEPH

Codeword

	W	I	M	P		H	U	G	E		R	A	Z	E
O		D		A		U		A		C		G		A
F	R	I	A	R		S		R	U	I	N	O	U	S
F		O		O	T	H	E	R		R				E
E	X	T	O	L		E		I	N	C	I	S	E	D
N		I		E		D		S		U		E		
C	I	C	A	D	A		J	O	U	S	T	E	D	
E			X			E		N			I			R
	P	R	E	T	E	X	T		S	K	E	T	C	H
		I		R		P		H		E		O		U
L	U	M	B	A	G	O		I		S	Q	U	I	B
O				G		N	I	G	H	T		S		A
R	E	S	T	I	V	E		H		R	U	L	E	R
R		O		C		N		L		E		E		B
Y	A	W	N		S	T	A	Y		L	U	D	O	

N	R	S	C	B	T	Q	L	U	X	D	A	F
O	Z	H	E	M	P	J	G	K	W	I	Y	V

DO THEY KNOW IT'S CHRISTMAS?

Sudoku

1	2	3	4
3	4	1	2
2	3	4	1
4	1	2	3

3	4	1	2
1	2	3	4
2	3	4	1
4	1	2	3

3	1	4	2
4	2	3	1
2	3	1	4
1	4	2	3

Riddle

The word is: BAGPIPES

Home Front

Janet – Door 3,
James – Door 1,
Beth – Door 4,
Craig – Door 2.

Kriss Kross

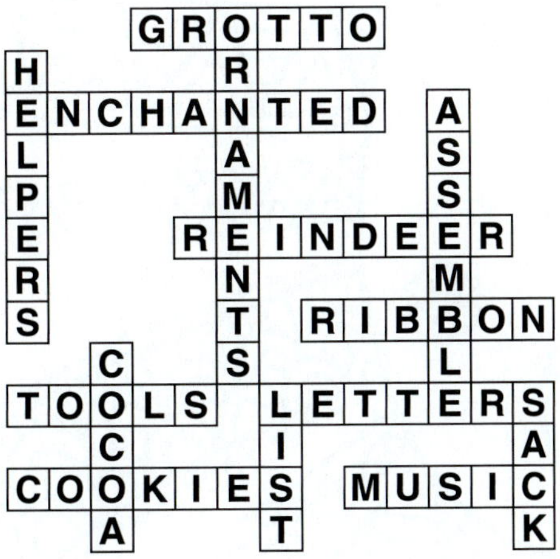

Logical

Beryl, Lisbon, 11 weeks
Olive, Nice, 9 weeks
Pearl, Majorca, 13 weeks

Pyramid

I
IS
SIR
RISE
PIERS
PRIEST
TRICEPS
PIECRUST
SCRIPTURE

Wordsearch

K	I	M	I	B	H	I	N	D
P	Y	E	A	R	S	L	E	R
U	O	D	E	A	I	T	B	E
R	N	A	O	C	S	U	T	B
Y	S	L	E	E	L	U	R	M
S	I	M	R	L	R	E	N	U
O	T	C	I	E	S	A	E	N
K	R	O	W	T	D	T	H	C
A	N	I	N	E	H	N	A	S
P	L	A	T	E	D	O	O	R
S	S	A	P	M	O	C	L	W

Missing Link

The words in the correct order are:

TAPE, SOUL, PIPE, PINK, SOAP, WINE, STUD, MALT, TIDY, ROAD

Reading down the shaded letters: POINSETTIA

Ladder

COAL, COIL, SOIL, SAIL, SAID, SLID, SLED

Hide and Seek

1 a3
2 b5
3 c6
4 d2
5 d5
6 f5

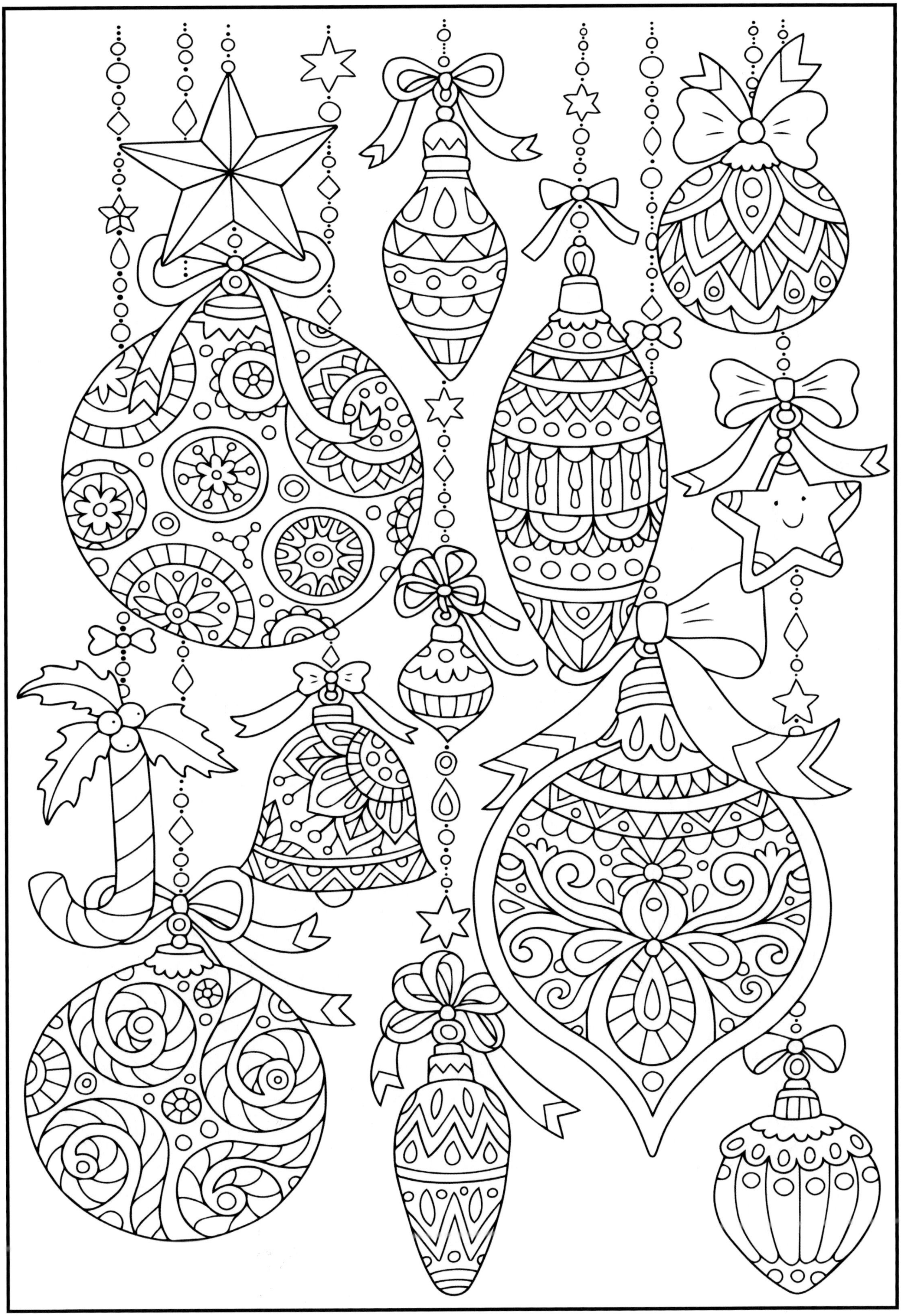

The People's Friend

Annual & The Friendship Book 2026

- 25 short stories from your favourite "Friend" authors
- Fascinating nature facts
- Delightful poems

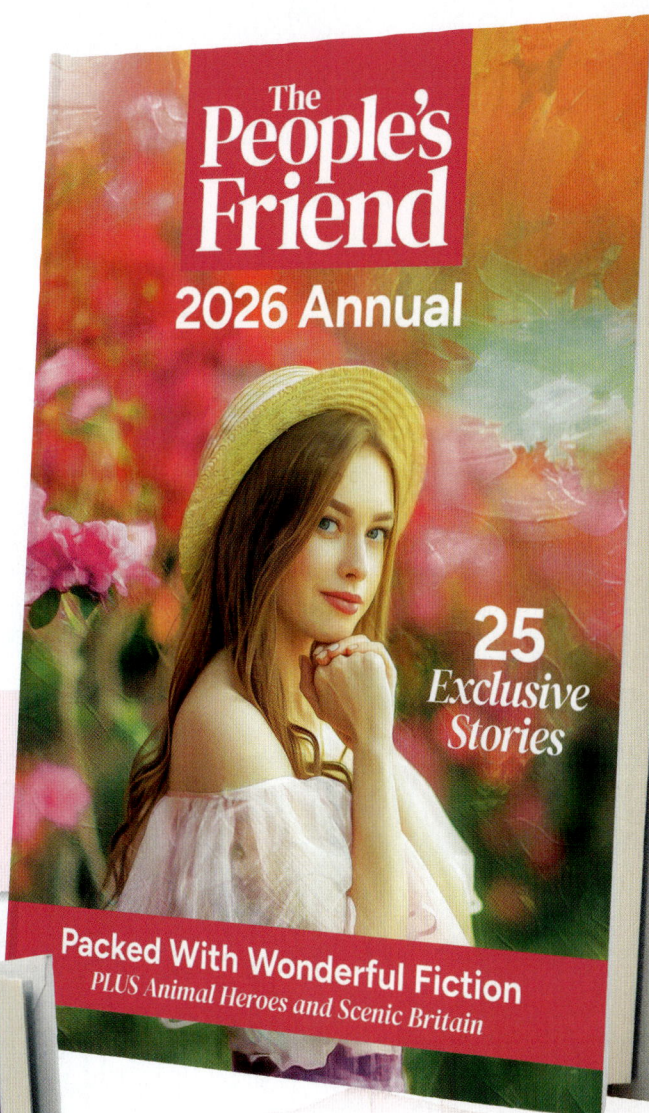

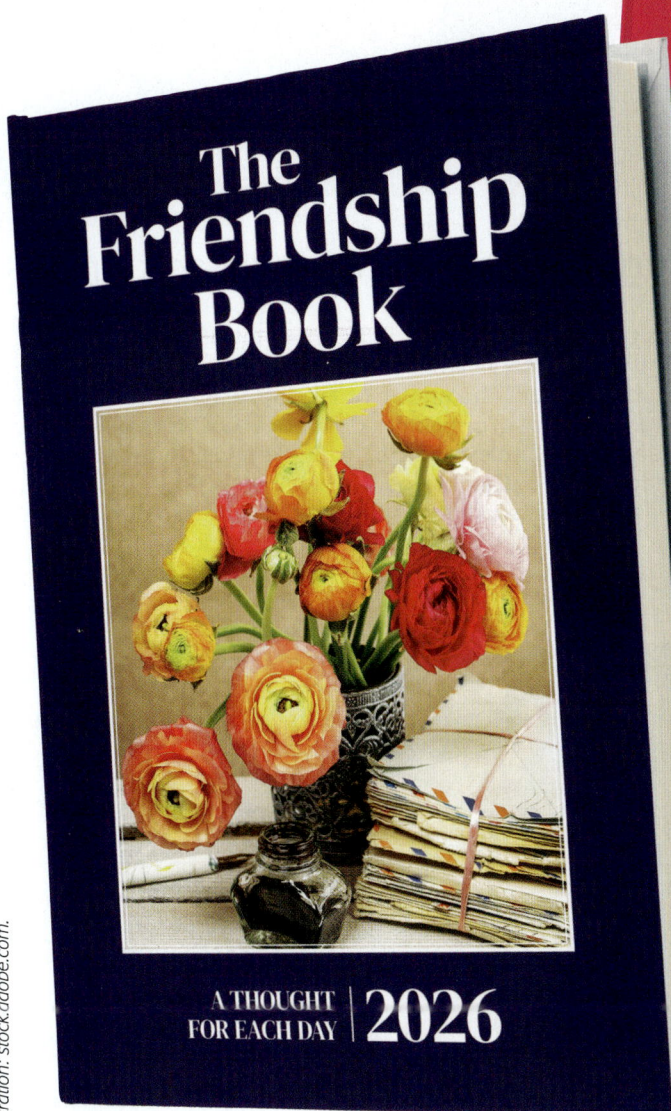

The People's Friend
2026 Annual

25 Exclusive Stories

Packed With Wonderful Fiction
PLUS Animal Heroes and Scenic Britain

The Friendship Book

A THOUGHT FOR EACH DAY | 2026

Hardback, 176 pages each.

Each annual is £11.99. Buy both for £20.50 and save £3.48 plus enjoy FREE delivery!

SCAN ME

"The People's Friend" Annual & Friendship Book Pack 2026, code: PFR26, £20.50.

- A thought for each day of the year
- Uplifting and life-affirming
- Perfect companion for the year ahead

@ **Visit www.dcthomsonshop.co.uk/ 2026annuals**

If you prefer to place your order by telephone, please dial 0800 318 846.

Also available on Amazon and in bookstores.

Illustration: stock.adobe.com.

Nine Lessons & Carols from
KING'S COLLEGE, CAMBRIDGE

Christmas at King's College.

At this famous chapel, Christmas Eve glows with song and tradition.

CHRISTMAS Eve, about two in the afternoon. A low murmur hangs like night traffic as people congregate. Subtle up-lighting gives the ceiling a soft ivory glow, and ripening colours are flooding through the stained glass as the sun sinks to the west.

Candles burn like stars among the peaty panels of the Choir and there's a hint of incense. Soon the whole world will be listening and the excitement scurries under your skin.

You want to savour every delicious moment but it's all so soporific; the warmth, the gentle light, the exquisite surroundings.

Organ music stirs, the mystical shades of Messiaen's "La Nativité du Seigneur", shifting and turning like a kaleidoscope in slow motion, carrying you away on their serene journey. Your thoughts drift, through the pillars and arches, up into the ceiling, around the vaults, the sound all the time dimming and narrowing until just a single note is left.

The inner chapel choir.

It's the voice of a lone chorister. The service has begun. It can only be one thing: the Festival of Nine Lessons and Carols at King's College Chapel, Cambridge.

Despite its association with Cambridge, the festival actually has its origins in Truro. In 1880, Edward White Benson, Truro's bishop, was concerned about the seasonal drunkenness in the local pubs.

He wanted to guide his people back to something more spiritual and came up with the idea of a new ceremony.

On December 24 of that year, about 400 people gathered in the temporary wooden hut that served as a cathedral to hear the first ever Festival of Nine Lessons and Carols.

Benson's son recalled, "My father arranged from ancient sources a little service for Christmas Eve — nine carols and nine tiny lessons which were read by various officers of the Church, beginning with a chorister and ending, through the

The pipe organ.

The inner chapel decani.

Gothic stained glass inside.

different grades, with the Bishop."

Though the festival has been celebrated at Truro every year since, it didn't come to Cambridge until 38 years later, when Eric Milner-White, an ex-student and army chaplain during World War I, was appointed Dean of King's College.

Milner-White believed that the Anglican Church needed more imaginative forms of worship and held his version of the festival at King's College Chapel on Christmas Eve, 1918. At that time the choir was made up of boy trebles, choral scholars and lay clerks.

There had been a choir at King's since the chapel's founding in 1441 but the quality hadn't always been good. As recently as the mid-19th century, choirboys were still indulging in rough initiation rites, street fighting and theft from local shops.

In 1876, the organist Arthur Henry Mann was appointed director of music with the specific aim of raising standards.

During his tenure, and reflecting the increasing importance of music, the college built a new choir school and house for the director of music's use.

Mann was music director for the first King's festival in 1918. It had a lukewarm reception, but Milner-White was undeterred.

He made revisions, re-arranging the readings, inserting a bidding prayer and opening with the carol, "Once in Royal David's City", and the second festival in 1919 was more successful.

The idea began to gain traction, with other churches adapting it for their own use, and when live broadcasting by the BBC started in 1928, its popularity increased further.

By that time, the choir was improving.

The last of the lay clerks had left in 1927 and it was now made up entirely of boy choristers and undergraduate choral scholars. The service was broadcast live again in 1929 though not in 1930, for reasons that aren't clear.

This may have been due to the chapel's acoustics, which were problematic for radio broadcasting, or insufficient confidence in Boris Ord, the inexperienced director of music who had only been appointed the previous year.

There had also been friction between Milner-White and the BBC over its religious broadcasting policy. Whatever the reason, by 1931 it was resolved and every year since, it has been broadcast live by the BBC.

Throughout the 1930s, the festival began to spread, featuring on the

BBC World Service. The first broadcast by an American radio company took place in 1938, with networks in Italy, France and Switzerland also relaying parts of the programme.

Neither did World War II prevent transmission, though throughout the conflict the name and location of King's College was kept secret. At the

WordS: Chris Franks. Images: Shutterstock.

outbreak of the war, Boris Ord was still director of music, assisted by a young David Willcocks as organ scholar. When they were called off to military service between 1940 and 1945, the music directorship was held by Harold Darke.

During the war years, it was necessary to remove the ancient stained glass from the chapel windows and substitute blackout tar-paper, which rustled in the wind and made live broadcasting even more difficult.

Ord and Willcocks resumed their positions after the war and Ord was still director of music in 1954, when the festival was first televised by the BBC.

A different pre-recorded version of the service, the television broadcast has been a regular feature ever since. As well as by

radio and television, the festival's fame was further increased by the popularity of LP records. By the time Willcocks succeeded Ord as director of music in 1957,

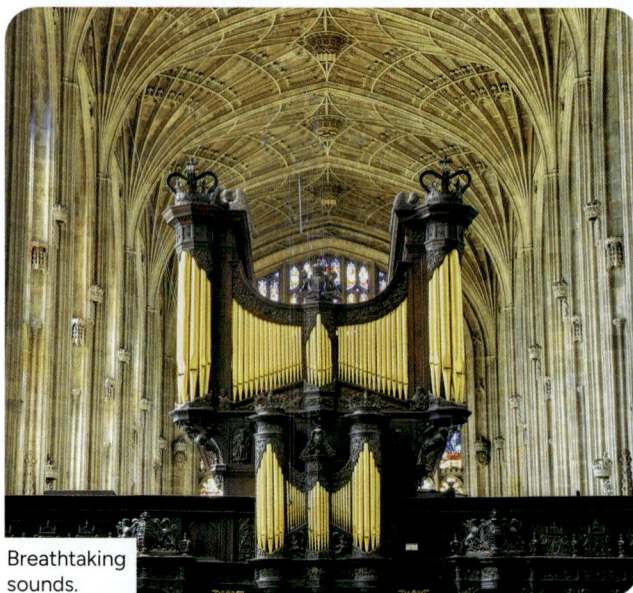

Breathtaking sounds.

it had become a global phenomenon, with people listening from locations as far-flung as deserts and the foothills of Everest.

Under Willcocks and his

successors, Philip Ledger and Stephen Cleobury, the reputation of the choir was further enhanced by numerous commercial recordings and tours.

The choir has worked with top record labels such as Decca and EMI and in 2012 formed its own label, The Choir of King's College. It is widely recognised as one of the finest and most famous choirs in the world.

These days, admission to the Christmas Eve Festival of Nine Lessons and Carols is by ticket only, with tickets distributed at 7am that day. This system only began in 2017, though, and prior to that the only way to gain entry to the chapel was to queue up outside all day.

The chapel is split into two parts by the rood screen, with the Ante-chapel on one side and the Choir and Chancel on the bright frosty day. Or huddle under soggy leaden skies if it wasn't.

Admission to the chapel starts at 1.30pm. The festival doesn't begin until 3pm but it takes over an hour to get everyone seated.

Once inside, you realise how cavernous the chapel is. At 289 feet long and 80 feet high, it boasts the largest fan vaulted ceiling in the world. Those with Chancel seats walk under the rood screen and through the Choir to their superior places.

And as you sit waiting for it all to begin, there's a curious fact to ponder: that because radio waves travel nearly a million times faster than sound and will span the globe in a fraction of a second, those at the far end of the Ante-chapel will be the last in the world to hear.

The festival always opens with the chorister solo of Once in Royal. It's an iconic moment, yet despite its colossal importance, with hundreds of millions around the world listening, the soloist isn't chosen until just seconds before the live broadcast.

This apparent madness has sound reasons behind it. The late Stephen Cleobury, director of music from 1982 to 2019, explained in a 2018 BBC documentary, "If you nominate a chorister a week or two before, he's got quite a lot of time to get wound up about it, which we don't want, and that particular boy might wake up on Christmas Eve with a sore throat.

"It's really down to who is in the best voice on the day. I make the selection in my mind and that is communicated to the chosen boy just as we go on air."

The director of music points his finger and the soloist steps forward as the music fades. The musically eared will notice how the organist always steers the tonality back to G major, the key of Once in Royal, to give the chorister his starting note.

The spectacular ceiling.

The chapel falls silent, the world waits. It's just seconds but for the chosen boy, it's a lifetime of nerves.

It is said that space is so dark you can see light through a keyhole on earth. So it is with that lone chorister's voice.

The chapel is so silent that the thread of sound fills every corner, the unique acoustic giving it a beguiling depth and resonance. Nothing stirs. Every soul is gripped. If ever there was a sound of Christmas, this is it.

The structure of the festival is built around the nine lessons, readings from the Old and New Testaments that tell the story of man's first fall from grace and his eventual redemption through the Nativity.

The lessons haven't changed since the 1919 service and are framed by an opening bidding prayer and closing prayer. Interspersed are the carols, one or two each time, so that in total there are eleven readings with roughly twice as many carols.

Milner-White maintained that the strength of the service came from the lessons, not the music.

The service unfolds and you sit, listening and pondering. There is something in the sound of the choir, in all the singers being so young, their voices charged with a rapturous

Leading the choir.

life force that knows nothing of disappointment or despair.

It warms and inspires and when it's time for the final Hark the Herald, you want to raise the roof.

From beginning to end, the entire service is less than two hours, but by the time it's over you feel like you have come on a journey.

And as you emerge from the chapel, you're filled with hope once more. You want to shake everyone's hand. You want everyone to be happy, to be safe and well on Christmas Day.

It is the very essence of Christmas and the Festival of Nine Lessons and Carols has captured it to perfection.

King's College also features on pages 62-66 where we discover the origins of Christmas carols and why we sing them.

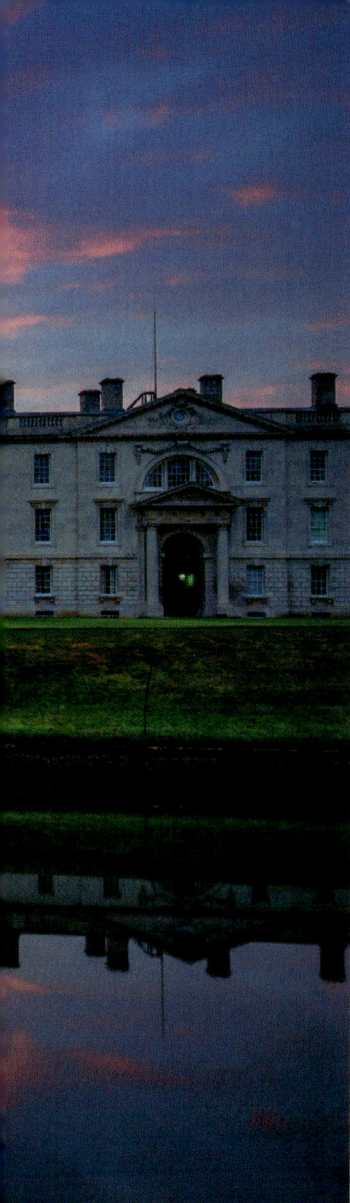
The chapel was built between 1446 and 1515.

other. The Choir is for the college dignitaries and the singers themselves, with visitors sitting either in the adjacent Chancel or in the Ante-chapel, from where the choir cannot be seen.

The Chancel seats are therefore the best, but to obtain one you had to be in the queue by 5am at the latest.

To get into the chapel at all, you had to be there by 9am and that was back in 1985. A news story from 2010 reported people queuing in King's Parade from the previous afternoon.

It was a long, cold day but you could talk to fellow queuers, or listen to fragments of the final rehearsal bursting through the chapel walls, or watch the long shadows cast by the low sun inching across the back lawn, if it was a

Luminous
LANDSCAPES

Festive light displays are appearing in gardens all over the country. Laura Coventry shares some of the best locations . . .

THERE was a time when the only Christmas lights that caught the public imagination in the UK were in London's Oxford Street, with the celebrity switch-on making national television news.

Now there are amazing Christmas light displays all over the country. You won't find them strung between lampposts in the high street, though; they're in some of our best-loved gardens, open to the public, and they create a festival of light that brings winter cheer to so many of us in the run-up to yuletide.

Christmas light trails in gardens are a relatively new phenomenon in this country, starting only about a decade ago, and getting bigger and better with every year.

Now our light trails are as much a part of the Christmas tradition as pantomimes and Father Christmas grottos – and tickets are just as highly prized. If you hope to kick off your celebrations with a walk through a fairytale land of light tunnels and fire gardens, you need to book now.

Here are some of the best to visit – but it's by no means an exhaustive list and there are bound to be more gardens and parks near your home where you can trip the light fantastic.

ROYAL BOTANIC GARDENS KEW, LONDON

There are few more dramatic sights than Kew's historic Palm House lit up and switching from one jewel-like colour to another — all reflected in the nearby lake.

It's the finale to the magical walk past massive trees with neon-lit canopies and through archways of colour along paths with more seasonal lights dotted among the bushes. This year's Christmas at Kew is being billed as "an unmissable opportunity to herald the start of the festive season".

The new 2025 trail promises new creations by artists from all over the world, displayed together for the first time in the UK. As well as the larger-than-life illuminations, look out for Father Christmas!

Time-slot tickets and parking must be booked in advance.

WHEN: Selected dates from November 14, 2025 to January 4, 2026; 4.20 pm to 10 pm (last entry times vary depending on which gate you arrive at)
PRICES: Non-member adult: Off peak £27.50 / Peak £34. Member adult: Off peak £23.50 / Peak £28. Family and child tickets available.
Note: On Christmas Eve, the event closes at 9 pm.
BOOK AT: kew.org/kew-gardens/whats-on/christmas

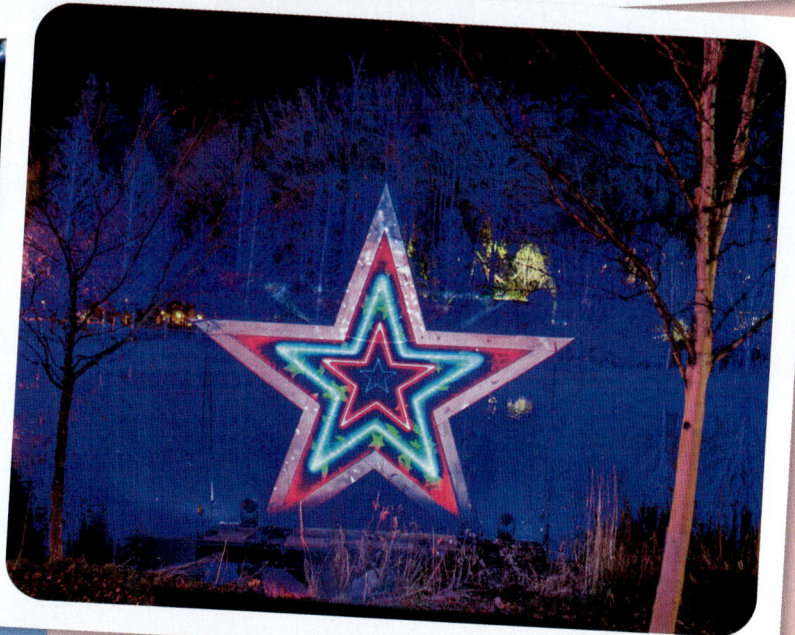

THE ALNWICK GARDEN, NORTHUMBERLAND

There's a double dose of happiness at the Alnwick Garden every Christmas season, as its Winter Light Trail also coincides with the start of Alnwick town's festivities.

This year, not only can you see the lights in The Alnwick Garden, you can also see the lights in the enchanting village of Lilidorei. So, you are getting to enjoy the festivities at two attractions, for one price! You can also book a slot to meet Santa at his magical grotto in Lilidorei.

Visitors can expect "an immersive experience of light and sound," an Alnwick Garden spokesperson says.

"This year is bigger and better than ever, with new installations set to a brand new soundtrack. See the garden and Lilidorei like never before and experience the perfect winter tradition this Christmas."

WHEN: November 20, 2025 to January 1, 2026
PRICES: see website
BOOK AT: www.alnwickgarden.com/events/winter-lights/

> ## WIMPOLE ESTATE, CAMBRIDGE

The lights trail at Wimpole is regarded as "one of the best Christmas events in the UK". This after-dark illuminated trail transforms the stunning National Trust Wimpole Estate into a dazzling display of twinkling lights and festive magic, making it an ideal seasonal day and evening out for families, friends and couples.

You are invited to wander through breathtaking Christmas light installations, including brand-new features for 2025. Tickets may be available on the day but booking advance tickets is recommended. National Trust members do not receive ticket discounts, but can park at the event free of charge.

WHEN: November 21, 2025 to January 3, 2026,
PRICE: Adult £25.00; Child (3-16 years) £18.50; Family (2 adults & 2 children) £84.00.
BOOK AT: nationaltrust.org.uk/visit/cambridgeshire/wimpole-estate/christmas-at-wimpole

WARWICK CASTLE, WARWICKSHIRE

Once home to the Earls of Warwick, the castle is one of the best-known in England. Its formal gardens, laid out in the 1860s, are now transformed each winter into the popular ice rink and Light Trail, with more than half a million twinkling lights illuminating 64 acres of its historic grounds.

But that's not all. The castle rooms are usually decorated with dazzling Christmas trees throughout, while Stories with Santa is a must-do experience as you enjoy storytime with Mr and Mrs Claus! This year, Warwick Castle has a brand-new ice rink, set against the stunning backdrop of Guy's Tower.

WHEN: November 22, 2025 to January 4, 2026
PRICE: Light Trail from £17pp; Ice Skating from £8pp; Stories With Santa £29pp
BOOK AT: warwick-castle.com/explore-1/events/christmas-at-the-castle/

DUNHAM MASSEY, CHESHIRE

Christmas at Dunham Massey will be full of light and laughter. It's a firm family favourite, with highlights this year including brand-new light installations transforming the historic grounds.

Dunham Massey is a Georgian house just outside Manchester with one of the finest winter gardens in Britain and a 3,000-acre deer park, so you can be sure there will be some special Christmas deer to see. As well as animals, visitors will also enjoy a wander through its magical illuminated mile-long trail filled with festive wonder, and you might even catch a glimpse of Father Christmas along the way. Seasonal treats and winter warmers will also be provided by hand-picked vendors.

The organisers warn that there is limited capacity, so it's best to book early in order to secure your preferred date and time.

WHEN: November 14, 2025 to January 3, 2026
PRICE: Adults around £27.50; Child (3-16 years) £18.50; Family (2 adults & 2 children) £88.00
BOOK AT: nationaltrust.org.uk/ visit/cheshire-greater-manchester/ dunham-massey/christmas-lights-at-dunham-massey

STOURHEAD, WILTSHIRE

Delve into a "new and reimagined" trail at this year's Christmas At Stourhead in a mile-long wonderland that will take around 90 minutes to navigate (at normal walking pace). The National Trust's world-famous landscape garden near Mere is known for its classical temples and Palladian house. Some of its historic architecture will be illuminated and, as in previous years, so may be the lake! Look out across the water for a breathtaking display of colour-changing reflections.

"You can enjoy a brand-new array of dazzling installations for 2025, including the mesmerising Star Show, a shimmering Sea of Light and spectacular lasers cutting through the night sky," a spokesperson says. As well as the new additions, for 2025, the returning favourites will also light up your world, including the ever-popular twinkling tunnel of light.

WHEN: November 28, 2025 to December 31, 2025
PRICE: Adults around £22.50; Child (3-16 years) around £16.00; Family (2 adults & 2 children) £74.00
BOOK AT: www.nationaltrust.org.uk/stourhead

CHRISTMAS AT THE BOTANICS, ROYAL BOTANIC GARDEN EDINBURGH

Christmas at the Botanics returns this festive season with an awe-inspiring after-dark illuminated trail – and you are invited. Head to the Scottish capital to create unforgettable memories with friends and loved ones as the world-famous Royal Botanic Garden comes alive with breathtaking light installations and sparkling displays to bring festive cheer to everyone. This year's trail will feature new, spectacular installations from international artists, designed to complement the Botanics' landscape. Don't miss Santa along the way!

If you're feeling chilly, then warm yourself up along the trail with seasonal delights from the on-site street food vendors. Toasted marshmallows, anyone? There are surely few things more Christmassy than sipping hot chocolate or mulled wine under the twinkling lights on a December evening!

Organisers advise you to book early to secure the date and time of your choice.

WHEN: November 20, 2025 to December 30, 2025
PRICE: Adults £25.00; Child £18.50 (4-16 years); Family £84.00 (special discounts are available for members)
BOOK AT: www.rbge.org.uk/whats-on/christmas-at-the-botanics-2025/

AGLOW, AUCKLAND PALACE, BISHOP AUCKLAND

It's become a real family tradition at Auckland Palace each year since AGLOW was first launched by the Auckland Project. Each winter, the organisers at the Auckland Project invite you to "step into a winter wonderland as the palace's dazzling light trail once again transforms the skies above Bishop Auckland".

Stretching over 1½ miles, the Bishop Auckland light trail is one of the largest in the country – and this year promises to be bigger, brighter, and more magical than ever before. Visitors are guaranteed Christmas sparkle and incredible illuminations, as well as another spectacular sight to see. It is also home to one of the tallest Christmas trees in the North of England – standing over 98 feet high! So, what are you waiting for? Book your tickets for the Tunnel of Light, the longest outdoor light tunnel in the region, and explore the installations as you go. "Whether it's your first visit or a returning festive tradition, AGLOW is a must-see experience for the whole family," a spokesperson says.

WHEN: November 21, 2025 to December 31, 2025
PRICE: Adult £22.50; Child £15.50; Family £68.50 (peak times)
BOOK AT: www.aucklandproject.org/event/aglow-25/

O come, all ye Carol Singers!

Christmas wouldn't be the same without carols!
Holly Crawford unwraps the origins of some festive
favourites and finds out why we sing them.

WHETHER sung by professional choristers in the sumptuous surroundings of King's College, Cambridge, or enthusiasts in cosy country churches, nothing says Christmas like carols.

But while classics like "Away In A Manger" re-tell part, or all, of the original Christmas story, this hasn't always been the case. ▶

Ancient Origins

Carols are rooted in a tradition that's thousands of years old. Originally, they were created to celebrate all the seasons. The name comes from "caroles", an old French word describing a circle dance with people holding hands and singing.

As harvest passed and winter deepened, further celebrations, including feasts and plays, took place to keep people's spirits up during the dark months.

During the winter, ancient Romans honoured the agricultural god Saturn with holidays and celebrations. They would eat lavish food, give gifts, hang wreaths and light candles – which all sounds rather familiar!

Carols became popular with th rise of Christianity.

St Francis was responsible for the medieval return of the carol.

At Your Service

Following Christianity's spread across Europe, the first carols pertaining to Christmas were written.

When a Roman Bishop included a song entitled "Angels Hymn" in his Christmas service, composers across Europe were quick to follow suit, penning their own carols.

However, these early efforts proved unpopular as they were written in Latin which most ordinary folk could not understand.

By the Middle Ages, carols had fallen from favour, mainly because people lost interest in Christmas.

A Triumphant Return

St Francis of Assisi was instrumental in restoring interest in carols.

He did this by writing nativity plays which included songs in regional languages so everyone could join in.

An early carol written in this way in 1410 was about Mary and Jesus meeting different people in Bethlehem.

Sadly, the title is unknown and only a fragment exists.

Upon reaching English shores, these plays inspired Franciscan friars to write their own which helped preserve this aspect of medieval music.

The concept of collecting carols for posterity was embraced by Shropshire Chaplin John Awdlay, who listed 25 "caroles of Cristemas".

These would have been sung by wassailers who went from house to house, wishing the occupants good health and prosperity for the coming year.

Entertaining Elizabethans

Carols from the first Elizabethan era tended to be only very loosely based on the Christmas story and were entertaining rather than religious.

This meant they tended to be sung in people's homes instead of churches. Canny minstrels would change the words of the carols from area to area to best favour the locals!

Christmas Is Cancelled!

Oliver Cromwell effectively cancelled Christmas by banning all festivities after coming to power.

Puritans considered Christmas celebrations excessive and sinful, preferring to focus on solemn observance.

Soldiers were deployed to enforce the ban – which included singing carols.

Christmas was re-instated when King Charles II, "The Merry Monarch", returned to the throne.

Visitors to Hampton Court enjoing a Tudor celebration.

Puritans treated Christmas Day as a regular work day.

The Tudors

"Carols for the Tudors were mainly religious in theme. At court, would be sung by the Children of the Chapel in specially arranged performances on or around Christmas and New Year's Day," Richard Fitch, historic kitchens manager at Historic Royal Palaces, explains.

Richard organises Christmas music performances at Hampton Court Palace.

"More secular tunes were probably sung by ordinary folk and a tantalising glimpse of what these were like survives in the single page of two carols remaining from Wynkyn De Worde's publication of 'Christmasse Carolles' from 1521, where the famous carol for 'bringing in the boars head' can be found along with a 'carol of hunting'."

Festive celebrations at Hampton Court Palace.

A Bonnie Song

One carol most modern audiences will know, and which is certainly still amongst the most popular, is "O Come, All Ye Faithful".

This carol was composed in the 1740s as "Adeste Fideles", with the lyrics originally written in Latin.

However, it has been suggested that it has a more complex meaning.

"The lyrics, written by John Francis Wade, an eighteenth-century hymnist, have Jacobite references to the restoration to the British throne of Charles Edward Stuart – the exile prince also known as Bonnie Prince Charlie," Professor Bennett Zon from the music department at Durham University suggests.

"While purporting to celebrate the birth of Jesus Christ, the hymns is strewn with references supporting the king, with 'O come, all ye faithful,' really meaning 'Come, faithful Catholics!'"

Meanwhile, "Joyful and triumphant, o come ye, o come ye to Bethlehem", is seen as a rallying cry for joyful and triumphant Jacobites to come to England.

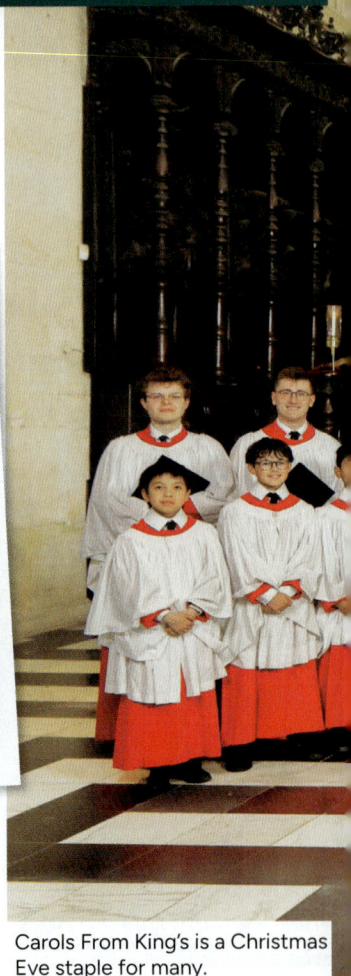
Bonnie Prince Charlie.

Carols From King's is a Christmas Eve staple for many.

Images: Truro Cathedral, Historic Royal Palaces, Leon Hargreaves, Shutterstock, Alamy, stock.adobe.com.

Victorian Celebrations

The Victorians re-vamped carols.

They put new words to old tunes, published collections and embraced singing them.

The carol "Good King Wenceslas" tells the story of a 10th-century duke known for his piety and charity.

The lyrics were penned in 1853 by hymn writer John Manson Neal, who set them to a traditional 13th-century tune.

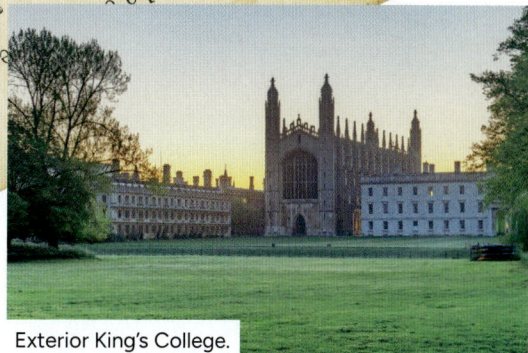

The Victorians revitalised Christmas celebrations.

Exterior King's College.

Carols From King's

As you may have read on pages 52-55, on Christmas Eve, 1918, choristers of King's College, Cambridge gathered to sing A Festival of Nine Lessons and Carols in the ornate surroundings of the chapel – the first time such a service had taken place there.

The idea of holding the service in the Chapel was that of newly appointed Dean of King's College, Eric Milner-White, who wanted to inject more creativity into the Church of England.

Carols from King's was first broadcast on radio in 1928, and on television in 1954.

It airs at 3pm on Christmas Eve starting with "Once In Royal David's City" and it remains a staple of the schedules.

Tradition dictates that the choirmaster chooses the soloist just seconds before the service.

This is done in an attempt to minimise pressure on the youngsters.

Truro Cathedral.

Did You Know?

• "Once In Royal David's City" was written to teach children about the birth of Christ.

• During World War II, the stained-glass windows of King's College, Cambridge were removed to protect them from bombings.

• "Silent Night" was penned in 1818 when an Austrian priest asked the church organist to write a melody for the guitar, probably because the organ was out of commission. It is one of the most frequently recorded Christmas carols.

• On Christmas Eve during the First World War, when the famous Christmas Truce took place between German and English forces, it's said the night was so quiet they could hear each other sing. The Germans sang "Stille Nacht" and encouraged the British to sing back in English.

• Although not a carol, "Rudoph The Red Nosed Reindeer" is a Christmas classic. Creator Robert L. May considered naming him Rollo or Reginald before settling on Rudolph. He was inspired to write the song because his daughter loved reindeer.

Carols From Truro

The Nine Lessons and Carols service actually originated in Truro during the 19th century.

It was devised by the first Bishop of Truro, Edward White Benson, as a more meaningful alternative to the kind of Christmas spirit found in public houses!

The first service was performed in 1880 inside a wooden shed – the temporary home of Truro Cathedral which was under construction at the time.

It was so successful that Anglican churches adopted it around the world.

"At Truro, we are extremely proud to be the origin of Nine Lessons and Carols," James Anderson-Besant, director of music at Truro Cathedral, says.

"Cornwall's culture and heritage are full of music and art. It is fitting that it was here that Benson created his magical concoction of carols and readings for Christmas.

"The cathedral is always packed for our Nine Lessons and Carols services, which continue to this day. The atmosphere in the building is electric.

"I will never forget the feeling of processing to the West End for my first experience of the service, awaiting the start of 'Once In Royal David's City'.

"As custodian of the music here at Truro Cathedral, it feels incredibly meaningful to be continuing this tradition."

Truro Cathedral has a magical atmosphere.

Fabulous
FOOD
FOR ALL

From simple and tasty, to
show-stopping and spectacular,
our stunning recipes are all
you need for your perfect
Christmas feast.

EASIEST-EVER CHRISTMAS DINNER

Take the stress out of your festive meal with these delicious dishes that are simple to put together, but still taste amazing.

Spiced Butternut and Red Pepper Soup

Ingredients (Serves 6)

25 g butter
80 g frozen chopped onion (or 1 large onion, chopped)
½ tsp ground cumin
500 g prepared butternut squash, chopped into chunks
2 vegetable stock cubes, dissolved in 1.2 litres hot water
2 roasted red peppers (from a jar, packed in brine), chopped
150 ml double cream
Fresh parsley sprigs, to garnish
Salt and freshly ground black pepper

1 Melt the butter in a large saucepan and fry the onion gently for 3-4 minutes, until soft but not brown. Stir in the cumin.
2 Add the butternut squash and vegetable stock and cook gently for 20-25 minutes, partially covered, until the squash is tender.
3 Transfer the mixture to a blender or food processor and add the peppers. Blend until smooth. Cool quickly, then freeze.
4 On Christmas Day, return the thawed soup to a saucepan and gently reheat. Stir in 4 tablespoons double cream. Season. Serve each portion topped with a swirl of the remaining cream, freshly ground pepper and a sprig of parsley.

Roast Turkey Crown

Ingredients (Serves 6)

1 turkey crown (choose appropriate size for your requirements)
1.5 kg frozen duck-fat or premium roast potatoes
12 bacon-wrapped cocktail sausages
500 g bag frozen carrot and swede mash
15 g butter
Cranberry sauce, to serve
Freshly ground black pepper

1 Cook the turkey crown according to pack instructions, according to the size chosen. Check that the turkey is properly cooked by inserting a skewer or sharp knife into the thickest part – the juices should run clear. Cook for a little longer if necessary. When cooked, remove from the oven, wrap with foil and leave to rest for 30 minutes (it will be much easier to carve). Keep the juices from the roasting tin to add to the gravy.
2 Meanwhile, increase the oven temperature to 230°C, 210°C fan oven, Gas Mark 8. Spread the potatoes on to a large baking tray and put them in the centre of the oven. Arrange the sausages on a separate baking tray and place above the potatoes. Roast for 25-30 minutes until the potatoes are crisp and golden, turning once.
3 Heat the carrot and swede mash according to pack instructions, then stir in the butter and season with black pepper.
4 Carve the turkey and serve with the potatoes, carrots, sausages and vegetables, with cranberry sauce, stuffing balls and turkey gravy.

Recipes and food styling: Sue Ashworth.
Images: Jonathan Short, stock.adobe.com.

MADE
easy

Sprouts

With Buttered Almonds

Ingredients (Serves 6)

**600 g ready-peeled
sprouts, trimmed
30 g butter
30 g flaked almonds
Salt and freshly
ground black pepper**

1 Put the sprouts into a large saucepan and cover with boiling water. Add a pinch of salt and simmer for 12-15 minutes.
2 Meanwhile, melt the butter in a frying pan and cook the almonds until pale golden brown. Drain the sprouts well and add the almonds and butter, tossing to coat. Serve.

Parsnips

With Honey & Mustard Glaze

Ingredients (Serves 6)

**6 parsnips, quartered
lengthways
2 tbs vegetable oil
1 tbs clear honey
1 tbs wholegrain mustard**

1 Cook the parsnips in lightly salted boiling water for 12-15 minutes, until almost tender. Cool quickly and freeze at this point.
2 On Christmas Day put the frozen parsnips into a roasting pan and add the oil, tossing to coat. Roast in the oven for 25 minutes.
3 Add the honey and mustard to the parsnips and turn them over to coat. Roast for a further 5-10 minutes until golden.

Turkey Gravy

Ingredients (Serves 6)

**2 x 350 ml pouches finest
turkey gravy
Reserved juices from the turkey
joint
Few drops balsamic vinegar
Few drops sherry**

1 Heat the turkey gravy according to pack instructions.
2 Stir in the juices from the roast turkey and add the balsamic vinegar and sherry. Check the seasoning, adding salt and pepper if needed. Serve, piping hot, with the Christmas dinner.

Herb & Lemon Stuffing Balls

Ingredients (Serves 6)

**Finely grated zest of 1 small lemon
1 tbs mixed dried herbs
150 g pork sausagemeat
100 g ready-made fresh white breadcrumbs
Salt and freshly ground black pepper
1 tbs vegetable oil**

1 Mix together the lemon zest, herbs, sausagemeat and breadcrumbs. Season. Form the mixture into 12 balls. Freeze at this point if making ahead.
2 On Christmas Day toss the thawed stuffing balls in the vegetable oil and roast with the sausages for 25-30 minutes, turning after 15 minutes.

Mince Pies With Toasted Marzipan and Orange Brandy

Ingredients (Serves 6)

6 luxury mince pies
100 g golden marzipan, grated
300 ml extra thick cream
2 tsp finely grated orange zest
1 tbs brandy

1 Preheat the oven to 180°C, 160°C fan oven, Gas Mark 4. Put the mince pies on to a baking sheet and heat them for 10 minutes.
2 Share the grated marzipan between the mince pies. Use a cook's blowtorch to lightly brown the marzipan, or brown under the grill for a few moments.
3 Stir the orange zest and brandy into the cream and serve with the warm mince pies.

MADE easy

Boozy Fruit Trifles

Ingredients (Serves 6)

100 g sultanas
100 g raisins
50 g dried cranberries
50 g glacé cherries, quartered
100 ml brandy or rum
12 sponge fingers
150 ml orange juice
2 x 400 g cans ready-made custard
200 ml double cream
Fine shreds of lemon or orange zest, to decorate

1 Several days before Christmas, put the sultanas, raisins, cranberries and glacé cherries into a bowl (not a metal one). Add the brandy or rum and stir well. Cover and refrigerate for up to 2 weeks.
2 To assemble the trifles, break up 2 sponge fingers into each of 6 serving glasses. Pour the orange juice on top, then share the soaked dried fruit mixture between them.
3 Spoon the custard into the glasses. Whip the cream in a chilled bowl until it holds its shape, then top the desserts with it. Decorate with lemon or orange zest and chill until ready to serve.

ALTERNATIVE ROASTS

Ding dong merrily! Ring the changes and serve up a delicious festive roast with a difference for your family gathering.

Recipes and Food Styling: Maxine Clark. Images: Stockfood, Alamy.

Christmas Roast Beef

Ingredients: (Serves 8)

1.8 kg rib of beef on the bone
3 tbs plain flour
Salt
Freshly-ground black pepper
2 tbs vegetable oil
4-5 carrots, quartered
1 red onion, cut into wedges
8 shallots
1 tbs chopped thyme
1 head garlic, divided into cloves

For the Yorkshire puddings:

150 g plain flour
2 large eggs
300 ml milk
3 tbs fat from the roast beef, or use beef dripping or vegetable oil

1 Heat the oven to 220°C, 200°C fan oven, Gas Mark 7.

2 Put the meat in a roasting tin and rub 3 teaspoons flour into the beef. Season with salt and pepper, rubbing the flour well into the flesh and fat.

3 Roast for 15 minutes, then reduce oven temperature to 180°C, 160°C fan oven , Gas Mark 4. Roast the meat for 15-20 minutes per 450 g, plus 20 minutes for rare, 20-25 minutes per 450 g for medium, plus 20 minutes or 25-30 minutes per 450 g for well done, plus 20min.

4 For the Yorkshire pudding batter, put the flour and a pinch of salt in a bowl. Add the eggs, then the milk a little at a time, beating to give a thick, smooth batter. Stir in 150 ml cold water. Cover and leave to one side until required. Toss the vegetables, thyme and garlic in the oil.

5 After about 30 minutes, place the vegetables and garlic around the meat and continue cooking until tender. While the meat is cooking, baste with the juices from time to time.

6 30 minutes before the end of the calculated cooking time, remove meat from the oven and pour off the roasting fat (if available, otherwise use melted beef dripping or vegetable oil) to make the Yorkshire puddings. Return the meat to the oven.

7 At the end of cooking time, remove meat from tin, wrap in foil, cover with tea towel and allow to rest on a serving plate. Transfer the vegetables to a warmed dish.

8 Increase oven temperature to 220°C, 200°C fan oven, Gas Mark 7 and pour 2 teaspoons fat into each of bun tin holes. Place tins at the top of the oven; the fat needs to be very hot before you add batter.

9 Stir batter. Remove tins from the oven, carefully pour in the batter and return to the oven. The puddings will take 20-30 minutes to cook.

10 To make the gravy, stir the remaining flour into the meat juices in the roasting tin and cook over a gentle heat until absorbed and browned. Whisk in 500 ml cold water and simmer until lightly thickened. Add gravy browning if you like your gravy to be dark in colour. Season. Remove the puddings from the oven, uncover the beef, pouring any juices into the gravy. Carve and serve with vegetables, Yorkshire puddings and gravy.

Christmas Roast Pork

Ingredients: (Serves 4)

2.5 kg boneless leg of pork
Salt
2-3 eating apples, cut into wedges
1 small bunch seedless white grapes
Seeds of 1 pomegranate

To garnish:
Sage sprigs

1 Rub the pork skin dry with kitchen paper and then cover with 3 tablespoons of salt, working it into the cuts. Leave at room temperature for at least 30 minutes. The salt removes excess moisture from the skin to ensure crisp, delicious crackling.

2 Preheat the oven to 220°C, 200°C fan oven, Gas Mark 7.

3 Rub off all the salt from the joint and from between the cuts and pat dry.

Lightly cover the rind with 1 teaspoon salt.

4 Put into a roasting tin and cook for 30min per 450 g, plus 35 minutes. After the first 25 minutes, reduce the oven temperature to 180°C, 160°C fan oven, Gas Mark 4.

5 Add the apple wedges to the roasting tin 15 minutes before the end of the cooking time. Remove the pork from the tin to a warmed serving plate, cover with foil and a clean tea towel and leave to rest for 20 minutes.

6 While the pork is resting, add grapes to the apples in the roasting tin and put back in the oven for 10-15 minutes until slightly soft and warmed through.

7 Arrange the roasted fruits and pomegranate seeds around the pork on the serving plate. Garnish with sprigs of sage and serve with potatoes and vegetables as desired.

MADE easy

The Perfect
Gingerbread House

This magical seasonal centrepiece is a joy to create – it's easy with our step-to-step guide – and even more sensational to eat.

MADE easy

Recipes and food styling: Sue Ashworth.
Photography: Jonathan Short.
Images: Shutterstock.

Ingredients
(Makes 1 house)

200 g dark muscovado sugar
250 g butter
7 tbs (150 g) golden syrup
650 g plain flour, plus extra for sprinkling
5 tsp ground ginger
2 tsp bicarbonate of soda
Several sheets of baking paper

Decoration:
1 egg white
250 g icing sugar
250 g pack flower and moulding paste (Renshaw Decor-ice)
Selection of small sweets, silver balls etc.

1 Put the sugar into a large saucepan. Cut the butter into pieces and add to the pan. Measure in the syrup. If you prefer, put the pan on to digital scales, zero them, and weigh in the syrup to exactly the correct amount. Heat gently to melt slowly, stirring occasionally. Do not allow the mixture to boil.

2 Sift the plain flour, ginger and bicarbonate of soda into a large mixing bowl, stirring to mix thoroughly. Pour in the melted mixture and stir together with a wooden spoon to make a stiff dough, using your hand to bring the mixture together. Preheat the oven to 200°C, 180°C fan oven, Gas Mark 6.

3 Put a sheet of baking paper on to a work surface and sprinkle it with a little flour. Take about a quarter of the dough and press it out with your fingertips until it's quite flat (this is easier than rolling, as it helps prevent it from cracking). Now take a lightly floured rolling pin and carefully roll out until about 0.5cm thick.

4 Cut out the first shape for your gingerbread house using a cutter or template. Remove the cutter or template, then slide the section, still on the baking paper, on to a baking sheet. Continue to roll out more of the dough, re-using the trimmings, until you have two side walls, two roof panels and two gable ends. Use trimmings to make a chimney, Christmas trees, snowflakes and stars, if you like.

5 You will need to bake the sections in batches, each for 11-12 minutes, until firm and a little darker around the edges. Before you cook the front gable end, use cutters or templates to remove the door and mark out two windows (these can be removed more easily once this section is baked). After baking, cool all sections on the baking tray for a few minutes before transferring to a wire rack to cool completely.

6 Thinly roll out the moulding paste on a surface dusted with icing sugar. Cut out 4 window frames. Use a small round or heart-shaped cutter to stamp out about 60 roof slates. Leave to harden for 20 minutes. Beat the egg white and icing sugar together to make a thick icing. Place in a piping bag fitted with a medium-sized plain tube. Use the icing to fix the window frames to the side walls and the slates to the roof panels.

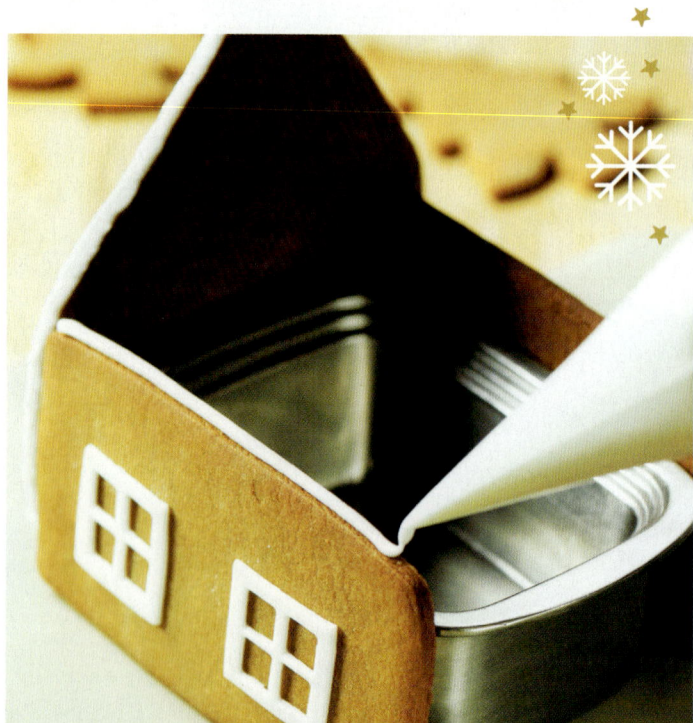

7 Construct the house: pipe icing thickly on to a cake board where each panel will stand. Put the first panel in place. Pipe icing thickly along the wall edge. Fix on the gable end, using a butter dish or bowl to support the pieces until 3 pieces are fixed. Remove the support and fix on the front gable end. Leave for 20 minutes, then fix on roof panels. Leave overnight to dry. Decorate with sweets as in the first picture, fixing in place with icing.

Added extras

Make up a batch of dough with half the quantity of ingredients, then use this to create these wonderfully festive biscuits for hanging from the tree or to fix to the house. Or make Christmas trees that can be used to stand around your gingerbread house!

Tree Decorations

Roll out the dough to about the thickness of two £1 coins. Stamp out cookies with a snowflake cutter, and arrange on a baking sheet lined with baking paper. Bake for 8-10 minutes. Cool, then decorate with small sweets, silver balls and edible glitter. Thread some ribbon or raffia around them for hanging on the tree.

Christmas Trees

Roll out the dough and use a Christmas tree cutter to stamp out shapes. Bake as above. Decorate with royal icing (as used for the house) and fix small sweets and silver balls onto the icing, with a star-shaped sweet at the top. Stand them up in blobs of white moulding paste or ready-to-roll icing. Scatter a little icing sugar on top to look like snow.

5 GOLDEN Rules

1 Be patient. This is not to be rushed! Create over 2-3 days if that suits you.

2 Measure ingredients accurately for failsafe results. This ensures that the gingerbread bakes without expanding.

3 Roll out and cut out each piece on baking paper – then slide onto baking trays. If necessary, trim baked pieces with a sharp knife for straight edges.

4 Get a helping hand when constructing the house. Make sure the icing "cement" is thick enough, and hold walls together for 2-3 minutes to set, before adding the roof.

5 Decorate as you wish – that's the fun part! Be as lavish as you like.

FESTIVE CHRISTMAS PANCAKES

These delicious variations on festive pancakes makes super treats for all the family.

MADE easy

Christmas Tree Pancakes

Ingredients (Makes 4)

150 g plain flour
Pinch of salt
2 eggs
350 ml milk
2 tbs unsweetened cocoa powder
A few drops of vegetable oil

To decorate:
Fresh fruit, such as peach, mango, blueberries or pomegranate seeds
Strawberry flavoured syrup or golden syrup

1 Put the flour, salt, eggs and milk into a mixing bowl and whisk together to make a smooth batter. Pour about one quarter of this batter into a separate bowl and beat in the cocoa powder to make chocolate batter.
2 Put the chocolate batter into a squeezy bottle (you could use a rinsed-out washing up bottle for this). Heat a non-stick frying pan and add a few drops of vegetable oil. Remove from the heat. Using the squeezy bottle, carefully "draw" a Christmas tree shape. Heat gently until just set.
3 Ladle plain batter over the surface of the "tree". Cook lightly until the batter just sets on the surface, then flip the pancake over to cook the other side. Make four pancakes like this, keeping them in a warm place as you make them.
4 Decorate the pancakes with fresh fruit, then serve drizzled with syrup.

Recipes and food styling: Sue Ashworth. Images: Jonathan Short.

Smoked Salmon Stars

Ingredients (Serves 6)

110 g self-raising flour
Pinch of salt
1 large egg
4 tbs low-fat natural
   yoghurt
100 ml milk
Few drops of
   vegetable oil
200 g medium-fat
   soft cheese
100 g smoked salmon,
   cut into strips
Dill sprigs and lemon
   slices, to garnish

1 Put the flour, salt, egg, yoghurt and milk into a mixing bowl and whisk together to make a smooth, thick batter.
2 Heat the vegetable oil in a non-stick frying pan and add tablespoons of the batter to make 12 drop scones, cooking them in batches until the batter is used up.
3 Cool the drop scones, then use a star-shaped cutter to stamp out star shapes from them.
4 Top each star with a dollop of soft cheese (or pipe it if you prefer), then arrange smoked salmon on top. Garnish with dill sprigs and serve with lemon slices.

Peach and Amaretto Pancakes

Ingredients (Makes 4)

3 peaches, pitted and sliced
50 g caster sugar
4 tbs Amaretto liqueur
Finely shredded zest and juice of 1 orange
110 g plain flour
Pinch of salt
1 large egg
200 ml milk
A few drops of vegetable oil
Whipped cream, toasted flaked almonds and icing
    sugar, to decorate

1 Put the peach slices into a shallow pan with
the sugar, liqueur, orange zest, orange juice and
2 tablespoons of water. Simmer gently for
4-5 minutes until tender.
2 Meanwhile, make the pancakes. Put the flour, salt,
egg and milk into a mixing bowl and whisk together
to make a smooth batter.
3 Heat a few drops of vegetable oil in a pancake pan.
Pour in a quarter of the batter, cook over a medium
heat until set, then flip over to cook the other side.
Cook 4 pancakes, keeping them covered in a warm
place (such as a low oven) until they are all cooked.
4 Serve the pancakes and peaches with whipped
cream, scattered with a few flaked almonds and add
icing sugar.

Christmas Pancake Brunch

Ingredients (Makes 4)

110 g self-raising flour
Pinch of salt
1 large egg
4 tbs low-fat natural yoghurt
100 ml milk
Few drops of vegetable oil
8 rashers streaky bacon
100 g Danish blue or Stilton cheese
100 g medium-fat soft cheese
2 tbs chopped fresh chives, plus extra to garnish
4 tomatoes, sliced
2 ripe avocados, pitted and sliced
Freshly ground black pepper

1 Put the flour, salt, egg, yoghurt and milk into a
mixing bowl and whisk together to make a smooth,
thick batter.
2 Heat the vegetable oil in a non-stick frying pan
and add tablespoons of the batter to make 8 drop
scones, cooking them in batches until the batter is
used up.
3 Grill the bacon until crisp. While it's cooking, mash
the blue cheese with a fork and mix it with the soft
cheese and chives.
4 Serve the pancakes with the tomatoes, avocados
and crispy bacon, with the blue cheese mixture on
the side. Sprinkle with black pepper and garnish
with chives.

Festive Waffle Bites

Ingredients (Serves 4-6)

125 g plain flour
½ tsp bicarbonate of soda
½ tsp salt
230 ml buttermilk
1 egg
A few drops of vegetable oil
80 g medium-fat soft cheese
80 g mature Cheddar, finely grated
1 fig, sliced into 8
100 g red pepper houmous
A few cucumber slices
30 g roasted peppers, from a jar
Herb sprigs, to garnish

1 Sift the flour, bicarbonate of soda and salt into a large bowl. Add the buttermilk and egg and beat with a whisk to make a smooth batter. Leave to stand for 20 minutes.

2 Brush a waffle pan or waffle iron with vegetable oil. Add about 2tbsp batter to each waffle section and cook for 1-2 minutes until the underneath is golden brown. Turn over to cook the other side. Repeat to make 4 waffles. Cool.

3 Cut each waffle into 4. Mix the soft cheese and Cheddar together and use to top half the waffle pieces, placing a piece of fig on top.

4 Top the rest of the waffles with houmous, cucumber slices and strips of roasted red pepper. Garnish with herb sprigs, then serve.

MADE easy

DELICIOUS DESSERTS

Fancy something lighter than pudding and posher than trifle? Try one of these indulgent puds – or all three!

MADE easy

Cranberry-Cinammon Ice Cream

Ingredients: (Serves 8)

225 g caster sugar
350 ml whipping cream
2 medium eggs, beaten
250 ml double cream
1½ tsp vanilla extract
1½ tsp ground cinnamon
250 g cranberries, washed
150 g redcurrants, washed
2 tbs pink dragée balls, to garnish

CAN BE FROZEN

1 Stir together the sugar and whipping cream in a saucepan set over a medium heat. When the mixture begins to simmer, remove it from the heat, and gradually but quickly whisk half into the beaten eggs in a heatproof bowl.
2 Pour the mixture back into the pan, and whisk in double cream. Continue to cook over a slightly reduced heat, stirring constantly, until thick enough to coat the back of a spoon. Remove from heat and whisk in vanilla and cinnamon. Set the saucepan in a bowl of iced water, giving it a stir occasionally.
3 As the custard cools, combine 100 g of the cranberries with 50 ml water in a saucepan. Cook over a medium heat, stirring occasionally, until soft and bursting. Crush the cranberries with a spoon and strain off any excess liquid. Stir the crushed cranberries into the cooling custard.
4 Once the custard is cool, churn in an ice cream machine according to the manufacturer's instructions. Alternatively, place in the freezer to set, stirring occasionally to break up any ice crystals. Once set and ready, spoon the ice cream into a 20 cm x 15 cm x 5 cm rectangular baking dish lined with cling film. Use a spatula to spread flat in the dish. Cover with cling film and freeze for at least 2 hours.
5 When ready to serve, let the ice cream stand at room temperature for 5-10 minutes to soften. Turn out from the dish and garnish with the remaining cranberries, redcurrants and dragée balls.

CANNOT
BE FROZEN

Red Fruit Jewels

Ingredients: (Serves 4)

For the red fruit puddings:
275 g raspberries, washed
150 g strawberries, hulled
600 ml cranberry juice
**5 sheets of gelatine, soaked in
  cold water**

For the sauce and garnish:
100 g white chocolate, chopped
2 tbs double cream
1 tbs unsalted butter
4 coated chocolate rings

1 For the fruit puddings: Combine
the fruit and cranberry juice in a
large saucepan. Cook over a
moderate heat until simmering.
2 Once fruit is soft and easy to
crush with a spoon, put into a food
processor. Blend for 30 seconds
and strain through a fine sieve into
a clean saucepan.
3 Warm the juice until simmering.
Squeeze the sheets of gelatine dry
and whisk into the simmering juice
until dissolved. Divide the liquid
between four serving glasses and
leave to cool to room temperature.
4 Cover and chill until set, at least
2 hours.
5 For the sauce: When the jellies are
set, prepare the sauce by combining
the chocolate, cream and butter in a
heatproof bowl set atop a half-filled
saucepan of simmering water. Stir
until melted and smooth.
6 Remove the bowl from the
saucepan and leave sauce to cool
and thicken. Spoon on top of jellies
and garnish with chocolate rings.

MADE **easy**

CAN BE FROZEN

Christmas Caramel with Almond Cream

Ingredients (Serves 4-6)

For the almond cream:
1 tsp almond extract
200 g almond nougat, chopped
500 ml double cream

For the caramel:
150 g caster sugar
110 ml double cream
2 tbs butter
2 Gala apples, cored and sliced
75g flaked almonds, toasted, to garnish

1 For the almond cream: Grease and line a 900 g loaf tin with a double layer of cling film. Combine the almond extract, chopped nougat and 250 ml of the cream in a saucepan. Cook over a medium heat, stirring frequently, until the nougat has melted. Set aside to cool.
2 Whip the remaining cream until softly peaked. Whisk one-third into the nougat cream, and then fold in the remainder, working quickly but thoroughly. Spoon the mixture into the lined loaf tin. Cover and freeze overnight.

3 For the caramel: Combine the sugar, cream and butter in a saucepan. Cook over a medium heat until the sugar has dissolved. Simmer for 4-5 minutes until thickened, stirring occasionally. Add the apples and continue to cook until softened. Set aside to cool.
4 To serve: Remove the almond cream dessert from the freezer. Leave to stand for 10 minutes and then turn out and cut into slices. Serve on plates with the caramel apple sauce, garnished with toasted flaked almonds.

Visit us at...
thepeoplesfriend.co.uk

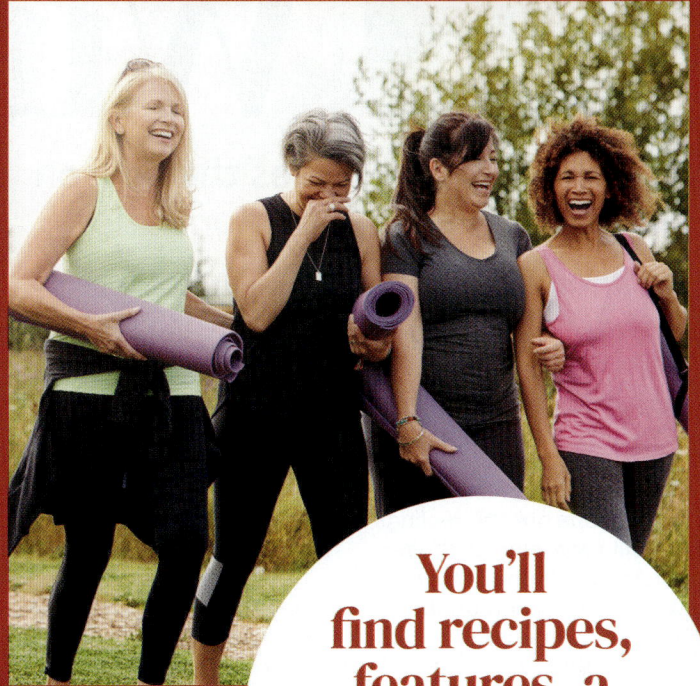

You'll find recipes, features, a daily serial and great subscription offers

f @PeoplesFriendMagazine

X @TheFriendMag

P ThePeoplesFriend

> A perfectly ice dipped branch hangs over the burn.

There is an old Japanese proverb – "One kind word can warm three winter months." It makes me think that during winter it becomes even more important to look after those less fortunate, particularly those who live alone and are incapacitated, and may find the season long and dark. And if they are unable to get out and about, we can share in words the beauty we have experienced.

In Praise of Winter

Polly Pullar celebrates the season of renewal and transformation.

WINTER is a season of quietude, of slowing down and stopping, a time for creativity.

The nights are long, but then there is a chance to read – gone are the feelings of guilt regarding all those outside tasks you feel you ought to be doing during the rest of the year. It's quite legitimate to sit by a fire and to put your thoughts in order.

It's a season for checking up on those who live alone, and particularly during harsh weather, to ensure they are managing. Often a visit can make all the difference.

From nature's point of view, winter is a time of renewal and transformation, just as it is for us. I have written often about the joy of bright, crisp days with snow or hoar frost, and of rushing out with my camera to see if I can capture the extraordinary beauty.

Winters are changing and snow is becoming a rare occurrence. So often it is short-lived.

Sun makes the scene dramatic, but then begins to melt away the beauty. Wet, heavy snow and slush make it far harder to get about and often cause chaos.

Often the best pictures are those I find right on our doorstep, but usually time is of the essence and there is no chance to wait until later.

Now is the moment to look at the little things and to see how a single frozen raindrop can bring an ethereal quality to a forgotten berry or seed, or how hoar frost etches a bare tree with silver.

Ice creates dramatic patterns and the little burn through our garden becomes a fascinating spot for closer study.

When it is frozen hard and there has been a sprinkle of snow on top, I might even find otter tracks with the telltale drag mark of the tail. Red squirrels leave their tracks too, and once I found those of a pine marten.

I love to go out early by myself, just for a few minutes. I go without the dogs, for then I can see the unspoilt tracks in the drive before they run up and down in excitement – for they love snow too.

There are many beautiful quotes regarding winter, and I am including a few here. I hope they may inspire you to write some of your own.

Snow begins to melt on swaying alder catkins.

"In seed time learn, in harvest teach, in winter enjoy."
William Blake

◄ This is one of my favourite trees. Close to our home, it sits high on the hillside above. Every year it becomes more gnarled but still produces large crops of berries. Too often the hawthorn is overlooked, but it is a valuable tree providing a rich food source, including gloriously scented blossom in spring.

▲ "Smoke" on the water at Wade's Bridge in Aberfeldy. As the temperature rises, steam swirling off the River Tay coupled with snow and hoar frost made this scene quite otherworldly.

▲ Hawthorn berries are an important food source for numerous species, from birds to red squirrels, foxes and badgers.

"Let us love winter, for it is the spring of genius."
Pietro Aretino

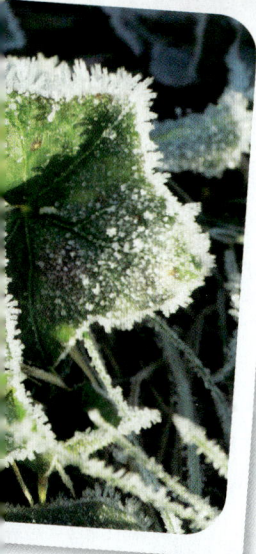

◄ Though ivy can spread madly around a garden, it's not only astonishingly beautiful, especially when etched in frost, but also it is one of the latest flowering plants and provides a rich source of nectar for bees and other pollinators.

▲ Hair ice is a particularly lovely and unusual phenomenon. Also sometimes called ice wool or ice beard, it forms on dead wood and is created as the wood oozes moisture in temperatures just below freezing when the weather is humid. A piece of wood that produces hair ice once is likely to produce it again, so it is worth looking out for this magic creation.

▲ View down the Tay valley towards the Glen Lyon Hills. A small snow-covered thorn bush becomes a thing of ultimate beauty.

"December has the clarity, the simplicity, and the silence you need for the best fresh start of your life."

Vivian White

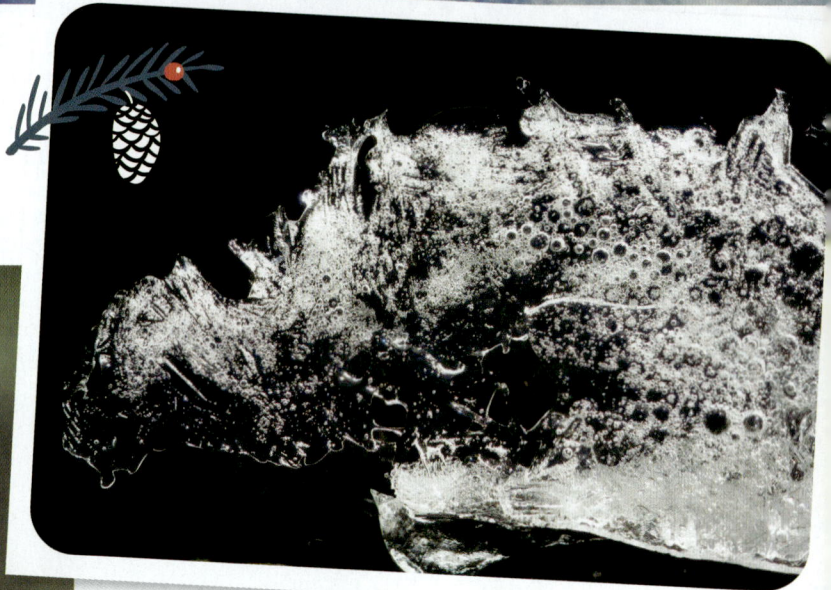

▲ I loved these patterns created by ice on the burn. Nature is perfection.

▲ Backlit and snow coated, a dried leaf undergoes a dramatic transformation.

"To appreciate the beauty of a snowflake, it is necessary to stand out in the cold."
Aristotle

➤ The dampness of the moss below has helped to create ice crystals on blonde grass stalks.

"Winter is a glorious spectacle of glittering fractals complete with a soundscape and atmosphere entirely its own."
Anders Swanson

What's In A Name?

• Christmas Cove, the US Virgin Islands. Legend has it that Christopher Columbus spent Christmas Day in the cove while sheltering from a storm, hence its name.

• Santa Claus in Indiana was originally called Santa Fi. However, the town's application for a post office was rejected because the name was already in use. A town meeting was called on Christmas Eve to pick a new one. During the session, a gust of wind blew the hall doors open, and the children excitedly exclaimed, "Santa Claus!"

• In 2005, the town of Santa, Idaho changed its name to SecretSanta.com for a year. This was part of a deal with an online gift company whereby the town received money in exchange for promoting the website.

• Carmarthenshire in Wales has a small village called Bethlehem. Its original name was Dyffryn Ceidrich but was changed by a nonconformist religious movement.

• No specific place in Wales is called Christmas. However, the Welsh word for Christmas is *Nadolig* and several places incorporate the word, including Pant Nadolig and Castell-nadolig.

• North Pole, Alaska has an official Santa who – aside from greeting visitors – conducts voluntary work to help underprivileged children across the world.

A Place Called
Christmas

Wizzard sang, "I wish it could be Christmas every day" but for the millions of people living in places inspired by the festive season, that's the case!

North Pole, Alaska

Since 1952, Santa Claus House in North Pole, Alaska has welcomed millions of visitors from across the globe to the place "where it's Christmas every day".

They can greet Santa's reindeers at the Antler Academy of Flying and Reindeer Games, send postcards with a special "Santa Claus, AK" postmark, see the toy workshop and pose with Santa all-year round, resulting in some sensational summer snaps!

The shop was originally a general store founded in 1952 by Nellie and Con Miller. During its construction, a child asked if they were building a new house for Santa, and the name stuck!

It is still run by the same family.

"It's a privilege to put smiles on the faces of millions of children all over the world, and know that our business has been doing so for over seventy years," operation manager Paul Brown says.

"We're now in the third and fourth generations of the family business and hopefully continue to bring Christmas cheer for visitors of all ages for the next seventy-five years."

Why the name North Pole? That was chosen by estate developers hoping to attract toy manufacturers to the area who could advertise products "Made In The North Pole".

While the endeavour failed to take off, their efforts were not in vain.

The name put the town on the map, leading to a thriving tourist attraction. It even has a 42-foot fibreglass Father Christmas – the largest in the world!

Christmas, Michigan

Christmas in Michigan got its name from a roadside factory which opened in 1938 producing Christmas-themed gifts. Today, the town makes the most of its festive connotations with themed shops and attractions. Even the casino has a Santa statue!

In 1966, the first Christmas stamp to feature religious symbolism was issued in Christmas, Michigan. It featured the painting "Madonna and Child with Angels" by Hans Memling.

It made history as it was the first time the US Postal Service had used Christian imagery on a Christmas stamp.

❯ Festive Names

England boasts festive names including Christmas Pie Wood in Kent, named after a prominent Tudor family called Christmas. The Saxon word *pightle* describes a small piece of arable land.

Christmas Island

Legend has it that Christmas Island (also known as Kiritimati Atoll Island) in the Pacific Ocean was named by Captain James Cook who spotted it on Christmas Day 1777 – although accounts vary.

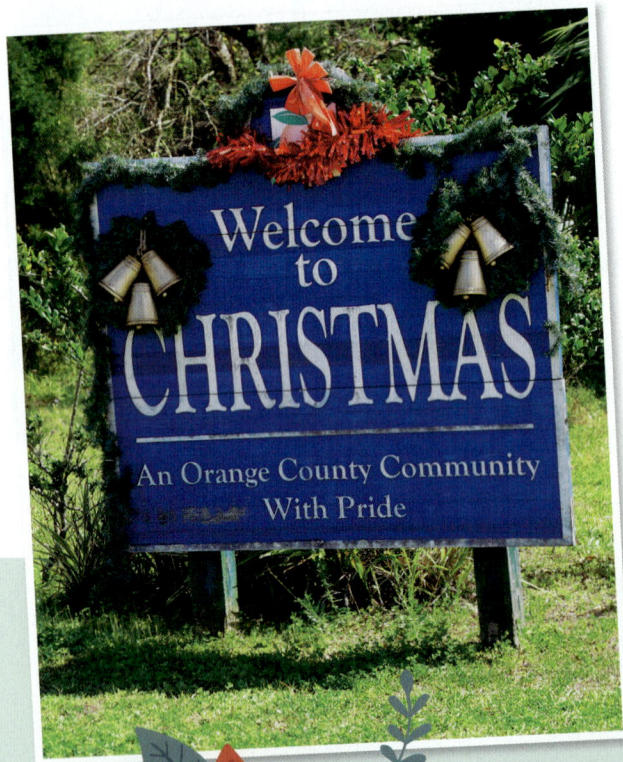

Cold Christmas, Hertfordshire

The legend of Cold Christmas is a sad one. The story goes that a terrible cold snap around Christmas time in 1802 took the lives of many children who are buried in a mass grave in the churchyard.

A Place Called Christmas

You won't find much snow in sun-soaked Florida, but you will find a place called Christmas. A 35-foot Christmas tree, nativity scene, Santa statue and decorations are on display 365 days a year. Even the streets are named after Father Christmas's reindeer!

The post office handles hundreds of letters sent to and from Santa throughout the year. The workload quadruples over the festive season, with thousands of Christmas cards sent daily. Even the postmark changes to "Christmas, Fl" during that period.

The town takes its name from a fort built by soldiers on Christmas Day, 1837, during the Seminole Wars.

North Pole, New York

Santa's Workshop, North Pole, NY inspired one of the biggest theme parks in the United States, and it all started with a story.

Lake Placid businessman Julian Reiss would entertain his daughter with tales of a baby bear who discovered Santa and his workshop. She longed to visit this magical place and her father endeavoured to make this "permanently frozen" North Pole a reality.

The theme park opened its doors in 1949 and immediately captured the imagination of visitors who could enjoy shows and a festive market, much like today.

The Christmas village was so authentic that Walt Disney sent his engineers to get inspiration for Disneyland!

It remains one of the oldest continuously running theme parks in the USA.

WELCOME TO
Bethlehem
PENNSYLVANIA

Bethlehem, Pennsylvania

Some 5,780 away from Bethlehem in Palestine is Bethlehem, Pennsylvania. The latter was christened by Bishop Nicolaus Zinzendorf during a Christmas Eve service in 1741.

It was the first city in the US to decorate a Christmas tree. Known as "Christmas City USA", preparations start in October when every street is decorated with a tree. Its epic Christkindlmarkt runs for five weeks.

Christmas Island, Australia

Christmas Island in Australia was christened by Captain William Mynors of the British East India Company.

He sighted it on December 25, 1643 while exploring the area and decided to name it in honour of the day of Christ's birth.

Easter Island was named under similar circumstances, when Dutch explorer Jacob Roggeveen saw it on April 5, 1722. He called it Paaseiland which translates to Easter Island in Dutch.

Christmas and Easter Island are thousands of miles apart, located in the Indian Ocean and Pacific Ocean respectively.

A Festive Feel

PLACE NAMES ASSOCIATED WITH CHRISTMAS

- Nazareth, Pennsylvania
- Bethlehem, Pennsylvania
- Rudolph, Wisconsin
- Santa Claus, Indiana
- Santa Claus, Arizona
- Dasher, Georgia
- Holly Springs, Mississippi
- Snowflake, Arizona
- Rudolph Street, Mansfield
- Christmas Common, Oxfordshire
- Christmas Hill, Warwickshire
- St Nicolas Drive, Scotland
- Hollybush, Scotland
- St Mary's Drive, Scotland
- Mistletoe Street, Durham

A special time of year for young Angela . . .

Angela Finlayson recalls the delights of a 1970s childhood Christmas . . .

Fun, Festivities & FIREWORKS

ISN'T it funny how memory works? You can have forgotten about something for years, but all it takes is one small reminder and the recollections come flooding back . . .

I was browsing a shop's post-Christmas sale when I saw it: a small orange and navy blue box emblazoned with the words Indoor Table Fireworks.

Suddenly, I was spinning back through the years to my childhood in the 1970s, when indoor fireworks just like these were a highlight of my family's festive celebrations.

Every year, a long, thin oblong box would be produced in the gap between main course and pudding.

We three children would watch, awestruck and a little afraid, as Dad lit the little fountains, snakes and torches with his cigarette lighter before we all sat well back to enjoy the show.

No matter that it was often more damp squib than firework, or that the acrid smell of sulphur made us cough.

What could be more thrilling than setting off fireworks indoors?

As for the miniature sparklers we were

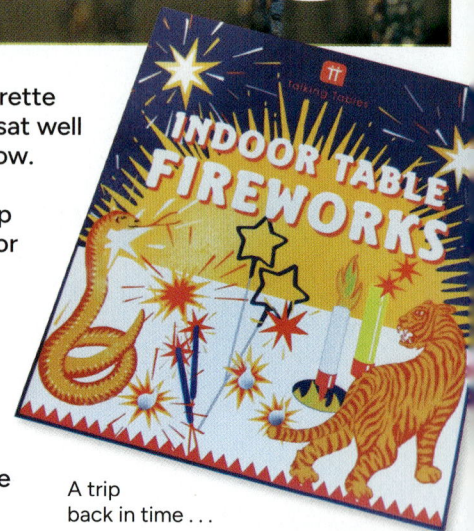

A trip back in time . . .

handed to wave around as they fizzed and burned – the excitement was almost too much.

The 1970s, for those too young to remember, was a time before domestic smoke alarms were a common feature in the home!

The table fireworks might have been the culmination of the festivities, but there were plenty of other sources of excitement for children celebrating Christmas in the 1970s.

Back then, the festive season didn't last for months.

In our house, Christmas preparations never started until after my sister's birthday at the beginning of December, but really, nobody thought about making plans until the very end of November.

Christmas trees were saved for even later, going up just a week or so before the big day.

The sense of anticipation and excitement was at fever pitch by the time the 25th rolled round.

Themed and colour co-ordinated trees were unheard of.

We threw everything at our faithful artificial tree, which was resurrected every year from its box in the basement looking a little more squashed and threadbare than before.

No matter – by the time we kids had draped tinsel and paperchains and hung baubles, stars and chocolate

A trip to Santa's grotto was a highlight.

Santas from every available branch, no more than the merest glimpse of green plastic could be seen.

Every year, Mum told the story of how, when she and Dad were first married, she bought expensive and elaborate chocolate decorations made to look like miniature pirates, musicians and courtiers for the tree in her new home.

She was aghast the next morning to find their little foil costumes and tiny feathered hats in the bin. Our sweet-toothed Dad had scoffed them all in one go!

No childhood Christmas in the 1970s was complete without a visit to Santa.

As we lived in Edinburgh, we always went to Goldbergs, a big department store near Tollcross.

We'd queue up for ages before finally getting a few precious moments with the great man himself to whisper our hearts' desires.

Presents

The trusty old hostess trolley.

when I was a child tended to be quite practical in nature.

There were always toys, but often your main present was a new winter coat or, on one memorable occasion, a home-made dressing table for my bedroom.

I was thrilled with it – it felt like the most wonderfully grown-up, sophisticated gift ever.

I'm not sure many modern children would be quite so happy to receive a piece of furniture, but those were simpler times and families couldn't always afford to spend lots of money on toys when so many other things were needed.

Every year, though, my favourite present of all was my stocking.

I can still remember that feeling of anticipation when I half-woke in the night and felt its weight at the bottom of my bed.

In our family, there was a strict rule that you had to wait until everyone had

eaten breakfast before any presents were opened.

But stockings were the exception. It was perfectly OK to open your stocking in your bedroom as soon as you woke up.

I'd dig down to the toe and eat both the tangerine and the chocolate coin I found there before I even got out of bed.

Christmas dinner was usually served in the early afternoon, and it was hosted at our house, with other family members joining us for the meal. Mum's hostess trolley would be wheeled in, and Dad would preside over the electric carving knife.

As it was such a special occasion, the coal fire would be lit in the "good" room, which was only used for visitors, and Nat King Cole's Christmas album would be playing softly on the stereo in the corner.

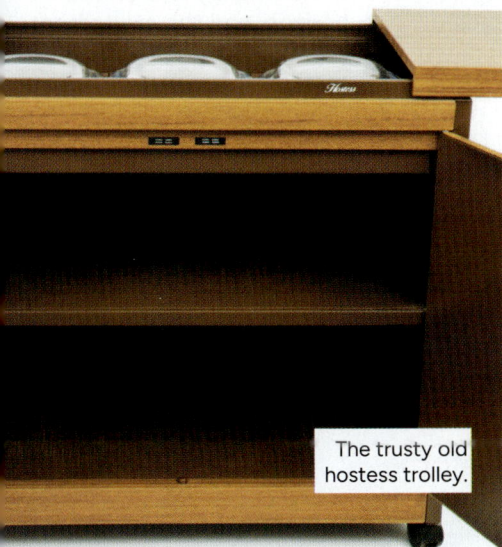

Christmas staples – "The Wizard of Oz" and, left, Morcambe and Wise.

every possible drop of enjoyment out of them.

For the whole of December, we pored over the bumper edition of the "Radio Times", circling in pen all the programmes we wanted to see.

Dad loved Morecambe and Wise, but for us, the highlight was the Christmas Day film. With no videos or DVDs, watching a movie that had never been on TV before was a massive treat. "The Wizard Of Oz", "Chitty Chitty Bang Bang" and "The Sound Of Music" were amongst our favourites.

We also loved the Christmas Specials of all our favourite shows like "The Generation Game" and "Celebrity Squares".

There was always a big tub of Quality Street to share, and a bowl of nuts, a special Christmas treat.

Cracking them with the big wooden-handled nutcrackers caused much hilarity as pieces of shell

shot across the floor in all directions, leaving very little nut to show for your efforts.

Eventually, after far too much food and excitement for one day, we were shepherded upstairs to bed.

I don't remember there ever being a sense of anti-climax that the big day was over, as we knew we had a whole week of festivities to look forward to in the run-up to New Year's Day.

Christmas Day was just the start of the festive season in the 1970s, certainly in Scotland, and in our house, Boxing Day was devoted to playing with all your new presents.

Subsequent days might feature visits to friends and family, or even a trip to the cinema.

Then, before we knew it, Hogmanay was on the horizon, and the excitement levels ramped up once more!

We kids, though, were only interested in one visitor – our uncle. Much younger than our dad, and without any children of his own, he was quite simply the most fun adult that we knew.

And he brought us such brilliant presents – even though the grown-up me can see how completely unsuitable they often were.

One memorable year, my sister, brother and I received a joint gift – a fully operational CB radio.

Our uncle spent the whole day getting it working for us, but it "broke" very soon after Christmas, never to be resurrected.

Little wonder, really, as the oldest of us was only twelve at the time!

After the meal and the presents, the next highlight was the TV.

We had three channels in the 1970s, but we wrung

12 CRAFTS
of Christmas

We all have to buy gifts and decorations, but nothing says you care more than the personal touch that comes from making your own. We hope you enjoy these lovely, creative projects.

TREATS For All

These dainty cones are perfect for filling with tasty goodies or little gifts.

You Will Need
(for four cones)

- Two 20.5 cm (8 in) diameter circles, one in pattern 1 and one in pattern 2 (use a dinner plate to draw circles)
- Four 25.5 cm (10 in) lengths of 5 mm (¼ in) wide ribbon
- 8 small buttons
- Coordinating sewing thread

Tools

- Iron
- Fabric scissors
- Pins
- Sewing machine
- Spray starch (optional)

Size

Approx. 6.25 x 10 cm (2½ x 4 in).

To Make

Note: If your fabric is a little too lightweight to hold its shape, use spray starch to add stability. Iron your fabrics to make sure they are smooth.

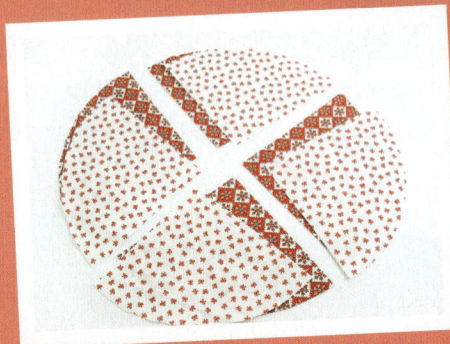

1. Cut the circles of fabric in half, then in half again to make quarters.

2. Take one quarter and pin a ribbon strip, facing inwards, 4 cm (1½in) in from each side of the curve.

3. Tack the ribbon ends in place and remove the pins.

4. Place a contrasting piece of fabric over the top, right sides together. Pin in place, and sew across the curved edge.

5. Open out joined piece of fabric and refold, with the right sides facing inward to create an elongated diamond shape. Pin straight sides together, then sew, leaving a gap of 5 cm (2 in) on fabric that will sit on the inside of your cone.

6. Trim the seam allowances at the points. Turn the right way out and stitch the gap in the lining closed. Push the lining of the cone inside the outer fabric.

7. Carefully press around the top of the cone, to leave a small band of the lining showing. Add a button at each end of the hanging ribbon for decoration.

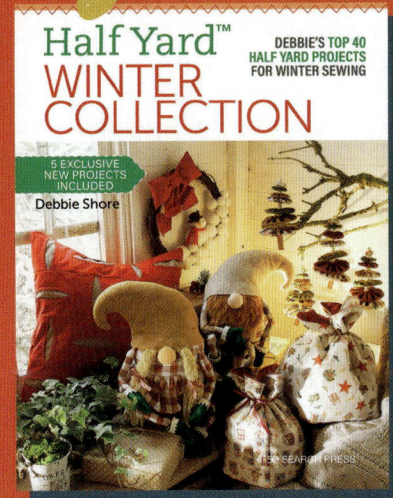

This festive design is taken from the book "Half Yard Winter Collection" by Debbie Shore, published by Search Press, ISBN: 9781782219293, RRP £14.99. It is available online and from all good bookshops or you can order direct from **www.searchpress.com** or telephone **01892 510850.**

Half Yard™
WINTER COLLECTION
DEBBIE'S TOP 40 HALF YARD PROJECTS FOR WINTER SEWING
5 EXCLUSIVE NEW PROJECTS INCLUDED
Debbie Shore

PICK A Poinsettia

The traditional seasonal flower is worked in crochet and given a fun look.

Skill Level : EASY

MATERIALS

Of **Drops Nord 4-ply**, 1 x 50 g ball in Red (14) **A** and Forest Green (19) **B**;
of **Stylecraft Special DK**, 1 x 100 g ball in Walnut (1054) **C** (small amount needed); lengths of Black and Yellow yarn;
2 x 4 mm safety eyes; 3 mm crochet hook; small bag of rice or lentils; polyester stuffing; chenille wire; floristry wire; small plant pot.
Drops Nord yarn can be ordered direct from **www. woolwarehouse.co.uk** or call **0800 505 3300.** For Stylecraft yarn stockists call **01484 848435** or e-mail **info@stylecraftltd.co.uk.**

ABBREVIATIONS

Ch(s) – chain(s); **dc** – double crochet; **dc2inc** – double crochet increase; **dc2tog** – double crochet 2 together; **rnd(s)** – round(s); **sl** – slip stitch; **st(s)** – stitch(es).
Size: Flower head is approx. 13 cm (5¼ in).

TO MAKE

PETALS (make 5) – With 3 mm hook and A, make a magic ring.
1st rnd – 1 ch, 4 dc into the centre of the ring.
2nd rnd – [Dc2inc] 4 times – 8 sts.
3rd rnd – [3 dc, dc2inc] twice – 10 sts.
4th rnd – [4 dc, dc2inc] twice – 12 sts.
5th rnd – [5 dc, dc2inc] twice – 14 sts.
6th rnd – [6 dc, dc2inc] twice – 16 sts.
7th rnd – [7 dc, dc2inc] twice – 18 sts.
8th - 13th rnds – Work 6 rounds straight.
14th rnd – [1 dc, dc2tog] 6 times – 12 sts.
15th rnd – [Dc2tog] 6 times – 6 sts.
Fasten off and leave a tail of yarn.

FLOWER FACE – With 3 mm hook and A, make a magic ring.
1st rnd – 1 ch, 6 dc into the centre of the ring, join with a sl st.
2nd rnd – [Dc2inc] 6 times – 12 sts.
3rd rnd – [1 dc, dc2inc] 6 times – 18 sts.
4th rnd – Work 1 round straight.
5th rnd – [1 dc, dc2tog] 6 times – 12 sts.
Remove the loop from the hook and place on a safety pin. Using the photograph as a guide, position the safety eyes. Use a strand of black yarn to embroider the mouth. Use a strand of yellow yarn to sew a few running stitches around the edge of the face. Fasten off and leave a tail of yarn.

FLOWER BACK – With 3 mm hook and B, make a magic ring. Work as 1st - 3rd rnds of flower face. Fasten off and leave a tail of yarn.

STEM – With 3 mm hook and B, ch 4 sts, sl st in first ch to create a loop.
1st rnd – 1 ch, 4 dc into the centre of the loop.
2nd - 16th rnds – Work 15 rnds straight.
Fasten off and leave a tail of yarn.

LEAF (make 2) – With 3 mm hook and B, make a magic ring.
1st rnd – 1 ch, 4 dc into the centre of the ring.
2nd rnd – [Dc2inc] 4 times – 8 sts.
3rd rnd – [3 dc, dc2inc] twice – 10 sts.
4th rnd – [4 dc, dc2inc] twice – 12 sts..
5th rnd – [5 dc, dc2inc] twice – 14 sts.
6th - 14th rnds – Work 9 rows straight.
15th row – [5 dc, dc2tog] twice – 12 sts.
16th & 17th rnds – Work 2 rounds straight.
18th rnd – [Dc2tog] 6 times – 6 sts.
Fasten off and leave a tail of yarn.

SOIL – With 3.5 mm hook and C, make a magic ring.
1st rnd – 1 ch, 4 dc into the centre of the ring.
2nd rnd – 2 dc into each st – 12 sts.
3rd rnd – [1 dc, dc2inc] 6 times – 18 sts.
4th rnd – [2 dc, dc2inc] 6 times – 24 sts.
5th rnd – [3 dc, dc2inc] 6 times – 30 sts.
6th rnd – [4 dc, dc2inc] 6 times – 36 sts.
7th - 11th rnds – Work 5 rows straight.
12th rnd – [4 dc, dc2inc] 6 times – 30 sts.
13th rnd – [3 dc, dc2inc] 6 times – 24 sts.
14th rnd – [2 dc, dc2inc] 6 times – 18 sts.
Place a small bag of rice or lentils in the base and then stuff firmly with polyester stuffing.
15th rnd – [1 dc, dc2inc] 6 times – 12 sts.
16th rnd – [Dc2tog] 6 times – 6 sts.
Using a tapestry needle, weave this yarn through the last dc sts of the round and gather the hole together. Fasten off and weave in ends.

To Make Up – Fold each petal in half and press it flat with your hand. Arrange the five petals to form a star and, using the tails of yarn, sew the end rows together to form a flat star.
Sew the flower face to the middle of the petals.
Fold a chenille wire in half and feed this through the middle of the flower stem. Position the stem so that it meets the centre back of the flower (see opposite). Place the flower back over the top of the stem. Use the yarn tail to whip stitch the flower back to the stitches at the base of the petals. Poke the stem into the centre of the soil.
Place a piece of floristry wire in the leaf so that you can bend and position the leaf to suit your arrangement. Sew the base of the leaves 2 cm from the bottom of the stem. With a few small stitches sew the base of the stem to the top of the soil. Place into a small pot filled with wadding or paper. ▣

Images: GMC Publications.

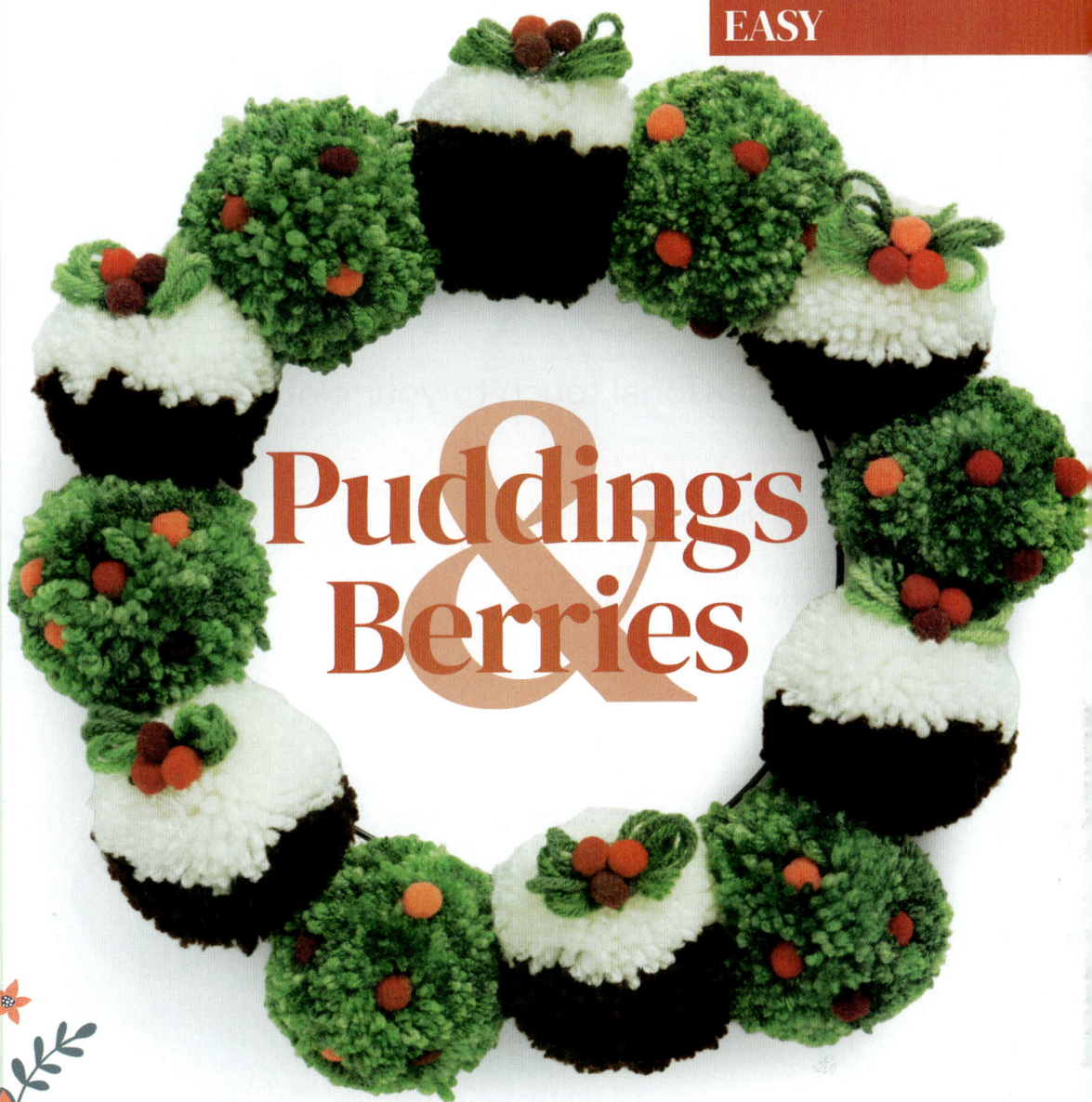

Puddings & Berries

Create a quick wreath with pompoms —
simple, seasonal and so soft!

MATERIALS
Of **Red Heart Super Saver,** 1 x 198g ball each in Soft White (0316) **A**, Coffee (0365) **B** and Green Tones (0629) **C**; 65 mm Clover pompom maker; wire or rattan wreath base measuring 25 cm (10 in) in diameter; Red craft pompoms 1.25 cm (½ in); glue gun and glue sticks.

This yarn is available from your local Red Heart stockist or you can order direct from **www.readicut.co.uk**, telephone: **01162 713759** or **www.woolwarehouse.co.uk**, telephone **0800 505 3300**.

Size: Approx. 25 cm (10 in) diameter.

TO MAKE
Pudding pompom (make 6) — Wind A around first half of pompom maker until full (see manufacturer's instructions). Wind B around second half of tool until full. Cut and secure, leaving a long tail for attaching pompom to wreath frame.

Trim to a smooth, round shape, but do not cut tails.
With colour 1, ch 4, join with sl st to first ch to form ring.

Leaves and Berries — Wind C around 3 fingers 5 times, then tie tightly in centre to secure. Trim ends to be even with loops. Glue 3 small red craft pompoms in centre of bow. Glue holly to pudding pompom on the white section.

Solid pompom (make 6) — Wind C around both halves of pompom maker. Cut and secure, leaving a long tail for attaching to wreath frame. Trim to a smooth, round shape, being sure not to cut tails. Glue on small red craft pompoms, nestling them into the yarn to look like berries.

To assemble — Using the long ends of the pompoms, tie them to the wreath frame. Using the photograph as a guide, alternate pudding pompoms and solid pompoms. Once in place, secure pompoms to wreath frame at the back using a glue gun.

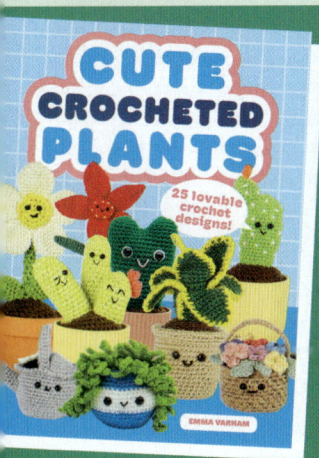

CUTE CROCHETED PLANTS
25 lovable crochet designs!
EMMA VARNAM

Stunning
SNOWFLAKES

Add a seasonal touch to your clothes with these festive buttons.

You Will Need
- Embroidery floss in white
- 18-count Navy Aida, approximately 10 cm (4 in) square per button
- 3.8 cm (1½ in) metal self-cover button for each snowflake

Tools
- Dressmaking scissors and sharp embroidery scissors
- Embroidery hoop (optional)
- Tapestry needle No. 24
- Pencil
- Cookie cutter (optional)
- Iron

Cross Stitch

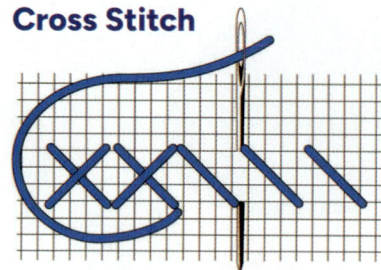

To Make

1. Use a 10 cm square piece of Aida for each design you choose. Following the chart, key to chart and stitch diagrams, stitch your chosen design, using two strands of thread throughout. You can stitch these designs on to the Aida without first putting them into an embroidery hoop if you prefer.

2. After you have stitched a snowflake, you will need to cut around it. You may find that drawing around a cookie cutter with a pencil first helps. Centre the snowflake in the middle of the cutter and draw around the outside edge. Cut out the snowflake following the pencil line. Iron on the wrong side if required.

3. Centre the snowflake, facing outwards, in the middle of the button front. Press two opposite edges of the Aida over the edges of the button, pushing firmly into the teeth on the edges. Flip the button over and make sure the snowflake is central.

4. Press the other two edges into the button back so the shape looks like a square. If you follow this process, you will keep the finish neat without any puckering around the button edge.

5. Now press the rest of the fabric edge into the teeth. Check that you don't have any pleated bits around the edge. If you do, rub your thumb over them towards the teeth and they should straighten out.

6. Press the button back into place to secure the fabric. Once this is done you cannot take the

backs off, so make sure you are happy with how the button looks before completing this step. If you would like to wear your button as a badge, attach a brooch pin to the back.

This decorative project is taken from the book "**How To Cross Stitch**" by Sian Hamilton, GMC Publications, RRP £7.99, available online and from all good bookshops. You can buy "How To Cross Stitch" from Gifts to Me for only £6.40 (+P&P). Visit **www.giftstome.co.uk** and use the offer code **R5939**. Offer ends December 31, 2025.

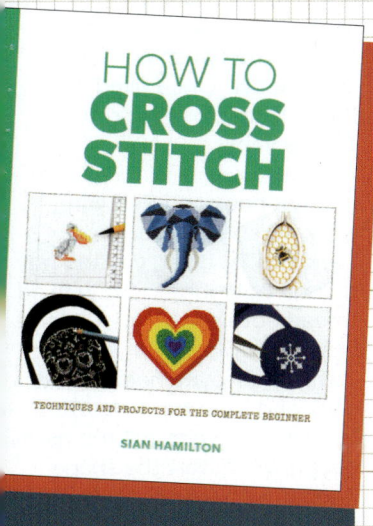

HOW TO
CROSS
STITCH

TECHNIQUES AND PROJECTS FOR THE COMPLETE BEGINNER

SIAN HAMILTON

Skill Level : EASY

Oh, Christmas TREE

Knit your own Scandi-inspired traditional tree baubles.

You will need: 50 g DK yarn in Red and White – we recommend a wool or alpaca yarn (this will be enough for approx. 5 baubles); set of five 3.5 mm knitting needles or circular needle; stitch markers if using circular needle; 20 g 100% wool wadding (or similar) per bauble in beige or white; 3 mm crochet hook; large-eyed yarn needle.

Abbreviations:

ch – chain; **dec** – decrease; **inc** – increase; **K** – knit; **rep** – repeat; **rnd(s)** – round(s); **st(s)** – stitch(es); **yrh** – yarn round hook.

Tension:

22 sts and 28 rows to 10 cm measured over st-st using 3.5 mm knitting needles (an accurate tension is not essential).

To Make: Note: Chart is repeated four times. When working more than one colour, use Fair Isle technique, stranding yarn not in use to the back.

1st rnd (right side) – With 3.5 mm set of needles and Red, cast on 12 sts (the bottom 3 squares on the chart). Distribute these 12 sts over four needles, 3 sts per needle.

2nd rnd – K12.

3rd rnd – ★K2, inc 1, K1 ★, rep from ★ to ★ on each needle – 16 sts.

4th rnd – K16.

5th rnd –★K1, inc 1, K2, inc 1, K1 ★, rep from ★ to ★ on each needle – 24 sts.

6th rnd – K24.

7th rnd – ★K1, inc 1, K4, inc 1, K1★, rep from ★ to ★ on each needle – 32 sts.

8th rnd – K32.

9th rnd – ★K1, inc 1, K6, inc 1, K1 ★, rep from ★ to ★ on each needle – 40 sts.

10th rnd – K40.

11th rnd – ★K1, inc 1, K8, inc 1, K1 ★, rep from ★ to ★ on each needle – 48 sts.

12th rnd – ★K2 Red, K7 White, K3 Red, rep from ★ to ★ on each needle. The last rnd sets chart.

13th - 15th rnds – Working each row of the chart four times, inc as before until there are 64 sts.

16th - 27th rnds – Keeping the chart correct, K64. Continue to follow the chart as before while working the dec rnds:.

28th rnd – ★K1, K2tog, K10, K2tog, K1 ★, rep from ★ to ★ on each needle – 56 sts.

29th rnd – K56.

30th rnd – ★K1, K2tog, K8, K2tog, K1 ★, rep from ★ to ★ on each needle – 48 sts.

31st rnd – K48.

32nd rnd – ★K1, K2tog, K6, K2tog, K1 ★, rep from ★ to ★ on each needle – 40 sts.

33rd rnd – K40.

34th rnd – ★K1, K2tog, K4, K2tog, K1 ★, rep from ★ to ★ on each needle – 32 sts.

35th rnd – K32.

36th rnd – ★K1, K2tog, K2, K2tog, K1 ★, rep from ★ to ★ on each needle – 24 sts.

37th rnd – K24.

38th rnd – ★K1, K2tog, K2tog, K1 ★, rep from ★ to ★ on each needle – 16 sts.

39th rnd – K16.

40th rnd – ★K1, K2tog, K1 ★, rep from ★ to ★ on each needle – 12 sts.

41st rnd – Cut yarn, leaving about 20 cm. Pull the yarn through the remaining 12 sts.

To Make Up – After closing the top, use the tip of your index finger to push the 12 stitches at the top of the ball smoothly together and under each other. Thread the yarn through all the stitches once more, then bring the needle down through the hole at the top towards the hole at the base, and fasten securely.

Steaming – It is important to achieve a good finish on the balls by steaming them. Place the ball on the ironing board and cover it with a wet towel, then press. If you've used natural fibres such as wool or alpaca, you'll see that the ball immediately takes on a rounded shape. You will need to press with the iron to flatten the ball. If using man-made yarns, check the ball-band before steaming and ironing.

To Complete – Once the ball is completely dry, turn upside down to fill. Loosen and separate the wadding so it is fluffier, then push fine layers into the ball. Once filled, sew the bottom closed and tie off the yarn.

Hanging Loop – With a 3 mm crochet hook and Red yarn, work 40 ch sts, insert hook back into 1st ch st, yrh and pull though both loops, cut yarn ad thread both ends through loop in hook. Tighten end yarns. Using large-eyed needle, sew each end from top to bottom to secure. Do not pull too hard or you will distort the shape. Repeat with the other yarn then trim as necessary. Hang your decoration on the tree.

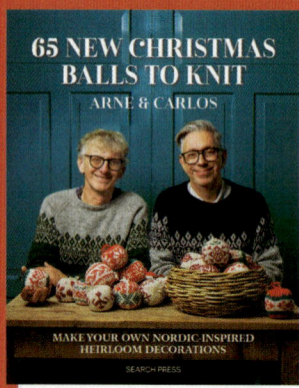

65 NEW CHRISTMAS BALLS TO KNIT
ARNE & CARLOS
MAKE YOUR OWN NORDIC INSPIRED HEIRLOOM DECORATIONS
SEARCH PRESS

This festive design is taken from the book, "65 New Christmas Balls To Knit" by Arne & Carlos published by Search Press, price £14.99 ISBN: 9781800923355. It is available from **www.searchpress.com**, telephone **01892 510850**, or from all good bookshops.

Skill Level :
EASY

A Festive FRIEND

This cute little gingerbread decoration is a lasting memory of a favourite seasonal treat.

You Will Need

- Felt for the bag measuring at least 18 cm x 12 cm
- Felt for the gingerbread man measuring at least 8 cm x 6 cm
- White and Red felt for the hearts and stars measuring 3 cm x 3 cm
- Dark brown embroidery thread
- 20 cm length of narrow gingham (or similar) ribbon
- 5 g toy stuffing
- 15 g dried lavender

Tools

- Fabric scissors
- Pins
- Embroidery needle
- Pen or pencil

Size

Approx 9 cm x 12 cm.

This adorable gift bag is taken from the book "A Year of Felt Decorations" by Corinne Lapierre, published by Search Press, ISBN: 9781800920477, RRP £12.99. It is available online and from all good bookshops, or you can order direct from www.searchpress.com, telephone 01892 510850.

TO MAKE

1. Trace and cut out the templates and transfer to the felt. Cut two rectangles of 9 cm x 12 cm for the bag plus one gingerbread man, two hearts and two stars.

2. Place your gingerbread man on one of the rectangles of felt. Sew in place with blanket stitch and two strands of thread. Make little curves for his eyes and mouth in back stitch using one strand. Add three cross stitches or French knots down his front.

3. Using the photograph as a guide, draw a curve above his head, going from one hand to the other, with a faint pencil line and embroider with backstitch using three strands of thread.

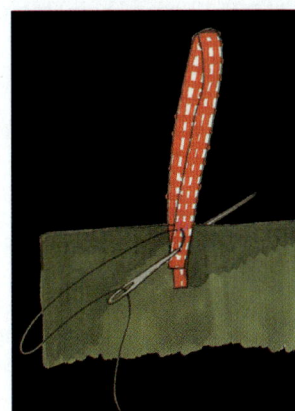

4. Add the stars and hearts and hold in place with a few running or back stitches. If you wish to personalise by adding a name, date or message, do so now, either on the front or back, using back stitch.

5. Once you are happy with the front, fold the ribbon in half to form a loop and pin the ends on the wrong side of the back piece at the top. Stitch in place. Do not cut your thread – simply position the front piece on top of the back piece with the ribbon ends sandwiched in between. Stitch round with blanket stitch, leaving a small gap to fill.

6. Add a little toy stuffing, pushing down to the base, then some lavender, then another small layer of toy stuffing at the top. Stitch the gap closed, make a secure knot and cut your thread.

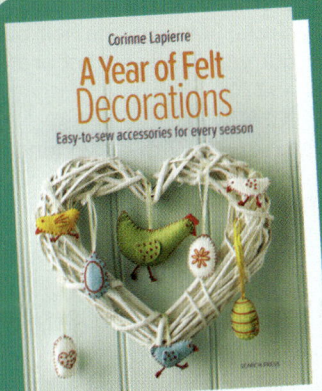

Images: Search Press.

Skill Level :
EASY

You will need:
1 x 50 g ball **Hobbii Rainbow Deluxe 8/4** in Winter White [04] **A**, Natural White [02] **B**, Light Malibu [18] **C**, Pineapple [43] **D** and 1 x 10 g ball **Ricorumi Lamé DK** Gold [002] **E**; length of Black embroidery thread; 2 mm crochet hook; toy stuffing; large-eyed sewing needle. For more information on Hobbii yarns, visit **www.hobbii.co.uk**.

Abbreviations:
BLO – back loop only; **ch** – chain; **dc** – double crochet; **dc2inc** – double crochet increase; **dc2tog** – double crochet 2 together; **FLO** – front loop only; **rnd[s]** – round[s]; **sl** – slip; **st[s]** – stitches.

Size: 12 cm (4¾ in) high.

To Make
NOTE: Figures in square brackets [ ] are worked the number of times stated.

BODY:
1st rnd – With 2 mm hook and yarn C, working into magic circle, 8 dc – 8 sts. Place marker for beginning of round and move marker up as each round is completed.
2nd rnd – [Dc2inc] 8 times – 16 sts.
3rd rnd – [1 dc, dc2inc] 8 times – 24 sts.
4th rnd – 1 dc, dc2inc, [2 dc, dc2inc] 7 times, 1 dc – 32 sts.
5th rnd – [3 dc, dc2inc] 8 times – 40 sts.
6th rnd – 2 dc, dc2inc, [4 dc, dc2inc] 7 times, 2 dc – 48 sts.
7th rnd – BLO 1 dc in each st around – 48 sts.
8th & 9th rnds – 1 dc in each st around.
10th rnd – [10 dc, dc2tog] 4 times – 44 sts.
11th - 15th rnds – 1 dc in each st around.
16th rnd – [9 dc, dc2tog] 4 times – 40 sts.

17th & 18th rnds – 1 dc in each st around.
19th rnd – [6 dc, dc2tog] 5 times – 35 sts.
20th rnd – 1 dc in each st around.
21st rnd – [5 dc, dc2tog] 5 times – 30 sts.
22nd rnd – 1 dc in each st around.
23rd rnd – [4 dc, dc2tog] 5 times – 25 sts.
24th rnd – 1 dc in each st around.
25th rnd – [3 dc, dc2tog] 5 times – 20 sts.
26th rnd – 1 dc in each st around.
27th rnd – [3 dc, dc2tog] 4 times – 16 sts.
Fasten off.
With E and the angel's body pointing away from you, pull up a loop in the FLO from 6th rnd, 1 dc in each st around.
Fasten off.

HEAD:
1st rnd – With 2 mm hook and yarn C, working into magic circle, 6 dc – 6 sts.
2nd rnd – [Dc2inc] 6 times – 12 sts.
3rd rnd – [1 dc, dc2inc] 6 times – 18 sts.
4th rnd – 1 dc, dc2inc, [2 dc, dc2inc] 5 times, 1 dc – 24 sts.
5th rnd – [3 dc, dc2inc]

6 times – 30 sts.
6th rnd – 2 dc, dc2inc, [4 dc, dc2inc] 5 times, 2 dc – 36 sts.
7th rnd – [5 dc, dc2inc] 6 times – 42 sts.
8th rnd – 3 dc, dc2inc, [6 dc, dc2inc] 5 times, 3 dc – 48 sts.
9th - 13th rnds – 1 dc in each st around.
14th rnd – [7 dc, dc2inc] 6 times – 54 sts.
15th - 18th rnds – 1 dc in each st around.
19th rnd – [7 dc, dc2tog] 6 times – 48 sts.
20th rnd – 1 dc in each st around.
21st rnd – [1 dc, dc2tog] 16 times – 32 sts.
22nd rnd – [2 dc, dc2tog] 8 times – 24 sts.
23rd rnd – [1 dc, dc2tog] 8 times – 16 sts.
Stuff firmly. Cut yarn and leave a long tail for sewing. Sew together the body and head.
With A, embroider a nose between 14th and 15th rnds. With Black embroidery thread, embroider eyes over 13th rnd.

HAIR:
1st rnd – With D, working into magic circle, 6 dc – 6 sts.
2nd - 8th rnds – As given for head.

9th rnd – [7 dc, dc2inc] 6 times – 54 sts.
10th - 12th rnds – 1 dc in each st around.
13th rnd – 16 dc, 4 htr, 3 tr, 1 htr, 1 sl st, 1 htr, 3 tr, 4 htr, 21 dc.
14th rnd – 24 dc, 1 sl st, 29 dc.
Cut yarn and leave a long tail. Sew on to head.

BUN:
1st rnd – With D, working into magic circle, 8 dc – 8 sts.
2nd rnd – [Dc2inc] 8 times – 16 sts.
3rd rnd – [1 dc, dc2inc] 8 times – 24 sts.
4th - 8th rnds – 1 dc in each st around.
Cut yarn and leave a long tail. Sew on top of the head, and stuff before closing the hole.
HEADBAND: With E, 26 ch, sl st into first ch to create a circle. Place on the hair bun, cut yarn, and sew securely.

ARMS [2]:
1st rnd – With A, working into magic circle, 8 dc – 8 sts.
2nd - 4th rnds – 1 dc in each st around.
Change to C.
5th - 16th rnds – 1 dc in each st around.
Flatten the arm, dc across

ANGEL ON HIGH

Crochet an angel as a symbol of love and friendship.

into both sides to close the arm. Cut yarn and leave a long tail.
Place and sew the arms just under the head to the sides of the body. Sew together the hands.

WINGS [make 2]:
1st row – With B, 6 ch, start in 2nd ch from hook, 1 dc in next 4 sts, 1 sl st in the next st, 1 ch, turn – 5 sts.
2nd row – Skip 1 st, 1 dc in the next 4 sts, 4 ch, turn – 8 sts.
3rd row – Begin in second ch from hook, 1 dc in next 5 sts, dc2inc, 1 sl st, 1 ch, turn – 8 sts.
4th row – Skip 1 st, dc2inc, 1 dc in the next 6 sts, 4 ch, turn – 12 sts.
5th row – Begin in second chain from hook, 1 dc in the next 10 sts, 1 sl st, 1 sl st in the 1 ch from the start – 12 sts.
Cut yarn and leave a tail. Sew on wings 5 rnds under the head on the back, with 5 sts in between.
OPTIONAL: With E, add a loop on top of the bun to use as a tree decoration.

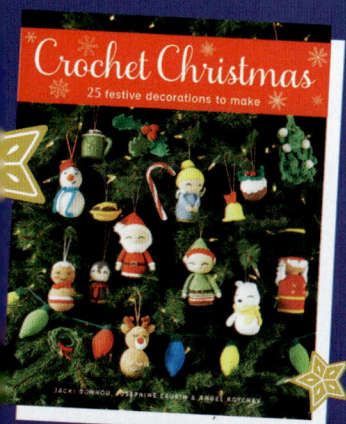

Skill Level :
EASY

Anyone For TEA?

Welcome friends with a hot cuppa from a pot with its own festive cosy.

MATERIALS
1 x 198 g ball of **Red Heart Super Saver** in Soft White (0316) **A**, Light Sage (0631) **B**, Tea Leaf (0624) **C** and Cherry Red (0319) **D**; one pair 5 mm (No. 6) knitting needles. This yarn is available from your local Red Heart stockist or you can order direct from **www.readicut.co.uk**, telephone **0116 2713759**, or from **www.hellocrafts. co.uk**, telephone **0116 2713131**.

TENSION
16 sts and 23 rows to 10 cm (4 in) measured over st-st using 5 mm needles.

ABBREVIATIONS
Dec – decrease; **K** – knit; **P** – purl; **rep** – repeat; **st(s)** – sts; **st-st** – stocking stitch (knit 1 row, purl 1 row); **tog** – together.

Important Note
Instructions are given for two sizes. Figures in brackets refer to the larger size. Figures in square brackets [ ] refer to both sizes and are worked the number of times stated.
Size: 46 cm (18 in) or 51 cm (20 in) in circumference to fit small or medium teapot.

TO MAKE
NOTE: Work 1st - 28th rows in 4-row stripe pattern of A, B, A, C, D, A, and C. With 5 mm needles cast on 36 (42) sts.
1st row (wrong side) – Knit.
2nd row – Knit.
3rd row – K2, purl to last 2 sts, K2.
4th row – Knit.
Rep last four rows six times more, keeping stripe pattern correct.
29th row – With B, knit.
30th row – Knit.
31st row – As 3rd row.
32nd row – K2, ★K2tog, K4, rep from ★ to last 4 sts, K2tog, K2 – 30 (35) sts.
33rd & 34th rows – With A, knit.
35th row – As 3rd row.
36th row – K2, ★K2tog, K3, rep from ★ to last 3 sts, K3 – 25 (29) sts.
37th row – With D, knit.
38th row – K2, ★K1, K2tog, rep from ★ to last 2 sts, K2 (3) – 18 (21) sts.
39th row – As 3rd row.
40th row – Knit.
41st & 42nd rows – With A, knit.
43rd row – As 3rd row.
44th row – Knit.
45th & 46th rows – With C, knit.
47th row – As 3rd row.
48th row – K2, [K2tog] 7 (8) times, K2 (3) – 11 (13) sts.
49th row – As 3rd row.
50th row – K3 (2), [K2tog] 3 (4) times, K2 (3) – 8 (9) sts.
Cut yarn leaving a 30 cm (12 in) tail. Draw tail through all sts, pull tightly to close and knot to secure.
To complete – Pin seams leaving openings for spout and handle (try on teapot to check). Sew seams above and below spout and handle openings.
With A, make a pompom approx 6 cm diameter. Sew to top securely. Weave in ends.

Image: Red Heart Yarns.

TABLE Topper

Create a stunning centrepiece with fresh poinsettias.

You Will Need

- Short length of plastic pipe (to hold candle)
- Bowl
- Chicken wire
- Cream and red poinsettias
- Selection of foliage (fresh or faux) – we used winterberry, anthurium, eucalyptus pods and protea
- Candle (wax or LED)

Tools

- Strong glue
- Household scissors/secateurs
- Florist's tape

To Make

1. Attach the plastic pipe to the bottom of the bowl using the glue.

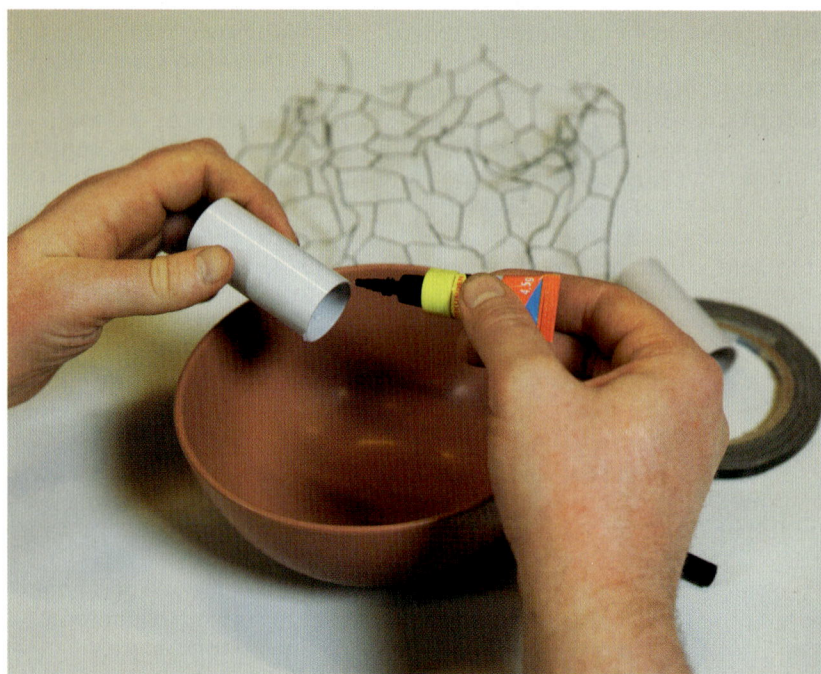

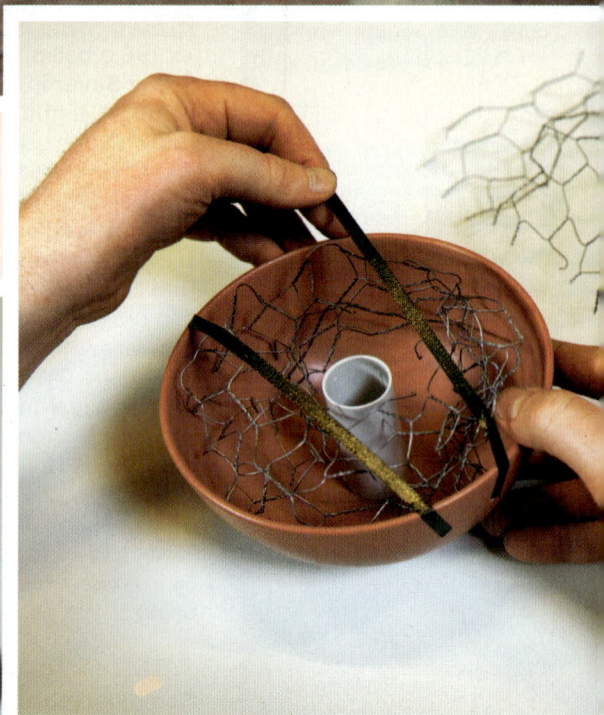

2. Cut a length of chicken wire to roughly the diameter of the bowl. Scrunch it up and place it inside the bowl around the section of tube. Fix it in place using florist's tape placed over the edge of the bowl.

3. Insert the cut poinsettias and the other florals close together into the chicken wire. Use the photograph as a guide and aim to create an interesting shape.

4. Place the candle into the plastic tube. If you are using a wax candle and plan to light it, make sure the foliage is clear of the flame and never leave the candle unattended.

5. When everything is in position, add water to the bowl.

Tip: Cut poinsettias will last for up to two weeks if you immerse the cut stem end in hot water (approx. 60°C) for a few seconds immediately after cutting, then in cold water. Finally, place the cut flowers in fresh water. 🏵

Gnome, SWEET Gnome

Create a tree with a difference – and chase that cheeky elf away!

You will need:

1 x 50 g ball of **cotton 4-ply** (Scheepies Catona or similar) in Bright Green **A**, Dark Green **B**, Ivory **C**, Green **D**, White **E**, Yellow **F**; 1 x 50 g ball of **King Cole Moments** in White (470) **G** or similar eyelash yarn (small amount needed); 3 mm and 4 mm crochet hooks; toy stuffing; tiny multi-coloured craft bells (around 50); orange star button; cardboard; sewing needle and thread; glue gun.

Abbreviations:

ch – chain;
dc – double crochet;
dc2tog – [Insert hook in next stitch, yarn over and pull up a loop] twice, yarn over and draw through all 3 loops on hook;
rep – repeat;
rnd – round;
sl – slip;
sp – space;
st(s) – stitches.

Size: 15 cm (6 in) high.

To Make

HEAD & BODY:

With 3 mm hook and yarn A, make 2 ch, 6 dc into second ch from hook, join with a sl st to form a circle.
1st rnd – 1 ch, 2 dc in each st to end, join – 12 dc. Place marker for beginning of round and move marker up as each round is completed.

2nd rnd – 1 ch, ★1 dc in next st, 2 dc in next st, rep from ★ to end, join – 18 dc.
3rd rnd – 1 ch, ★1 dc in next 2 sts, 2 dc in next st, rep from ★ to end, join – 24 dc.
4th rnd – 1 ch, ★1 dc in next 3 sts, 2 dc in next st, rep from ★ to end, join – 30 dc
5th rnd – 1 ch, ★1 dc in next 4 sts, 2 dc in next st, rep from ★ to end, join – 36 dc.
6th rnd – 1 ch, 1 dc in each st BUT working into back loop only, join.
At this point, using the base of the body as a template, cut a small circle of card

and insert it into the base.
7th - 12th rnds – 1 ch, 1 dc in each st to end, join..
13th rnd – 1 ch, ★1 dc in next 3 sts, dc2tog, rep from ★ to last st, 1 dc in last st, join – 29 sts.
14th - 20th rnds – 1 ch, 1 dc in each st to end, join. Break off A, join in yarn C.
21st & 22nd rnds – 1 ch, 1 dc in each st to end, join.
23rd rnd – 1 ch, ★1 dc in next 2 sts, dc2tog, rep from ★ to last st, 1 dc in last st, join – 22 sts.
24th & 25th rnds – 1 ch, 1 dc in each st to end, join.
26th rnd – 1 ch, ★dc2tog, rep from ★ to end, join – 11 sts.
27th rnd – 1 ch, ★dc2tog to last st, 1 dc in last st, join – 6 sts. Fasten off.

NOSE:

Using 3 mm hook and yarn C, make 2 ch, 6 dc in second ch from hook, join with a sl st to form a circle.
1st rnd – 1 ch, 2 dc into each st to end, join – 12 sts.
2nd rnd – 1 ch, 1 dc into each st to end, join.
3rd rnd – 1 ch, ★dc2tog, rep from ★ to end, join – 6 sts. Fasten off.

BEARD:

With 4 mm hook and yarn G, make 18 ch.
1st rnd – 1 dc in second ch from hook, 1 dc in each ch to end, turn – 17 sts.

2nd rnd – 1 ch, 1 dc in each st to end. Fasten off.

ARM (make 2):

With 3 mm hook and yarn C, make 2 ch, 6 dc into second ch from hook, join with a sl st to form a circle.
1st rnd – 1 ch, 1 dc into each st to end, join.
2nd rnd (right side) – 1 ch, ★1 dc in next st, 2 dc in next st, rep from ★ to end, join – 9 sts.
Break off yarn C, join yarn A.
3rd & 9th rnds – 1 ch, 1 dc in each st to end, join. Fasten off.

HAT:

With 3 mm hook and yarn B, make 2 ch, 6 dc into second ch from hook, join with a sl st to form a circle.
1st - 4th rnds – 1 ch, 1 dc in each st to end, join.
5th rnd – 1 ch, ★1 dc in next st, 2 dc in next st, rep from ★ to end, join – 9 sts.
6th rnd – 1 ch, 1 dc in each st to end, join.
7th rnd – 1 ch, ★1 dc in next 2 sts, 2 dc in next st, rep from ★ to end, join – 12 sts.
8th rnd – 1 ch, 1 dc in each st to end, join.
9th rnd – 1 ch, 2 dc in each st to end – 24 sts.
10th - 15th rnds – 1 ch, 1 dc in each st to end, join.
16th rnd – 1 ch, ★1 dc in next 2 sts, 2 dc in next st, rep from ★ to end – 32 sts.
17th - 19th rnds – 1 ch, 1 dc

This delightful design is taken from the book "Gnomes to Crochet" by Val Pierce, published by Search Press, price £12.99 ISBN: 9781800922174. It is available from www.searchpress.com, telephone 01892 510850, and from all good bookshops.

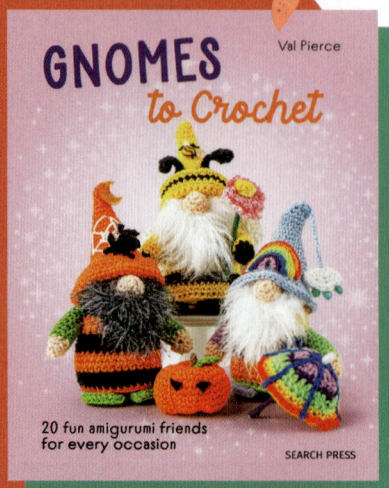

GNOMES to Crochet
Val Pierce
20 fun amigurumi friends for every occasion
SEARCH PRESS

in each st to end, join. Break off B, join in yarn E.

20th rnd – 1 ch, work a round of dc from right to left to create a twisted stitch (also known as a crab stitch), join. Fasten off.

LARGE BRANCH:

Make one in yarn B and one in yarn D.

With 3 mm hook, make 41 ch, join with a sl st to form a circle.

1st rnd – 1 ch, 1 dc into each st to end, join – 41 sts.

2nd rnd – 1 ch, 1 dc in first st, ★miss 1 st, [3 tr, 2 ch, 3 tr] into next st, miss 1 st, 1 dc in next st, rep from ★ 9 times – 10 clusters.

Break yarn B or D, join in yarn E and work the edging as follows:

1st rnd – 1 ch, 1 dc in first st, ★1 dc in next 3 tr, 3 dc into 2-ch sp, 1 dc in next 3 tr, 1 dc in next st, rep from ★ to end, join. Fasten off.

MEDIUM BRANCH:

Make one in yarn B and one in yarn D.

With 3 mm hook, make 33 ch, join with a sl st to form a circle.

1st rnd – 1 ch, 1 dc into each ch to end, join – 33 sts.

2nd rnd – 1 ch, 1 dc in first st, ★miss 1 st, [3 tr, 2 ch, 3 tr] into next st, miss 1 st, 1 dc in next st, rep from ★ 7 times – 8 clusters.

Break yarn B or D and join in yarn E. Work the edging in the same way as large branches. Fasten off.

SMALL BRANCH:

Make one in yarn D.

With 3 mm hook, make 21 ch, join with a sl st to form a circle.

1st rnd – 1 ch, 1 dc into each ch to end, join – 22 sts.

2nd rnd – 1 ch, 1 dc in first st, ★miss 1 st, [3 tr, 2 ch, 3 tr] into next st, miss 1 dc, 1 dc in next st, rep from ★ 4 times – 5 clusters.

Break off yarn D and join in yarn E. Work the edging in the same way as large branches.

HAT BRANCHES:

Make one in yarn B and one in yarn D.

With 3 mm hook, make 17 ch, join with a sl st to form a circle.

1st rnd – 1 ch, 1 dc into

each st to end – 18 sts.

2nd rnd – 1 ch, 1 dc in first st, ★miss 1 st, [3 tr, 2 ch, 3tr] into next st, miss 1 dc, 1 dc in next st, rep from ★ 3 times – 4 clusters.

Break off yarn B or D and join in yarn E. Work the edging in the same way as large branches. Fasten off.

STAR:

With 3 mm hook and yarn F, make 4 ch, join with a sl st to form a circle.

1st rnd – ★[3 ch, 1 tr, 3 ch, 1 dc] into ring, rep from ★ 4 times. Fasten off.

TO MAKE UP:

Weave in any loose ends of yarn. Add some stuffing to the arms and sew them to either side of the body. Using a fine needle and toning thread, sew the craft bells on to each point of every branch.

Pull up the branches on to the gnome's body under the arms in the following order: medium in yarn B, large in yarn B and large in yarn D.

Glue these in place or secure with a few stitches. Then take the second set of medium-sized branches (in yarn D) and pull them over the gnome's head so that they sit on top of the arms and sew or glue in place.

Gather the base of the nose and add a little stuffing before sewing it to the face. Sew the nose so the bottom of it sits where yarn C begins.

Attach the beard so it curves around underneath the nose; you can sew or glue this in place. Slide the first mini ring of branches in yarn D over the top of the hat and glue or sew the piece so it sits halfway between the top and bottom of the hat.

Take the second mini ring of branches in yarn B and secure the piece in the same way so it sits approximately 2.5 cm (1 in) away from the tip of the hat. Glue the star on to the top of the hat, and then sew your star button in the middle of the piece.

In The BAG

Add a personal touch and stay environmentally friendly with these re-usable fabric gift bags.

You Will Need

- Hobbycraft Festive Fabric Fat Quarters
- Selection of plain fabrics in Christmas colours (optional)
- Sewing thread to match fabrics
- Toning ribbon or twine, to tie

Tools

- Iron
- Ruler
- Temporary fabric marker
- Craft scissors
- Pins
- Sewing machine
- Sewing needle

Stockists

All products are available from Hobbycraft. For details of your nearest Hobbycraft store or to order direct, visit **www.hobbycraft.co.uk** or telephone **0330 026 1400.**

TO MAKE

1. Take the two fabrics you wish to use. One will be your outer fabric and the other fabric will line your gift bag. Iron to make sure fabric is perfectly smooth. Beginning with your main outer fabric, use a ruler and marker to measure out a rectangle. You can choose any dimensions you wish, but we chose 26 cm (10 in) length x 16 cm (6 in) width. Once you have drawn this with a fabric marker, cut out your rectangle.

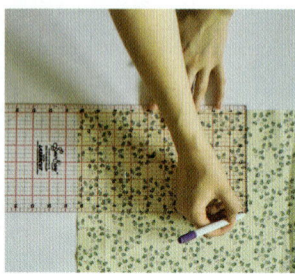

2. Place your cut fabric on top of the same fabric and use it as a template to cut out another rectangle.

3. Repeat step 1 and 2 again with the lining fabric, but this time keep the width as before but make the length 1 cm shorter. This will ensure that your lining sits inside your bag without too much bulk. You should now have 2 rectangles for your outer fabric and 2 rectangles for your lining fabric.

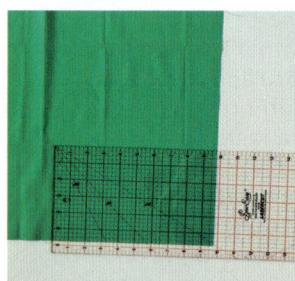

4. Place the right sides of your outer fabrics together and pin around 3 edges, leaving 1 shorter edge unpinned. This unpinned edge will become the opening of your bag. Place right sides of lining fabrics together and pin around 3 edges, leaving 1 shorter edge unpinned.
On the shorter edge that IS pinned, mark a 9 cm (3½in) gap, as shown in the photograph. This gap remains unstitched. Stitch around your bags with a 1 cm (⅜ in) seam allowance.

5. Once both bags are stitched, press all the seams facing away from each other, making sure the gap you've left on your lining is pressed out well.

MAKE & create

Skill Level :
EASY

7. Using the gap at the bottom of your lining, pull your fabric bag from the inside out.

6. Turn your outer fabric bag outside in, so that the pattern on the fabric is now on the outside. With your lining fabric bag still inside out, push your outer fabric bag inside the lining bag, all the way until the open ends meet. Make sure you are matching your side seams with both bags and pin all around the top edge. Stitch all around the top with a 1 cm (⅜ in) seam allowance.

8. With a pointer, push out your corners using the gap in the lining bag. Take particular care with the 4 corners, as once the bag is closed you won't be able to do this.

9. Hand stitch the gap in the bottom seam closed using ladder stitch.

TO FINISH

Add a gift, use ribbon or twine as ties and decorate with Christmas tags, floral picks or as desired.

10. Once you've closed the gap in the lining, push your lining bag into the other bag. Push all the corners into the corners and smooth out your bag. You might need to give it a light press.

Skill Level : EASY

You will need:

Red Heart Super Saver, 1 x 198 g ball in Buff (334) **A**, Cherry Red (309) **B**, Aran (385) **C**, and Royal (385) **D** (Note: small amounts are needed of each shade); yarn or embroidery thread for hanging; 3.75 mm crochet hook, and toy stuffing. If you have difficulty finding the yarn used, you can order directly from **www.woolwarehouse.co.uk**, telephone **0800 505 3300**.

Tension:

4 dc and 4 rounds to 2.5 cm (1 in) using 3.75 mm hook.

Abbreviations:

ch – chain; **dc** – double crochet; **dc2tog** – [Insert hook in next stitch, yarn over and pull up a loop] twice, yarn over and draw through all 3 loops on hook; **rep** – repeat; **rnd** – round; **sl** – slip; **st(s)** – stitches.

Size:

16.5 cm (6½ in) tall excluding pompom.

To Make

HEAD: Beginning at top, with A, ch 2.
1st rnd – Work 6 dc in 2nd ch from hook – 6 dc. Place marker for beginning of round and move marker up as each round is completed
2nd rnd – Work 2 dc in each dc around – 12 dc
3rd rnd – ★Dc in next dc, 2 dc in next dc, rep from ★ around – 18 dc.
4th rnd – ★Dc in next 2 dc, 2 dc in next dc, rep from ★ around – 24 dc.
5th rnd – Dc in each dc around.
6th rnd – ★Dc in next 3 dc, 2 dc in next dc, rep from ★ around – 30 dc.
7th - 11th rnds – Dc in each dc around.
12th rnd – ★Dc2tog, rep from ★ around – 15 dc.
13th rnd – Dc in each dc around, join with slip st in first dc. Fasten off, leaving a long tail.
With D, embroider French

knot eyes on 10th rnd (use photograph as a guide).
BODY: Work from the bottom up. With B, ch 2.
1st & 2nd rnds – As 1st & 2nd rnds of head – 12 dc.
3rd rnd – ★Dc in next 3 dc, 2 dc in next dc, rep from ★ around – 15 dc.
4th - 8th rnds – Dc in each dc around.
9th rnd – ★Dc in next 3 dc, dc2tog, rep from ★ around – 12 dc.
10th rnd – Dc in each dc around. Stuff body.
11th rnd – ★Dc2tog, rep from ★ around, join with slip st in first dc – 6 dc. Fasten off, leaving a long tail. Weave tail through last round and pull closed.
ARM (make 2): With B, ch 2.
1st rnd – Work 6 dc in 2nd ch from hook – 6 dc.
2nd rnd – ★Dc in next dc, 2 dc in next dc, rep from ★

around – 9 dc.
3rd - 6th rnds – Dc in each dc around.
Join with slip st in first dc. Fasten off, leaving a long tail. Do not stuff.
BEARD: WIth C, ch 2.
1st row – Work 2 dc in 2nd ch from hook, turn – 2 sc.
2nd row (right side) – Ch 1, 2 dc in each dc, turn – 4 dc.
3rd & 4th rows – Ch 1, 2 dc in first dc, dc in each dc across to last 2 dc, 2 dc in last dc, turn – 8 dc.
5th row – Ch 1, dc in each dc across, turn.
6th rnd – Ch 1, dc2tog, dc in next 4 dc, dc2tog, ★working in ends of rows, work 6 dc evenly spaced ★ down first side; working in opposite side of foundation ch, 3 dc in ch, rep from ★ to ★ up other side, join with slip st in first dc. Fasten off, leaving a long tail.

BELT: With C, ch 18.
1st row – Dc in 2nd ch from hook and in each ch across. Fasten off, leaving a long tail for sewing.
HAT: With C, ch 5.
1st row (right side) – Dc in 2nd ch from hook and in each ch across, turn – 4 dc.
2nd - 29th rows – Ch 1, dc in back loop of each dc across, turn.
30th row – Rep last row, change to B, turn.
Shape crown –
1st row (right side) – Ch 1, working in ends of rows, dc in each row across, turn – 30 dc.
2nd row – Ch 1, ★dc in next 3 dc, dc2tog, rep from ★ across, turn – 24 dc.
3rd row – Ch 1, dc in each dc across, turn.
4th row – Ch 1, ★dc in next 2 dc, dc2tog, rep from ★ across, turn – 18 dc.
5th row – Ch 1, dc in each dc across, turn.
6th row – Ch 1, ★dc in next dc, dc2tog, rep from ★ across, turn – 12 dc.
7th row – Ch 1, dc in each dc across, turn.
8th row – Ch 1, ★dc2tog, rep from ★ across, turn – 6 dc.
Fasten off, leaving a long tail for sewing.

To Make Up

Arms: Weave tail through last round and pull stitches closed, then sew in place.
Head & Body: Stuff head. Sew beard (see photograph). Push 13th rnd of head on to top of body and sew to join. Sew on belt. Weave tail of hat through last row and pull closed. Working through ends of rows, sew back seam. Working in ends of ribbing, sew hat on head.
Pompom – Cut a 38 cm (15 in) strand of C and set aside. Wrap C around 4 fingers 50 times. Slide loops off and tie strand tightly around centre. Cut loops open and trim. Thread ends of tie through top of hat and secure pompom. Cut embroidery floss for hanging loop, thread through hat, and tie in a knot. Weave in ends.

Santa, BABY

Brighten up your tree with this jolly little fella.

Image: Red Heart Yarns.

TALES
of Yuletide Joy

It's time to relax with our
selection of wonderful new stories,
filled with seasonal magic,
from your favourite "Friend"
writers.

That Festive Feeling

The approach of the big day had emotions riding high – how would Maisie keep everyone happy?

BY GABRIELLE MULLARKEY

MAISIE had forgotten her key again.

Sighing, she rang the doorbell.

No answer, but no pounding music either to suggest that her fifteen-year-old daughter Nadine might not have heard her.

After a few more bell presses, she lifted the letter box.

"Nads, it's me!" she hollered, shivering in the winter cold. "Can you let me in and help with the shopping?"

At last, footsteps on the stairs. Nadine opened the door, talking into the phone wedged under her neck.

"Yeah, all right. Later, I s'pose," she said in a flat tone, turning away from Maisie.

"Nads? A hand," Maisie insisted, indicating the shopping bags. "Unless you want all the Christmas food you've specially requested to defrost out here on the doorstep?"

Nadine flipped her phone shut, picked up the smallest bag.

"Well, there can't be a turkey defrosting for me, seeing as I'm vegan."

"No, the turkey's for me and your gran," Maisie confirmed.

In the kitchen, Maisie unpacked the turkey, frozen veg, a mound of spuds, vegan mince pies, red onion tarte tatin, vegan cheesecake and vegan Christmas pudding.

Maisie had already sampled some of Nadine's choices and couldn't taste much difference from the "real" thing.

She just hoped the same was true for her mum, who was coming for Christmas Day.

"Who was that on the phone?" she asked her daughter, flicking on the kettle. "Your dad, by any chance?"

Since her divorce from Graham last year, Maisie was greatly relieved that he and Nadine talked so much.

It was just that Nadine seemed to be the one always ringing him and Maisie knew from experience that Graham was an "out of sight, out of mind" kind of guy.

Of course, he loved Nadine and would throw himself in front of a snow plough for her, it was simply that . . .

"Where's Luna?" Maisie asked suddenly, glancing round the kitchen.

Usually, their chocolate Labrador was dancing round her when she came through the door with shopping.

"Huh?" Nadine looked up once more from her phone.

"Oh, I let her out the back door to snuffle round the garden," she explained, gesturing vaguely in that direction.

Maisie felt exhaustion and irritation flood up from her toes in equal, non-festive measures.

"Nads, I told you to take her for a proper walk!" She tutted. "I wish you'd be a bit more responsible. Our fence is wobbly and if Luna gets out . . ."

"Chill, Grinchy." Nadine shrugged. "Can't go far, can she? Not with her bad paw."

Maisie wasn't worried about Luna's slight limp, which she'd had since birth.

It was why she and Graham had chosen her from the dog rehoming centre, the sweetly determined runt of her mother's litter.

No, Maisie was worried, specifically, about her next-door neighbour, Arthur.

He was not a dog person. Or a Nadine person. Or possibly even a Christmas person.

It was three weeks to the big day and Maisie had yet to glimpse any sign of festivity in his windows, front or back.

Mind you, this was her first Christmas in Copper Close, so she didn't really know her neighbours well or what they got up to.

She hurried to open the back door and peer into the bare, wintry garden, fighting a sudden lump in her throat.

In their last house – the now-sold "marital home" a few miles away – Graham had decorated the garden each year with white fairy lights.

Christmas had been a big deal, with lots of laughter, wobbling on stepladders, lifting up Nads to put the star on top of the tree.

Her garden fence creaked in a gust of wind.

Seconds later, she heard a shout.

"Get off those, you insolent mutt!"

It was followed by a sharp bark.

Oh, heck!

Maisie, still wearing her coat and boots, hurried into the back garden and popped her head over the fence.

There she saw Arthur Wells glaring down at a sheepish Luna.

Scattered around man and dog were the remnants of what resembled white confetti. The dark-green bush behind them, spiked with ragged bits of white petals, told the true story.

"She's ruined my camellia!" Arthur said bitterly. "Shaken off every flower while digging under the bush."

"I'm so sorry!" Maisie gasped. "She has this digging instinct whenever she sees a bush."

"A Snow Flurry camellia is prized for its pure white,

semi-double blooms," Arthur said in the same monotone Maisie had heard Nadine use on the phone a short time ago.

Now, she recognised that tone for what it was: the flatness of suppressed emotion.

"I'll get you another one!" Maisie yelped, indicating the bush. "Um, how did Luna get through?"

He pointed to a gap under the wobbly fence, clearly also tunnelled out by Luna.

"They could've used a dog like that in 'The Great Escape'!" he said with a snort, then sighed. "Never mind the bush. I'll plant something with colour for next year."

"I'm still happy to pay for the replacement," Maisie offered. "Luna, come here at once!"

The dog obeyed reluctantly, forcing her generous proportions into the gap she'd already carved out beneath the fence.

"Never mind about replacing the bush, just get that fence fixed." Arthur sniffed. "It belongs to you."

"I will." Maisie nodded. "So sorry again."

He stalked off into his house, as Maisie returned to the kitchen with Luna trotting to heel.

It occurred belatedly to Maisie that she'd never given Nadine a chance to answer that question about who she'd been talking to on the phone.

She found Nadine squinting at a packet of vegan stock cubes.

"I mean, no offence, Mum, but I don't bother with the concept of gravy, even when made out of onion powder. You know?"

"Was it your dad on the phone before I came in?" Maisie asked.

Nadine looked up, biting her lip.

Oh, poor love, Maisie thought. She'd probably rung Graham to ask what time he'd be popping round with her Christmas present and he'd smacked his forehead and said,

"Presents! Yes, er, of course. I'll get back to you."

Knowing Graham, he'd leave it all to the last minute.

"Dad happened to ring me while you were out," Nadine said. "About the baby."

Maisie focused on stroking Luna's head while saying briskly, "Oh, yes?"

Graham and his new partner Beth were expecting an early spring baby.

Ironically, Beth had once been a casual friend of Maisie's.

She'd met Graham soon after his divorce from Maisie, and it had been a whirlwind romance.

Maisie found Beth impossible to blame or dislike for all that had happened, but she'd shied away from close contact.

Nadine had met her in due course on visits to Graham's flat.

Last month, Graham had come round to Copper Close with a bunch of garage forecourt flowers and revealed the news of the baby.

Looking at his bald spot and the bags under his eyes, Maisie had almost felt sorry for him.

Poor bloke didn't know what was about to hit him, or else clearly suspected it.

Same must be true for Beth, a slightly older than usual first-time mum.

Now Maisie had a guilty tweak of conscience.

"I hope everything's all right?" she asked anxiously, scanning Nadine's face.

Her main concern up to now was that Nadine would feel displaced by the newcomer, who was understandably going to take up a lot of her dad's time and attention.

"It's all good," Nadine assured her, pausing. "Dad wanted to ask if I'd consider being godmother to the kid. When it's born."

"Goodness," Maisie said, taken by surprise and slightly annoyed.

Graham might have run the idea past her first.

"Are you even allowed to be a godmum?"

Nadine nodded.

"Dad looked it up. As long as you're a 'responsible young person', there's no age limit. What do you reckon, though? It's true what you said, I can't even be responsible for Luna!

"'You have to be a role model,' Dad said. What sort of one would I be?"

"Oh, love!" Maisie half-laughed and half-groaned. "Any little one would be lucky to have you as a role model!

"Why don't you think it over? I'm sure Dad didn't need an answer straight away."

Relief flooded Nadine's face. She nodded again and gave one of her rare, sweet smiles that reminded Maisie poignantly of the little girl she'd been a short time ago.

It also softened Maisie towards Graham.

He should've consulted her first, but he was impulsive, a bit thoughtless. That was just the way he was.

"Remember Dad told us that he and Beth don't want to know the baby's sex in advance?" Nadine said. "If it's a girl, I'm going to teach her never to eat anything with a face!"

Maisie laughed. Good for Nadine. And good for Graham too, she decided.

He'd found the perfect way to include Nadine in the life of her new sibling.

And next Christmas, Maisie realised, there'd be a little one to introduce to the magic of the season!

● ● ● ●

Two nights later, after a carol service, Maisie and Nadine paused outside Arthur's house.

His window now blazed with hand-torn paper chains – stars, stable and three camel-riding kings repeating in rainbow loops.

"That's so cool!" Nadine gasped.

Arthur came to the window just as they passed. On impulse, Maisie waved.

"I'm asking where he got

them," Nadine said, already knocking.

He opened the door. "Left the horticultural vandal at home?"

"She's chewing a bone. Did you make those chains?"

"I did – paper tearing. Come in for a look," he said, eyes brightening.

Over tea by his tree he explained he'd once toured theatres, tearing shapes while keeping up a jokey patter – skills learned years ago in Shanghai.

Nadine stared, rapt.

"You should demo it on TikTok," she burst out. "CraftTok would love you. I'll film and edit."

"You could do your 'patter' as well," she added.

"Only now it's called banter. Loads of people are into this sort of old-school stuff. You'd have a new audience!"

Arthur regarded her thoughtfully, as did Maisie.

It was a while since she'd seen her daughter so animated.

Usually, Nadine would never have knocked on Arthur's door out of artistic curiosity.

But Graham's request had boosted her confidence and sense of responsibility.

Last night, for instance, she'd actually washed up without being asked!

"I'll think it over, young lady," Arthur said. "Perhaps after Christmas. I've a lot to do between now and then. Expect we all have."

Maisie sipped her tea and wondered. Arthur hadn't mentioned how he was spending Christmas Day.

With gentle questions over the next few days, she might find out – and maybe invite him to their partly-vegan feast.

That way she'd know if he'd be up for sharing not only his paper-tearing skills with the wider world, but also a dinner with two other adults, an undisciplined dog and a phone-addicted teenager.

After all, Maisie mused, it was the most wonderful time of the year.

Rise To The Challenge

Could Maureen convince the others that festive baking was a piece of cake?

BY REBECCA HOLMES

BUY your Christmas cake ingredients here and avoid waste.

Sally paused by the sign outside the shop on a cold, late-November Saturday morning.

It was one those places that sold loose rather than prepacked goods.

With a frontage hardly larger than a terraced house, it was typical of the myriad little independent shops that thronged the bustling market town set on a hill, near the edge of the Peak District.

The contrast with Sally's larger hometown's flat terrain and modern shopping centre couldn't have been starker.

She'd known things would be different when she'd moved here, but hadn't realised the extent, along with other challenges.

The sign gave her an idea on that last point, so she took a deep breath and went in.

Inside, shelves groaned with jars of dried fruit, nuts, rice and even coffee beans.

Wooden drawers had labels for herbs and spices, while containers of eco-friendly cleaning products lined the floor. The sole customer, who looked in her fifties, in a warm, red coat and cream scarf, was reading from a list.

Behind the counter, a middle-aged woman with braided brown-grey hair and a rainbow-coloured sweater, measured out dried fruit into paper bags.

"Six ounces of raisins, next. Do me some extra, Sahira. The blackbirds love them."

"When will you convert to metric, Maureen? I know it's your mother's recipe, but even so . . ." Sahira smiled at Sally. "I'll be with you in a second. Have a mince pie while you wait. They're freshly made."

Maureen looked at her with barely disguised curiosity.

"I haven't seen you before. Are you new?"

● ● ● ●

Maureen chided herself for jumping in as the young woman, obviously unused to local ways, hurriedly swallowed her mince pie and explained she had recently moved to start a new job teaching history at the town's comprehensive and join her boyfriend, who already lived in the area.

"It's much better, not having to travel thirty miles to see each other, and I'm in a more senior post, but . . ."

She hesitated, looking surprised at herself for saying so much.

"But?" Maureen prompted.

"Well, Martin's parents have invited me for Christmas. They're nice, but they're rather . . ."

"Proper?"

"Posh?" Sahira suggested.

Sally nodded.

"I want to make a good impression, but I'm not sure how. When I saw the sign outside, I thought I could perhaps make a Christmas cake – except I've never made one before. My parents aren't keen on fruit cake."

It was Maureen's turn to be surprised.

She looked up as a fair-haired teenage girl came in.

"Hello, Laura. How's your mum? I heard she's in hospital."

The poor girl looked pale, and no wonder.

"Me and Dad are going to visit her this afternoon. I've got her Christmas cake recipe here. She usually buys the ingredients about now.

"I thought I'd make it as she probably won't be able to this year."

"What an excellent idea," Sahira said. "Sally, here, is next, but I'm sure she won't take long. Have you got your list ready, Sally?"

"I'm afraid I don't have one. You could serve, erm, Laura, while I find a recipe on my phone."

"Borrow mine. It's never let me down." Maureen smiled. "How's your dad coping?" she asked Laura as Sahira measured out more ingredients. "He must be very busy with his job, and everything."

She sometimes saw Laura's mother, Sylvia, in town, so knew that Laura was almost sixteen and the other children eleven and eight.

"Finding out that we're expecting another child was a shock but a happy one," Sylvia had told her. "It'll be nice to have January birthday to brighten winter up. The house will be a squeeze, but we'll manage."

Now, with complications leading to her recent hospital admission, there seemed even more to "manage".

"He is busy, but I'm helping. Dad says, with luck, we'll have Mum home by Christmas. The new baby will be born by then, though it won't know what's going on."

"But you'll still enjoy the magic, and the baby will old enough to appreciate it next year," Maureen assured her.

"Right, that's done," Sahira announced. "Your turn, Laura."

Sally handed back the list.

"Thank you so much. Do I put everything in a bowl and mix it up? I'll need to buy one."

"Am I right in thinking you haven't done much baking?" Maureen said. "There's a nice coffee shop round the corner.

"We'll go there, and I'll talk you through it."

"Can I come, too?" Laura asked shyly. "I've done some baking but haven't made a Christmas cake before."

This was turning out to be a morning of surprises.

•   •   •   •

Normally Laura would never dream of doing something like this, yet the way everyone had chatted in the shop made her want the moment to last.

Also, she really wanted this cake to be special and suspected she'd need all the help she could get.

"Pippa's Pantry" had holly sprigs in glass jars on each table, and a range of cakes and pastries. Her heart skipped a beat when Isaac, a boy in her year, came to take their order.

With a thick mane of hair and a winning smile, most girls at school fancied him, and she was no exception.

"Hey, Laura. How's things?"

She tried to sound cool.

"Not bad. You?"

"Same. We're busy, but that's good. Pippa's made mince pies and they're amazing. The perfect way to start the run-up to Christmas, especially with a splash of cream."

Both drinks and mince pies lived up to expectations.

Laura's worries seemed to drift away like the steam from the impressive coffee machine which Isaac operated like a true professional.

She learned that Maureen was personal assistant to the senior partner at a firm of solicitors in one of the big Victorian houses on the main road.

Her job sounded more interesting than Laura would have imagined.

Maureen seemed genuinely fond of her boss, who actually sounded like a normal human being.

On the subject of normal human beings, who would have thought of teachers in those terms?

She listened as Sally described her nervousness on starting a new job and worries about how to get along with her boyfriend's parents.

When Maureen jotted down cake-making instructions for Sally, Laura typed the main points into her phone.

"How are things with you, Laura?" Maureen asked gently, when she'd finished.

"I don't know the details, but the baby might need to be born soon, even though it isn't due till the new year."

She fumbled in her sleeve for a tissue.

"Oh, my goodness, Laura. I didn't know about that," another voice cut in.

Laura hadn't realised Isaac was nearby. How much had he heard?

"Is she in the Royal? My aunt Clara's a nurse in their maternity unit. She says the stuff they do there is amazing. What's your mum's name? I'll ask her to look out for her."

Maureen paid the bill, waving away the others' attempts to contribute.

"We should meet up again, to check on progress with our cakes.

"How about eleven o'clock, next Saturday?"

•   •   •   •

That Thursday, Sally went into town again after school, with a list of the utensils she needed.

Although Maureen had offered to lend her the various items, she would have felt awful if she broke something.

It made sense to buy her own equipment, anyway.

After seeing how much everything cost, she tried some charity shops and was pleasantly surprised to find what was available.

As well as mixing bowls, scales and a large storage tin, she bought a pretty teapot, a dress that would be perfect for wearing on Christmas day, and a set of three ceramic snowmen, skiing, skating and dancing a reel.

The woman behind the counter's face lit up when Sally mentioned she was making a Christmas cake.

"A lot of people are making theirs about now. With that, and the lights switch-on, tomorrow, it really is beginning to look a lot like Christmas."

Not long ago, such a conversation would have seemed unusual to Sally.

It was surprising how something so simple could make such a difference.

Last Saturday she'd almost walked past that sign, convinced the idea was a waste of time. Now, she was glad she hadn't.

"If felt like a turning point," she'd told Martin.

He'd been delighted, even admitting he'd been worried she was struggling to settle.

"You'll ace making the cake," he insisted encouragingly.

She would make the cake tomorrow, after school, then they would go to the switch-on while it baked for a few hours in a low oven.

Hopefully it would be ready when they got back, and she could tell the others about it on Saturday.

Thinking about Saturday reminded her of Laura.

Sally didn't teach her, but had seen her in the corridor, and wondered how she was coping.

When her baby brother or sister was born, it sounded as if they would be tiny.

An all-in-one suit would be a nice present, but they all seemed to be for "normal" sized babies.

The poor mite would be swamped.

She was pondering the problem when she came across yet another shop she hadn't noticed before.

This town had an uncanny knack of knowing exactly you what you needed.

The window displayed a range of babywear in colours far more imaginative than any she'd seen so far, arranged around a twinkling, silver tinsel Christmas tree.

Even better, it included clothes "For the Extra Tiny and Precious".

•   •   •   •

Maureen always made the cake several weeks before Christmas, booking a day off for the purpose.

It was a reassuring annual ritual, needing the house to herself and the right ambience.

She could doubtless make a perfectly good cake without all the "fuss", as her husband, Derek, jokingly called it, but that wouldn't have the same happy tingle of Christmas peering over the horizon like a golden sunrise.

That reassurance felt even more important this year, since their eldest son, Sam, had phoned when she got home on Saturday.

"Kate might not join us for Christmas dinner. We had a bit of an argument about bills. I said we could save more towards a house deposit if she bought less clothes.

"She got huffy, complained that I'm paying extra to subscribe to a sports channel, and even compared me to Scrooge not letting Bob Cratchit put coal on the fire when I turned the thermostat down."

"I know it isn't unusual for couples to argue about money, but this sounds serious," she'd told Derek.

"They've only been married a few months. They're still finding their way," he'd replied.

"What if they don't?"

"Then they don't. You can't sort everyone's problems out for them."

Despite his advice, the conversation niggled at her all week.

Now it was cake-making day. Nothing was allowed to spoil that.

As she sifted flour and spices into a bowl, the kitchen began to smell of Christmas.

Mixing the butter and dark brown sugar, she dipped her finger in to savour the concoction, before adding eggs, flour and a generous dollop of black treacle.

Next came her favourite part, stirring in the big bowl of dried fruit, soaked overnight, before placing the cake tin almost reverentially in the oven.

Soon, the comforting scent of rich fruit cake began spreading festive promise around the house.

Cakes didn't need to be perfect. The intended recipients would surely appreciate the thought as much as the finished result.

She hoped Sally and Laura had gone ahead with their Christmas cakes, if only to experience the healing balm of the process.

There had been something special about the way the three of them had come together.

Would they turn up again tomorrow?

• • • •

Without that chance meeting, Laura wasn't sure how she'd have got through the following week. She told Mum about it, the same afternoon, while Dad and a doctor had "a quiet word".

Mum thought the cake was a great idea, and seemed to brighten up at the prospect.

It was an almost-good day until the drive home, when Dad broke the news.

"They're planning to deliver the baby by caesarean tomorrow."

"Does that mean they'll both be home soon?"

The house felt wrong without Mum. Even the chaos of a new baby would be better than the current atmosphere.

"Probably not for a while."

Seeing his hands tighten their grip on the steering wheel, Laura told her father what Isaac had said.

"And Christmas is coming up. That always brings its own magic," she added.

She hoped so.

On Monday, she struggled to concentrate at school.

When Ivy, who sat next to her in Geography, asked if she was OK, Laura blurted out everything.

She hadn't even done that with any of her friends beyond the bare details.

It was as if talking with Maureen and Sally had unlocked something in her.

Instead of looking uncomfortable, Ivy hugged her. "If there's anything I can do, let me know. It won't be much, but it might help a bit."

She got home at the end of the day to find Gran there. Ben and Jessica were watching television in the living-room, but she could sense their tension.

Gran poured her a mug of the special milky coffee that only she knew how to make.

"You've got a new little sister. Holly. Your dad's sent me a photo. He didn't want to contact you at school, but he told me to show you as soon as I could."

The swell of emotions surging through Laura almost overwhelmed her.

Cradled in Mum's arms lay the tiniest person, with even tinier fists raised as if she wasn't ready for the real world to intrude yet, while Dad's hand hovered protectively nearby.

That evening Gran took her to the hospital.

Laura was almost overwhelmed again at the sight of her little sister attached to wires and monitors.

One of the nurses approached.

"Laura, isn't it? I'm Clara. I'm Isaac's aunt. Isn't your sister beautiful? So dainty."

"She looks so lost," Laura's voice broke.

Clara squeezed her shoulder.

"Holly's a fighter, and we're taking good care of her."

"Will she be home for Christmas?"

"We'll see. Your mum's been telling everyone that you're making the Christmas cake. Save a piece for me!"

• • • •

Sally unwound her scarf as she joined the others on the last Saturday before Christmas. "Sorry I'm late. It's busy out there."

Even Isaac looked rushed. "Hi, everyone. The usual?"

"Oh, yes please. I'm going to miss Pippa's mince pies, although my waistline won't," Maureen replied.

"Wait till you taste the scones she's planning for January!" Isaac laughed.

"Are you ready for Holly and your mum coming home tomorrow?" he asked Laura.

They had exchanged numbers and Isaac had already suggested a trip to the cinema in the new year.

"About as ready as we can be. Ben and Jess are already in love with Holly, though they might feel differently when we don't get much sleep! It's just as well the holidays have started."

"You must be so relieved," Sally said, after Isaac had confirmed their orders. "Some of your teachers have mentioned you're looking a lot better. They all send their congratulations."

"People have been really kind. Ivy, who sometimes sits next to me, gave me the sweetest little cardigan knitted by her sister, and my friends have brought rattles and tiny booties. With those, and Christmas presents, my school bag's been full to bursting."

"Speaking of presents . . ." Maureen leaned down and reached into her bag.

Sally gasped.

"You haven't!"

"I have. It is Christmas, after all."

She laughed as the others delved into their bags, too.

Maureen had bought woolly hats from a craft stall on the farmers' market.

Sally had opted for pretty notebooks, while Laura had bought bath bombs.

The two older women also presented Laura with tiny, all-in-one suits from the shop Sally had come across.

"Holly's going to be the best-dressed baby in town."

Laura wiped away happy tears.

"Time for official Christmas Cake Club business," Maureen announced. "Have we all put on our marzipan?"

"Mine isn't exactly neat," Laura admitted.

"That's fine. It'll be covered in icing. Don't worry about making it smooth and even, just say it's a snow scene and add a sprig of holly."

"But not my Holly." Laura giggled.

"Absolutely not. Make sure you take photos for us to share later, but also to celebrate what you've achieved because, make no mistake, it is an achievement! Do that as soon as you can.

"You won't have time, come Christmas, given the number of people we'll all have round the table."

"Did you sort out your son and his wife?" Sally asked.

"They sorted themselves out, after Sam asked us and Kate asked her parents how we coped with money and other disagreements. Things might still be bumpy, but they'll get there."

Advising Sally and Laura over the weeks had reminded her of her own early married years, when she'd asked her mother for advice on making the cake.

That, in turn, brought back memories of the many arguments she and Derek had had before rubbing the rough edges off each other.

Derek was right. Sam and Kate did have to find their own way, and they had.

Outside, as the trio hugged, snowflakes were drifting down.

"I used to laugh when people said this, but there's definitely Christmas magic in the air," Sally said.

"What are we going to call ourselves in January?" Laura asked. It was unthinkable they wouldn't keep meeting.

"The Simnel Cake Club? The Easter Bonnet Club?" Sally suggested.

"I'll tell you in January." There was a glint in Maureen's eye.

Sally struggled not to laugh. Whatever was decided, the three friends were already looking forward to it. ■

Room At The Inn

THE school had decided to revert to putting on a traditional nativity play.

Miss Hackett, who was in charge of all the music at Harriot Primary, was relieved.

The contemporary plays of recent years, with their new tunes and bizarre characters, had tried her patience.

Christmas was Christmas, not an opportunity to moralise about environmental damage or the dangers of mobile phones.

Last year's effort, which involved half of year two dressing up as pebbles (for reasons Miss Hackett had forgotten) had been incomprehensible.

No, Christmas needed the nativity story – shepherds, wise men and all.

The headteacher approached Miss Hackett one cold morning in late November.

"Miss Hackett," he said. "I know I can rely on you."

She knew this meant trouble.

Teachers, teaching assistants, admin staff and even the lunch monitors, all called the headteacher Mr McCall "Rely-On-You" behind his back.

The phrase always came before a request to work more than one's normal hours, or to manage a child with a nose bleed or stomach bug until their parents were summoned.

"Of course," Miss Hackett said. "Anything to help."

Ducking these approaches was impossible.

The children came first, and to be fair to Mr McCall, he was all about the children.

"Ofsted are almost certainly on their way in December," he said. "Mrs Rogers and Mr Dyer are

Miss Hackett was determined that the school nativity play would go without a hitch this year . . .

BY ALISON CARTER

running about like headless chickens getting ready."

Now Miss Hackett knew exactly what was coming.

Nina Rogers and Ben Dyer put on the Christmas show each year.

They were both young and keen. Miss Hackett was sure this influenced their choices of play.

The head was about to ask her to do the play, not just to accompany on the piano and rehearse the songs.

"It's nearly December already," she said.

"I know! A narrowing window in which the inspectors might turn up."

"No," Miss Hackett said, "I mean that if you want me to do the Christmas play, you've not left me much time."

Mr McCall looked crestfallen.

"It would save my life," he said, his voice rising to wheedling pitch. "Ben and Nina will be spending every spare minute making the place look like we're sharp as tacks."

"Some of us are already sharp as tacks," Miss Hackett said.

She prided herself, after 30 years in the job, on consistency and excellence. She had never had a bad word from a schools inspector.

"Yes, of course," Mr McCall said hurriedly.

A bead of sweat bubbled on the man's forehead.

"Full editorial and directorial control?" Miss Hackett narrowed her eyes.

"Full."

• • • •

The carols were not hard to choose – all the proper carols matched the story.

"Away In A Manger" was an obvious choice.

The children always enjoyed singing "We Three Kings", although some wag would no doubt try to insert "one in a taxi, one in a car", and have to be sent to stand in the hall until they appreciated the importance of choral singing.

The casting was trickier.

"Casting the roles can be fraught," Miss Hackett told her friend Ruth that evening.

They had got together at Miss Hackett's flat to listen to some Mozart.

"Parents get offended, or one ends up casting a child with no attention span to be narrator, resulting in huge gaps opening up in proceedings."

Miss Hackett knew that she had to be swift and firm in this task.

The narrator would be Yolanda Canning, she of the clear, sharp, bossy voice and remarkably advanced reading skills.

The lower years would all be sheep, a bold option which would sort out all manner of arguments in one fell swoop.

They could sing a verse of "While Shepherds Watched" on their own.

It would take days of practice to get all 26 of them to get it right, but it was a wise decision.

She would offer wholesale prices to parents on cotton wool for their costumes once she'd been to the cash and carry.

Having found roles, in performance, backstage and (nerve-racking) front-of-house for lots of the middling years, she set to work allocating the leads.

Once again, practicality was the name of the game.

They were a small group – the year had lost several pupils to private schools, and a few moving abroad.

Miss Hackett chose the shepherds and wise men, the angel and the innkeeper, with ease.

These were the reliable children.

Mary was an obvious choice, too, although Anabel Browne was far from being a likeable child.

She had an unfortunate side to her character which Miss Hackett had observed in music lessons, a tendency to do other children down via tittle tattling and snide remarks.

But she was tall, had long brown hair. She had a decent memory for lyrics and a strident tone.

Her friend Tom Freeling would play Joseph.

He was something of a thug. Miss Hackett was well aware that such terms were not used in modern education, and she only used them in her head, but he was – a boy who ploughed his way through life, not looking to right or left.

But he was clever, would manage the lines that the part involved, and got on with Anabel.

Miss Hackett looked at her list. She had to fit all the children in.

There at the bottom was Darcy's name.

Darcy Tanner, shy, sweet, and hard to get much out of in a music class of 21 pupils.

Darcy was clumsy.

Miss Hackett reminded herself of the dyspraxia diagnosis she'd recently been given.

Darcy's fine motor skills were poor, and she was always muddling up her knife and fork at lunchtimes.

Miss Hackett remembered watching her give up on cutlery and resort to eating with her fingers.

She remembered Anabel and Tom mocking her for doing it.

They could be poisonous to little Darcy, and she didn't fight back.

"The donkey," she said.

Darcy would play the donkey. Miss Hackett would write in a line for the part, or maybe just a moment in the drama when the donkey does something charming, such as nuzzling the baby Jesus' blanket.

Darcy would be fine with that, and she deserved

her moment of fame. She wasn't well-liked at school, and that tore at Miss Hackett's heart. Children could be cruel.

Sleeves were rolled up and the task tackled.

Miss Hackett toured the classrooms, telling the children who would be doing what.

Anabel and Tom preened when they heard they would be playing Mary and Joseph.

Miss Hackett sighed as they began talking to their friends about what they'd wear and how they'd have so much more to say that everyone else.

Miss Hackett pointed out firmly, as she stood at the front of the class with her clipboard, that the play was a joint effort, and every child was a vital cog in the machine, but the two with the lead roles weren't listening.

She itched to give them a piece of her mind, but there was so little time; everybody simply had to get on with it.

• • • •

Darcy's dad asked for a five-minute chat with Miss Hackett a few days later.

He wanted some hints about a costume.

"I mean, Miss Hackett, are the standards high? Am I expected to create something that actually looks like a donkey?" His eyes widened. "This isn't a pantomime horse situation? It's not two of them?"

"Should I be calling the other parent to discuss –"

"Not at all," Miss Hackett interrupted. "Mr Tanner, we are a small primary school with limited resources. Anything that gives the impression of a donkey will be marvellous. Ears, perhaps?"

Mr Tanner relaxed visibly. He was a single parent, and had a son, too, in the reception year.

He was obviously dedicated to his children, doing everything he could to smooth their way.

They both had special

needs. The little boy, Miss Hackett remembered, was waiting for a sight impairment statement.

She made a note to place him at the front of the sheep, so he could give his dad a big smile.

Darcy and her brother were adored by their father, but this did not stop Darcy from being the butt of jokes if she tripped over or dropped something.

Miss Hackett worked with the lead characters and discovered to her dismay that the nativity story in all its charming and poignant detail, was, astonishingly, not familiar to several of the children.

"That's the result of too many Christmas plays about melting ice caps," she muttered to the teacher standing beside her, before realising it was Mr Dyer, who had bought that particular script at some detriment to the school budget a couple of years ago.

She didn't have time to teach a whole school the nativity story, and ploughed on, coaching the final year students as they rehearsed.

The animals to be arranged around the crib were not required for this rehearsal, and they stayed in their classroom.

Nor were the sheep, who would simply be herded on to the area in front of the stage, ready for the scene with the shepherds and the angel host, and their verse of the carol.

But Darcy Tanner appeared just as the rehearsal came to a close, standing nervously in the doorway between the hall and the corridor from which all the classrooms opened.

"Sorry, Miss Hackett. Mrs Davis says can she make a start on decorations now?"

Miss Davis was the final year teacher, and custodian of Christmas decorations.

Annually, she dumped her class with someone else while she had fun with tinsel.

"Yes, Darcy," Miss Hackett said. "We will be done soon,

but if we could have just a few – ah, Mr McCall."

The head had come up behind Darcy.

He was carrying a small Christmas tree (tightly swathed in netting) which he now propped against his long body.

Harriot Primary's hall was modestly proportioned, and did not have space for a giant tree.

"Mr McCall," Miss Hackett said, in the voice she used when in front of the children but wishing to reprimand a colleague. "I wonder if we could just complete rehearsal of the innkeeper section before the decorating work begins?"

The head looked suitably contrite.

"Of course, Miss Hackett." He noticed Darcy Tanner beside him in the doorway. "Ah, Darcy. Off you trot and ask Mrs Davis to wait five minutes before bringing in her boxes."

Darcy turned and bumped heavily into the Christmas tree.

Giggles erupted from the children in the hall, and Miss Hackett turned towards them in a flash.

Tom and Anabel were obviously leading the mockery.

She heard Tom say, "She's caught her brother's blindness."

Anabel was shaking with laughter.

Somebody – Miss Hackett could not tell if it was Tom or some other little brute, began to make donkey noises.

As Darcy untangled herself from the netting and ran off along the corridor, the head propped the tree against the door jamb and marched into the hall.

"May I have five minutes, Miss Hackett?" he said.

She nodded. The headteacher was wishy-washy when it came to HR, but he knew how to deal with pupils.

He pointed to the tree.

"Is that what Christmas is about?" he asked.

There was a silence,

punctuated only by a few sniffs from the ones who had colds.

"What can you tell me about Christmas?" Mr McCall insisted. "Give me some words."

These children, Miss Hackett reflected, were at least ten and could be expected to have some coherent ideas.

"Is it the tree?" Mr McCall said. "The cake, the turkey, the crackers?"

"It's baby Jesus," piped up a girl at the back.

"That's a good start," Mr McCall said. "Think about this play you're putting on, for instance."

Miss Hackett felt that it was mainly her putting it on, but didn't say so.

"Giving presents?" Anabel Browne said sulkily.

"Giving, yes. But not just presents. Christmas reminds us of people that need our help. People volunteer at Christmas, they give things to those who are not necessarily in their immediate family.

"And it's about kindness, and hope."

He gestured towards Miss Hackett.

"I'd like you to pay attention to the words of the lovely carols that Miss Hackett had been practising with you.

"You might get some clues about how we treat each other. Start with 'Good King Wenceslas'."

Miss Hackett saw Tom Freeling's mouth move again, and was sure she heard Anabel say something derogatory about the sheep, and their attempts at "While Shepherds Watched".

For a moment she considered taking Tom and Anabel's parts away from them, depriving Anabel of her blue gown, and Joseph of his oaken staff, but it was far too late for that.

The head left, and the rehearsal came to an end.

• • • •

The day of the performance arrived horrifyingly quickly, and

Miss Hackett's nerves began to fray.

She hadn't had a moment to really rehearse the ox and other animals that would surround baby Jesus, but they had an easy cue for their few lines, and surely most of them knew the story.

They would, she hoped, sit quietly as they waited for Mary and Joseph to come knocking on the innkeeper's door.

The stage had been divided into two halves – the stable represented on one side, and the street scene on the other.

She stood in the "dressing room" (a large classroom) and surveyed her cast.

The parents could be heard in the hall, jostling for a front seat.

Miss Hackett called out, "First act beginners, please."

Nothing happened.

"All right then," she said. "Mary and Joseph first, for the journey to Bethlehem."

It all went well, to start with. Tom Freeling and Anabel Browne comported themselves with just enough dignity, though Anabel could be heard hissing "Don't!" when her husband laid a hand on her shoulder.

She wriggled.

"You'll crease the dress!"

The two of them managed to mime knocking on the door of the inn and the innkeeper, a solid child by the name of Rory, appeared on cue.

The enormous grin on his face wasn't quite right. He hadn't done that in rehearsal.

Miss Hackett realised that he was looking out at the audience to find his mum.

"Yes?" Rory said, after a very long pause during which his mum waved at him.

"We seek lodging," Tom said.

"No way," Rory said.

That wasn't quite the line in the script, but it worked.

"But we have asked all over the town," Anabel said, getting a surprising amount of pathos into her voice.

"The inn is full," Rory said. "Chock-a-block, mate."

He'd added the final phrase, and Miss Hackett glowered at him from the wings.

"We have travelled far a long way and my wife is very tired," Tom said.

He seemed to be taking a cue from Anabel, and he sounded pretty exhausted.

Miss Hackett felt that her coaching had not been in vain.

"No room at the inn," Rory declared firmly.

He too was getting into the spirit of it. He even raised a hand, palm outward, and the audience practically moaned with the sadness of it.

The animals, whom Miss Hackett had taken her eyes off, were restive now.

Some of them were children who struggled to keep still. Luckily little Darcy, always well behaved, was still, very still indeed, gazing up from under her floppy brown ears.

Rory stamped his foot unnecessarily.

"She is heavy with child and must lie down," Tom said. He pointed at Anabel's blue dress. "Have you no small corner for us?"

The innkeeper seemed to have forgotten his next line.

Miss Hackett let five seconds go by, and then she whispered loudly, "Begone!"

"Begone," Rory shouted, and the entire audience jumped.

Joseph put his arm around Mary.

Slowly they turned to go, towards the wings and Miss Hackett, who waited with a smile.

"No!"

A thin cry was heard from behind Mary and Joseph, on stage.

They turned to look. Darcy was scrambling up from the floor, her brown sacking costume catching under her feet.

"That's so mean!" she cried. "Rory! Let them in!"

She was crying.

Miss Hackett thought fast. If she allowed Rory to wing it, to turn aside and let

actually them into the inn in some way undecided, then the rest of the performance would collapse.

The story was ruined.

But Darcy's expression was so intense, so tragic, so . . . caring. And every other child in the school, including all the sheep crammed on gym benches along the sides of the hall, were gazing at her.

Miss Hackett saw Mr McCall shake his head in wonderment, and then a smile break out on his face.

Darcy had been ill treated by both these small actors, many times over.

She struggled, but she kept going, and here she was urging kindness; here she was showing an entire hall how a human behaved, and what Christmas was, in the end, about – love.

She had done it at completely the wrong moment, but it was kindness nevertheless, and courage – in front of 175 parents.

Miss Hackett caught the head's eye. He walked up to the stage and turned.

"Well, I for one think that's a very good idea, Darcy. Let us welcome Mary and Joseph, and the baby Jesus, into the inn, where the ox and ass and camel can come and worship.

"What a lovely way for our play here today to reflect what Christmas is all about. Miss Hackett, can you tell us what the next carol is?"

"It's 'Away In A Manger', Mr McCall."

"Perfect."

She came out from the wings and sat at the piano.

The carol began, and Darcy beamed.

Miss Hackett made a mental note to tell Mr Tanner what a very good job he was doing.

Then she played the introduction to the carol and began furiously to work out what to do next with the play.

But it would be OK.

The parents knew the story already and the true meaning of Christmas.

Say It With Flowers

The Christmas Window competition had all eyes on Avril and Flora . . .

BY BECCA ROBIN

ALL the small, independent shops along Hibberton's high street were going to town on their window displays, and with good reason.

In a few days, the judges of the annual Best Christmas Window competition would be along with their score sheets, giving marks out of ten for festive appeal, style and originality.

Of course, it seemed a foregone conclusion that one of the two florists would win.

One or other of them usually did.

Last year it was Flora's turn, although it wasn't unknown for first prize to be awarded to the same establishment two years in a row. It remained to be seen whether Posies in Bloom or Flora's Ark would win the coveted first place trophy this year.

As soon as Avril, the proprietor of Posies in Bloom, returned from her morning trip to the wholesaler's, her young assistant Chloe grabbed her chance of a break.

For most of the year, Chloe loved working for Avril, but the added Christmas pressures were getting to her.

It was a relief to slip over the road to the relative calm of the Busy Stitches wool shop, where owner Wendy was always happy to put down her needles and pop the kettle on.

"Avril says she's had a new idea for our window display," Chloe said. "I have to steel myself before finding out what it is."

"Oh dear."

Wendy tutted and offered her young friend a gingerbread biscuit.

Normally, Chloe would never have moaned about her employer, but Wendy was like an unofficial agony aunt to the locality and Chloe knew it wouldn't go any further. Wendy was also well aware of the problem, having witnessed this rivalry between the two florists over many years.

"I haven't seen Avril in ages," she remarked.

They took their coffees and sat at the table in the middle of the shop.

"Yesterday she was unhappy, because Flora did that." Chloe pointed at the window of the other flower shop, which was four shops down from their own.

"The new sign?" Wendy checked. "Eye-catching, isn't it?"

A word, spelled out in golden fairy lights, had been temporarily inserted above the usual two words on the signage, with a little arrow below.

It changed "Flora's Ark" into "Flora's Festive Ark".

Inside, Chloe noticed that Flora's new delivery driver had been roped into helping with the window display, which was also under construction.

"I wish Avril and Flora would cool down a bit. It's only a small, local competition," Chloe said.

"In its own way, it's as important as winning an Oscar to them both," Wendy said. "They've been friends for years, but there's no rivalry like friendly rivalry."

They chatted for a bit, then Chloe checked her watch and downed the rest of her coffee.

"I must get back," she said. "Thanks for listening."

"No problem." Wendy smiled. "I hope this new idea of Avril's works out, whatever it is."

"We'll see."

Chloe returned to find the expected flurry of activity.

Amidst the new stock, Avril was kneeling on the floor wrapping empty cardboard boxes with Christmas paper, although screwed-up balls of paper lay about, which she must have attempted to use and discarded.

"It needs to be perfect. No wrinkles at all." Avril was frowning in frustration.

"Shall I have a go?" Chloe offered.

"If you could. We need lots of boxes at different levels and they're lying on their sides, so they must have paper inside, too."

"What's the idea?"

"Oh of course, I haven't told you yet." Avril rose to her feet. "It came to me this morning.

"'The Language of Christmas Flowers'. What do you think?"

Chloe didn't say anything. She was hoping Avril would go on to explain.

"You have heard of the language of flowers?" Avril checked.

Chloe shook her head.

"The Victorians were very keen on it. Each flower had its own meaning, and you could put them together in a bunch, to send a sophisticated message to the recipient."

"Oh, I see. So, our display's going to be about the meaning of Christmas flowers?"

Avril nodded. Her eyes were shining with excitement now.

"You can look them up on the internet. Lilies mean purity, carnations mean devotion and so on. It works for single plants, too.

"For example, a poinsettia symbolises goodwill and celebration."

Chloe was just starting to appreciate the idea, when Avril went completely over the top as expected.

"So, we're going to build a huge, ornate Victorian fireplace at the back of the display, and it'll look like Santa's dropped his presents down the chimney and they're all spilling out of their boxes, with a sign explaining the meaning of each floral gift."

"Sounds amazing." Chloe took a deep breath. It also sounded like an awful lot of work at what was already a very busy time at the shop.

"Come on then." Avril chivvied her to take over wrapping the boxes, saying she was going to ring her friend Helen who was good at calligraphy and could make signs in beautifully sloping, Victorian-like script.

● ● ● ●

A couple of days later, Chloe grabbed her chance to pop over to Busy Stitches.

"Your window looks lovely," Wendy observed. "You've worked very hard."

"Yes, although the theme won't be obvious until the signs go up," Chloe said.

"I won't ask." Wendy chuckled. "I imagine you're sworn to secrecy."

As they munched through Wendy's home-made mince pies, they gazed across at the Posies in Bloom window.

It did look very impressive.

Avril had hired a carpenter to build the enormous fireplace, which acted as a backdrop to Chloe's beautifully wrapped boxes lying around all higgledy-piggledy. They were now constructing some showstopping arrangements of Christmas flowers to place in the boxes.

"Flora's display is coming along nicely, too," Chloe remarked.

A red-painted sleigh filled the window of Flora's Ark and there were splendid floral arrangements both on the sleigh and amidst the drifts of artificial snow.

Avril had sent Chloe on errands to the postbox several times, so she could report back on how their rival's display was shaping up.

"She's obviously been hard at it," Chloe said.

"Oh, I see everything from here," Wendy said. "She and Adam haven't stopped."

"Is that her new delivery driver?"

"Yes. He built the sleigh."

"He did a good job."

So far, they'd only talked about the florists' displays, but Chloe was keen to praise Wendy's own efforts.

"I love your window display," she said. "It's really effective."

"Oh, I wasn't sure what to do this year. I thought it might raise a smile."

Wendy had used a pair of hugely oversized knitting needles to knit an enormous Christmas stocking in chunky red, white and green wool.

It was hanging in the centre of her window still attached to the needles and enhanced by twinkling fairy lights.

A speech bubble coming out of the mouth of a tiny, knitted mouse read, "Please fill by Christmas Eve!"

Chloe was just about to ask how long it had taken to knit the stocking, when the bell above the shop door tinkled.

Turning, she recognised the delivery driver they'd just been talking about.

He clearly recognised her, too, because he looked uncomfortable.

For a moment he hovered in the doorway as though unsure whether to enter or not.

"I don't know if you two have been introduced?" Wendy jumped in. "Adam from Flora's Ark, meet Chloe from Posies in Bloom."

"I've seen you in the shop," he said with a half-smile. "Great display, by the way."

"Thanks," Chloe said. "I've seen you popping in and out of Flora's shop, too. And we were just talking about your fantastic display."

"Come in, it's freezing with the door open," Wendy interjected. "Tea? Coffee? The kettle's just boiled."

Adam fumbled for an answer, but Wendy was already at the door, closing it with one hand and offering him a chair with the other.

"You're both on a break," Wendy said. "Why not sit and have a chat? I think you'll find you have plenty in common."

Adam thanked Wendy and said he'd have a coffee.

She went through to the back room where the kettle was.

After a few awkward moments sitting side by side, Chloe caught Adam's eye and they both smiled.

"It's this window display competition." He shook his head. "I can't believe how seriously they're taking it. Apparently, it's the same every year. That's why I sometimes pop over here, to de-stress."

"You as well?" Chloe said.

Wendy hadn't mentioned it. Then again perhaps she wouldn't, given the circumstances.

"Thank goodness our display's nearly finished," Adam said. "All that remains is to put our signs up and we're done."

"We're more or less finished, too," Chloe said. "Avril thinks it's the best idea she's ever had."

"It's going to be hard, picking the winner."

"Too right."

The initial reserve between them was beginning to break down.

"I've noticed you going backwards and forwards to the postbox several times a day," Adam said, on a slightly different tack. "You seem to have lots of cards to post."

There was a meaning in his cheeky smile and Chloe laughed at the fact she'd been caught out.

"They're Avril's cards," she said with a wry smile of her own.

He lowered his voice, conspiratorially.

"I've been sent on a few missions past your window, too, although you were probably too busy to notice."

"Perhaps you're better at spying than I am."

Wendy returned with Adam's coffee, and they all carried on chatting.

Chloe returned to work with a very favourable impression of the young delivery driver.

She hoped they'd have further chances to meet, especially once the competition was over.

When Helen delivered the signs, Avril was delighted and gave her friend a lovely bouquet as a thank you.

She and Chloe set about arranging the signs in the window and then went out on to the pavement to admire their work.

Each of the bouquets and potted plants spilling out from their gift boxes was accompanied by a sign explaining their meaning and a large sign over the fireplace in beautiful cursive script, said "The Language of Christmas Flowers".

"There, finished!" Avril beamed. "A winning window display without doubt. This'll knock the socks off the judges, and everyone else."

She took a quick glance up the street and Chloe knew very well who she meant. "It's fabulous," Chloe agreed. "Do you mind if I go for my break now?"

While Wendy put the kettle on, Chloe peered past the giant stocking at the shops opposite.

The window of Posies in Bloom really did look good, as did that of Flora's Ark where some signs had also gone up that morning although they were mostly too far away to read.

The larger one on the sleigh said "Christmas Floriography". It sounded typically fancy, and Chloe wondered what it meant.

"Any idea what floriography is?" she called through to Wendy in the back room.

"Never heard of it," Wendy called back.

With that, the door opened, and in came Adam with a strange look on his face: a mixture of amusement and astonishment.

"Watch out. It's all about to kick off," he said with a nervous laugh.

"What do you mean?" Chloe said.

"Someone's told Flora about the signs on your display. She's on her way to have it out with Avril."

"I don't understand," Chloe said. "What's wrong?"

Over his shoulder, she could see Flora walking briskly up the street towards Posies in Bloom, as though she wasn't taking any prisoners.

"Our display's about floriography, too."

"Flori . . .? Oh!"

Chloe had just worked out what the word meant.

Wendy came through from the back room.

"What's the matter?" she asked.

"You'll never believe this," Chloe said. "Avril and Flora have chosen the same theme for our window

displays. Floriography and The Language of Flowers must be the same thing."

"We've got printed labels explaining the meanings behind all the flowers, just like you," Adam said.

"Oh, heck!" Wendy exclaimed. "And there they both are now."

Under cover of the giant stocking, they witnessed what was taking place across the road in Avril's shop.

As they worked their way through a plate of Wendy's home-made stollen, they saw the disagreement peak, then subside until at last, Flora left the shop sniffing into a hankie.

"How sad to see pride get in the way of friendship," Wendy said.

"I'd better go and see how Avril is." Chloe sighed.

When Chloe entered the shop, Avril's eyes were still moist.

She thought it best to let her employer tell her the problem, rather than reveal she'd just witnessed the scene with Flora.

"Flora was here just now." Avril sniffed. "She asked me to change our display! Can you imagine the nerve of that woman? I said she should think about changing hers."

In all honesty there was no time to change either display, with the judges expected the following day.

"I suppose great minds think alike." Chloe winced, thinking it wasn't the best thing she could have said, but Avril didn't seem to have heard, lost in the fug of her own thoughts.

She eventually calmed down but remained in a mood for the rest of the day.

Chloe was sorry. She liked Avril and wished she could stop letting this competition consume her, because it really wasn't what Christmas was all about.

• • • •

The results of the competition were always announced during the Christmas lights switch-on.

From where she stood, Chloe could see the glittering trophy, which would grace the winner's window for the next 12 months.

There were oohs and ahhs from the crowd when the lights came on.

They enhanced all the magnificent displays, though two elaborate ones stood out.

Hibberton's resident celebrity Martina Mason, who'd once been a runner-up on a television talent contest, had the task of announcing the results. Chloe stood next to Avril, who was bristling with anticipation.

"This year's results were very close," Martina said. "The judges want to thank everyone. You've all done Hibberton proud."

Applause followed.

"I wish she'd get on with it," Avril muttered.

Several windows were announced as highly commended. Then came the top three places.

"The judges were very impressed with two entries – Posies in Bloom and Flora's Ark," Martina said.

"They both scored equally for festive appeal and style but lost marks for originality, so they come in joint second place."

Neither could score highly for originality with identical themes.

But who had won?

Avril and Flora approached the stage together and had their photo taken.

Chloe spotted Adam in the crowd. He winked and she looked away to stop herself laughing.

"Who's won?" she mouthed. He shrugged.

"Now we come to the moment of truth," Martina said.

"The judges were delighted by the festive flair, stylish simplicity and amusing originality of the winning window.

"The award goes to . . . Busy Stitches!"

Adam's mouth dropped open, but Wendy looked

even more surprised. She had to be led to the stage amidst clapping and cheering.

She nearly dropped the trophy, but her grin said it was sinking in.

Chloe could see Avril and Flora applauding – this time, genuinely.

Wendy was clearly a worthy and popular winner.

• • • •

The following morning, Chloe was alone in the shop when Adam popped his head in.

"I'm on another mission," he said. "Flora's sent Avril a present."

Entering, Adam brought from behind his back a beautiful bunch of chrysanthemums and lilies.

"The symbols of friendship and new beginnings," he said with a smile.

"Great minds really do think alike." Chloe patted the flowerpot on the counter which had a big silver bow tied around it.

"As soon as Avril returns, I'm supposed to take this over to Flora, although I'm not sure where she's gone or how long she'll be."

"A Christmas cactus?"

"Symbolising hope and renewal," Chloe said with a delighted smile of her own.

Hopefully, these gifts would mark the end of Avril and Flora's rivalry, once and for all.

"Actually, I know where your boss is because mine's with her. I think they might be there a while longer."

Adam pointed across the road at Busy Stitches where the tiny, knitted mouse was now sitting atop a large, shiny trophy.

Beyond the giant stocking, Chloe could see three figures sitting around the table, chatting and laughing.

Where better to hold a peace summit, accompanied by Wendy's home-baked tasty treats?

After this, they could all settle down and enjoy a happy, friendly Christmas. ■

A New Chapter

A cosy evening dedicated to reading was more than Kelly could ever hope for . . .

BY FIONA THOMSON

JOLLY what?" Kelly paused, fork in mid-air, looking at Anna across the canteen table.

"Jólabókaflóð," her colleague said, grinning. "My mum and dad had no idea either."

She laughed.

"It's an Icelandic tradition on Christmas Eve. Everyone gives books and spends the evening reading. My idea of heaven – and this year I'll be doing it!"

"Oh, that sounds perfect," Kelly said. "I'm picturing a comfy chair . . ."

"Hand-knitted blanket."

"And hot chocolate," Kelly added, holding up her mug. "Twice the size of this."

"Don't forget the roaring fire!" Anna smiled. "Jonah and I are going for three days. It's expensive, but as he said, we're only young once."

Kelly nodded. Anna, twenty-one, had been in the office six months. She and her boyfriend had already visited Vietnam and taken a Berlin mini-break.

"Do it now," Kelly said. "Once you settle down, it gets harder to get away."

Anna sipped her coffee.

"So what are your Christmas plans?"

"Make a long list and tick everything off!" Kelly laughed. "I love it, but there's so much to do.

"Phoebe's asked for too many toys – no five-year-old needs that many – and Kai still prefers the wrapping to the gift.

"My parents come for Christmas dinner, then Joe's family on Boxing Day, so no time for reading."

• • • •

"Jolly what?" Joe said, loading a bulging shopping bag into the boot.

"That was my reply, too." Kelly lifted the last bag from the trolley. "Jóla-bóka-flóð.

It means 'Christmas book flood' in Icelandic.

"Jonah and Anna are flying to Reykjavik, two wrapped books in their suitcases ready to exchange."

Joe shut the boot.

"Can't remember the last time I read a book of my choice. Bluey and unicorns every night – I know them all off by heart."

Kelly laughed.

"So do Phoebe and Kai. When I tried skipping a page, they were so quick to notice. Remember how I was late on our second date because I was reading and missed the bus?"

"I thought you'd stood me up!" Joe kissed her. "Glad I waited."

That evening, Kelly paused by the bookcase in the hall.

Every shelf was packed – childhood favourites, student reads, plus many she'd been gifted but never opened.

Marian Keyes, Mick Herron, Richard Osman. She loved them all, but when did she have time to read?

• • • •

"How many hours until Santa comes?" Phoebe raced round the kitchen, Kai toddling after her.

"Lots," Kelly said, putting fish fingers in the air fryer. "But first it's tea, then Christmas Eve boxes when Daddy gets home."

There'd been nothing like that when she was little, but now it helped distract the kids so she could finish things off.

Even better, it was something Joe handled without needing to be asked.

Kelly sorted the new pyjamas, but Joe chose the extra treats and picked the film.

When he got in, she smiled at his excited face.

He loved this family time.

"Right, you two." Joe carried the boxes into the living room. "Time to see what's inside!"

When Phoebe and Kai had opened theirs, Joe handed Kelly another box.

"I thought you deserved one, too."

"What?" Kelly looked surprised. "But I haven't got one for you."

Joe shook his head.

"I didn't expect one. Please, open it."

Inside were two chocolate bars, a scented candle, and a wrapped parcel.

Her smile faded. Books. Just more to gather dust.

She looked at Joe and tried to sound upbeat.

"I think I might have guessed," she said, unwrapping it.

Richard Osman, Marian Keyes, Kate Atkinson.

Even worse – duplicates of books she already owned but had never read.

"I don't know what to say," she whispered.

"There's an envelope in the bottom," Joe said.

Kelly pulled out two bookmarks – Phoebe's decorated with flowers, Kai's with smudgy fingerprints – and a handwritten card.

"We promise you time to read in 2026. Love, Joe, Phoebe and Kai x"

She looked at the bookcase – where could she squeeze them in? Then she noticed the gaps.

"Yes, they're your own books," Joe said. "I wrapped them after work. I hoped you wouldn't notice!

"You always say you're too busy to start one. But I heard that if you read for just fifteen minutes a day, you can finish a book in a month.

"We'll make time after dinner, when the kids are in bed. Coffee and a book. That's my promise to you."

"Oh, Joe!" Kelly hugged him tight, tears in her eyes. "I love you so much."

• • • •

Later, with stockings hung and excited children asleep, Kelly heard a ping on her phone. A photo of Anna and Jonah curled up with books, hot chocolate and blankets by a roaring fire.

Kelly smiled. No need to travel to Iceland.

She had everything she wanted right here. ◼

Kindred Spirits

Doug and I just can't agree about the best way
to mark the festive season . . .

BY ALISON WASSELL

HE'S behind you!" Several hundred schoolchildren point towards the stage, shouting at the tops of their voices and I join in enthusiastically.

For me, a visit to the pantomime is the perfect start to Christmas.

I haven't missed a year since I was a little girl, back in the '60s.

At first, it was an annual treat with my grandparents, but as an adult I have always grabbed any child I can find to accompany me: a younger cousin, a neighbour, a nephew, a great-niece and, on several memorable occasions, a

whole troop of Brownies. Today though, I'm with Doug. I don't quite know how to describe him.

Since we're both retired, "boyfriend" doesn't seem right, and neither does "gentleman companion", which is how my friend Marcia insists on referring to him.

She has known Doug for years and introduced us at a local history talk she dragged me to. Since then, we've been on several dates, taking it in turns to choose the location.

This is his Doug's first pantomime and, I suspect, his last. I can sense that he hates everything I love;

the wobbly sets, the corny jokes, the minor celebrities neither of us have ever heard of, the audience participation. His tastes are definitely more highbrow.

The small child sitting next to him accidentally showers him with Maltesers and he visibly flinches.

"It was interesting," he says, later, over a glass of wine in a nice quiet pub, which is far more to his liking.

I tell him there's no need to pretend he didn't hate it.

"Maybe going to a midweek matinee performance packed with school parties wasn't the best idea," I add.

He smiles at me, looking much more relaxed now than he did in the theatre, where I'm sure I saw him clutching the arms of his seat in abject terror when they asked for "volunteers" to go up on to the stage.

"Honestly, Janice, I found it interesting. The pantomime has a fascinating history, you know." He starts to explain how it originated from the Italian Commedia dell'Arte, which featured the same kind of slapstick comedy and stock characters.

"And have you ever noticed that the baddies always enter from stage left, and the good guys from the right?" he says, warming to his subject.

I love the fact that he's taken the trouble to do some research, but I can't resist teasing him.

"How do you feel about going to one of the bigger shows, in the new year? I believe there's a great production of 'Jack And The Beanstalk' in Manchester."

It takes him a few seconds to realise I'm not serious. He holds up his hands.

"OK, I admit it. Pantomime's really not my thing. But I loved watching you having such fun."

It's a good answer, I suppose, although I'm a bit sad that he doesn't share my enthusiasm.

• • • •

"I can't believe you've never been to a classical music concert," he says, the following week, as we sip our mulled wine before the performance.

The truth is, I like my music to be accompanied by words. Preferably ones I can sing along with. Doug is dressed more formally than I've ever seen him in a suit and tie, and I'm wearing my best "going out" dress.

An hour ago, twirling around in front of my wardrobe mirror, I felt a million dollars.

Now, looking at several ladies in full-length evening gowns, I feel somewhat underdressed.

"I didn't realise it would be so grand," I whisper.

Doug grins, as though he regards grandness as a good thing rather than a cause for concern.

"Well, it's a far cry from the local theatre, that's for sure," he says, as he ushers me into the auditorium.

Despite feeling out of place, I can't help but be impressed by the beautiful domed ceiling and the ornate woodcarving.

An enormous, tastefully decorated Christmas tree adorns the stage.

We take our seats and Doug hands me the programme.

At least there are a few names I recognise.

There's to be an excerpt from Tchaikovsky's "Nutcracker Suite" and pieces by Rimsky-Korsakov and Liszt.

Most things have Christmas in the title, which is a good sign. I prepare to feel festive as the members of the orchestra file on to the stage.

• • • •

"It was lovely," I say, afterwards.

It was, although on at least two occasions I very nearly embarrassed myself by clapping in the wrong place and, towards the end, I felt a bit fidgety.

I longed to have some knitting or crochet to occupy my hands, the way I always do when I'm watching television.

I have a low boredom threshold, and I'm not used to just sitting still and silently, scared to even rustle the pages of the programme.

I was glad when the concert came to an end.

I could tell that Doug was loving it, though. Several times, when I glanced at him, his eyes were closed, and he was nodding away in appreciation, a beatific smile on his face.

"I'd love to learn more about classical music," I say, not having the vocabulary to enter into a more meaningful discussion.

"You'll have to recommend some pieces suitable for a complete ignoramus like me."

Doug helps me on with my coat.

"Thanks for coming with me. I know it's not really your cup of tea," he says.

It seems pointless, and dishonest, to deny it.

• • • •

With each day that goes by, we seem to discover another difference in our approaches to the festive season.

"Oh my word, it's like Santa's grotto in here," Doug exclaims, when he comes for a meal at my house.

It doesn't exactly sound like a compliment.

Even though I have lived alone for most of my adult life, I have never skimped on Christmas decorations.

My tree always goes up at the beginning of December and I throw on every bauble I have ever owned, including some I inherited from my parents, a set of hand crocheted snowmen made for me by my neighbour and, my absolute favourite, a small pig in a tutu.

A carol-singing teddy bear sits on my coffee table and all my cushion covers are temporarily replaced by seasonal ones.

"Don't squash Rudolph!" I say, as Doug lowers himself on to the sofa.

He retrieves a cuddly reindeer with a flashing red nose from behind him and, clearly not knowing what else to do with it, cradles it on his knee.

"Sorry mate, didn't see you there," he says.

I take Rudolph from him and place him under the tree next to a rabbit in a duffel coat and a mouse who can play "We Wish You A Merry Christmas" on a tiny piano.

"I expect your decorations are a bit more sophisticated," I say.

Doug says he's never really bothered, since his wife passed away.

"Mary liked a real tree, but I was never keen. We

were always still picking up the needles in June. And I usually spend Christmas Day at my daughter's house, so I've never really seen the point in going to any trouble myself."

"Don't you put up anything at all?" I say, failing to keep the note of horror from my voice. I can't imagine Christmas in an undecorated house.

"I put any cards up on the mantelpiece," he replies "Although hardly anyone seems to send them, these days. I certainly don't.

"I expect you think I'm a bit of a Grinch."

He looks ever so slightly embarrassed.

I assure him that I don't think any such thing, which isn't entirely true.

"I go a bit over the top with all this stuff," I say. "Maybe I should be a bit more restrained. Less is more, as the saying goes."

He says it's all very cheerful and welcoming, although his face tells me something different.

• • • •

"He doesn't even like mince pies! I made a fresh batch, and he took one bite and left the rest on his plate."

Marcia jokingly agrees that there's definitely something wrong with a man who doesn't consume at least three of my famous mince pies, which I make following a secret recipe passed down to me by my grandmother.

"Seriously though, Janice, what a boring world it would be if we were all the same? I'd never have introduced you to Doug if I hadn't thought you'd be perfect for each other." She blushes, realising what she's said.

I've long suspected that we didn't bump into him by chance that day at the talk, and now my suspicions are confirmed.

I'm constantly telling her that I'm perfectly happy being single, but it doesn't stop her trying to matchmake.

It used to annoy me, until

I realised it was her way of showing me she cared.

"He's a lovely man," I say. "But we have absolutely nothing in common. I honestly can't see much of a future for us."

Marcia looks so disappointed that I promise to give the relationship a bit more time.

• • • •

For our next date we decide to go to the cinema. It almost becomes the venue for our first argument.

I insist that Doug should choose which film we see and he is adamant that I should.

I suggest a French film with subtitles, thinking it looks like something he would love.

"They're showing 'Miracle On 34th Street'. The original black and white version," he says. "Wouldn't you rather see that?"

It happens to be one of my all-time favourite films and, of course, I would.

"But I don't like to think of you sitting through something you won't enjoy," I say.

"Same here," he replies.

There's a bit of a standoff until we both see the funny side and burst out laughing.

"Let's see something neither of us would normally choose," I suggest.

Doug agrees that this is an excellent idea.

"Well, that's two and a half hours of our lives that we'll never get back," he says, when we emerge from an action-packed blockbuster with lots of shooting and blowing things up, but no discernible plot.

"Well, at least we've found something we agree on," I point out.

We're both still giggling about the awfulness of it when he drops me off at home an hour later.

• • • •

"What did I tell you? You're definitely making progress," Marcia says, when I report back to her.

I'm surprised at how much ➤

I want her to be right. But I still have my doubts.

"If only we could find something we both enjoy," I muse.

Determined to help, Marcia finds a pen and paper and proceeds to make a list of activities that will, as she puts it, "take you both out of your comfort zones."

The first one is ice-skating. Apparently there's a rink in the grounds of a nearby stately home.

"Not only would it take us out of our comfort zones, it'd most likely put the pair of us in hospital," I protest.

I plead weak ankles and eventually Marcia concedes that it might not be one of her brightest ideas.

I disappoint her again by rejecting a wreath making workshop.

"I told you, Doug and decorations don't mix. It does sound good, though. Maybe you and I could go together," I say.

Marcia promises to book online for us as long as I choose something else from her list for Doug and me to try.

Ten minutes later I have dismissed something called a "Santa Dash" charity race where all the participants dress up as Santa, a Christmas karaoke night and a "Sleigh Ride Experience".

The only thing left is a tea dance at the town hall.

"Perfect!" Marcia says. "There's a live orchestra, which is right up Doug's street. And if you both enjoy the Christmas one, I happen to know that they hold them every month."

• • • •

"Well, I'm game if you are," Doug says, after only a short pause, when I suggest it.

I'm not much of a dancer, but I can just about manage a waltz.

Doug, on the other hand, is a revelation. He skilfully guides me around the dancefloor in the foxtrot, the quickstep, even the tango.

The orchestra is marvellous, with everyone wearing Santa hats and there's even a singer who entertains us with a medley of Christmas songs as we enjoy a delicious afternoon tea.

I can't remember when I last had so much fun.

On the drive home, though, Doug is quiet, and when I say it would be nice to make the tea dance a regular date, it takes him a long time to reply.

When he does, I detect a tremor in his voice.

"Ballroom dancing was Mary's favourite thing. She would have loved this afternoon.

"I need to be honest with you, Janice. I've really enjoyed today, but dancing with someone else has stirred up a lot of emotions for me.

"I'm just not sure I'm ready yet."

I can't decide whether he means he's not ready to go dancing with me, or not ready for a new relationship.

I'm afraid to ask, because the better I get to know him, the more I want things to work out for us.

When we reach my house he politely declines the offer of coffee and a slice of Christmas cake.

"I'll phone you in the New Year," he says, giving me a peck on the cheek.

• • • •

There are only a few days to go until Christmas, and we both have separate plans.

Doug will be staying with his daughter, Susan, and her young family for a few days while I'm planning to spend Christmas Eve helping Marcia with a party she organises every year for young carers.

On Christmas Day itself she'll be coming to my house, as usual.

She's an unenthusiastic cook, while I love an opportunity to show off my culinary skills.

I'm looking forward to it, although I can't help feeling a bit sad not to be seeing Doug.

In my experience, though, things rarely go according to plan.

At eight in the morning on Christmas Eve I'm woken by the phone.

It's Marcia, and she sounds as though she's on the verge of tears.

"Janice! There's been a disaster! In fact, there have been three disasters! We'll have to call the party off."

Knowing that my friend has a tendency to overdramatise. I tell her to take a few deep breaths.

"I'm sure it's nothing we can't sort out," I reassure her.

For once, she isn't exaggerating.

"There's been a break-in at the village hall and it's been left in a real mess. The caterers have no record of my booking, so there'll be no food.

"To top it all off, Father Christmas has 'flu."

I've often been told that I'm a good person to have around in a crisis.

But perhaps my greatest strength lies in recognising that I can't do everything on my own.

I tell Marcia to round up as many friends and neighbours as she can to sort out the hall.

Then I make a phone call of my own.

"Doug, I need your help." I say.

In less than an hour he arrives at my house with Susan and his two grandsons in tow, the boot of his car filled with bags of party food and baking ingredients.

There's no time for introductions as I get cracking on a batch of sausage rolls and some mini quiches.

Susan makes some fairy cakes while Doug supervises the sandwich making.

I put on some Christmas music to get us in a festive mood and, before long, we're all singing along, even Doug, who has a beautiful baritone voice.

The sausage rolls and quiches are still warm when we all pile into Doug's car to make our way to the village hall. Marcia and her band of helpers have managed to get the place looking shipshape.

Doug and I set about putting up some decorations while Susan helps Marcia put up trestle tables and cover them with festive tablecloths.

Susan's two boys make a general nuisance of themselves and get under everyone's feet until Doug gives them the task of counting out the right number of plates and cups and setting them out on the tables.

It's heartwarming to see their bond.

By some miracle, everything's ready as the guests arrive. Twenty young carers, aged seven to eighteen, enjoying a rare moment of carefree fun.

"It's wonderful to see them just being children," I say, noticing Doug has disappeared.

He reappears in a Santa suit, ho-ho-hoing with gusto. The teens pretend they're too cool, but I see their smiles.

"Well, that was out of my comfort zone," Doug says later.

I apologise for roping him in.

"Don't be silly, it's the most fun I've had in years," he replies — and I believe him.

• • • •

"We're going to look at volunteering opportunities, maybe involving working with young people, I tell Marcia, the following day, over our Christmas dinner. "It'll be something we can enjoy doing together." My friend sets down her knife and fork and claps her hands.

"You two have more in common than you think, you know," she says. "You'll both do anything to help someone in trouble.

"That's how I knew you were right for each other."

We raise our glasses in a toast.

"To the future, and to friendships, old and new."

O LIVER stared glumly around the empty café which was festooned with fairy lights and red and gold bunting.

The place should have been bustling by now.

There should be happy customers excitedly chatting about their Christmas plans, sipping hot drinks and enjoying good food. Where better to while away an hour on such a cold, damp December morning than the Cosy Café?

Oliver's phone pinged.

"Please don't be another negative review," he muttered, picking it up from the counter.

"More grumbling?" his Spanish wife enquired as she carried through a plate of freshly baked mince pies from the kitchen.

Oliver nodded silently.

"What do they say this time?" María asked. "More complaints about the thirty pence price rise for a latte, or the colours we chose to repaint the café?"

Sighing, her husband read out the latest comment on their Facebook page.

"'It sounds as though the new owners have ruined what was once a lovely little café in the village. Thanks for saving us a wasted journey.'"

"Wait – they have not even visited us?" María cried, slamming the plate of mince pies down on the counter.

"Careful! You spent ages making those," Oliver said.

"I begin to wonder why I bothered," María grumbled. "Besides, they are probably . . . what was it Señora Ambrose wrote in her review about my cakes?"

"I don't remember," Oliver lied, determined to avoid eye contact with his wife.

He just knew she was standing there, hands on hips, giving him the look.

María cleared her throat.

Oliver sighed.

"'All style over substance and decidedly dry, but thankfully . . .'"

"Sí, I remember now,"

Just Desserts!

Could María's pies make mincemeat of the café's unfair reviews?

BY GRAEME EDWARDS

María said, her voice rising, "but thankfully we serve such small portions customers do not have to endure the horrible dry cake for long!"

She paused suddenly.

There, standing in the doorway, was a middle-aged couple staring open mouthed at her.

"Come in, come in!" María cried, flashing them a smile.

"Err, I think we've left the car headlights on," the man said.

"Gosh, I think you're right!" the woman replied. "We'd better go and turn them off. We'll be back shortly."

"That is a relief," María said, watching as they hurried out. "I thought we had scared them off."

Oliver smiled sadly. His wife always took people at face value.

It was one of the many things he loved about her. "They're not coming back," he said.

"How can you be so sure?" María asked.

"Trust me. You know, I hadn't realised just how dependent we'd be on the locals during the winter months.

"Hardly any of them have visited since we re-opened."

"But we still serve everything that was on the old menu and more," María protested. "Our portions are just as generous, and my cakes were always popular when we ran our pop-up café.

"I do not understand why Señora Ambrose and the rest of the village hate us so."

"Your cakes are delicious," Oliver said, giving his wife a hug, "and I don't think they hate us – just the changes we've made."

"Most of which they have imagined. Perhaps things will improve in the summer when the tourists visit?" María suggested, hopefully.

"Perhaps," Oliver replied. "That won't help pay the mortgage or the bills in the meantime though. So much for thinking we'd have to take on extra staff.

"At this rate we'll be out of business by January."

A sudden thought struck María.

She picked up two mince pies and offered one to her husband.

"This is the first batch I have made this year," she said. "We must make mince pie wishes like your mamá taught me!"

Oliver smiled.

Closing their eyes, they bit into their pies and each made a wish.

• • • •

When the opportunity to buy the café had come along earlier that year, Oliver and María couldn't believe their luck.

Having run a pop-up café from their increasingly unreliable old van for several years, they were keen to buy their own place.

The young couple had been driving to a county show when their van had broken down in the picturesque village.

While they waited for the breakdown recovery man to arrive, they popped into the Cosy Café for a bite to eat.

Grabbing the last remaining table, Oliver and María soon found themselves enjoying a tasty cooked breakfast.

They then decided to sample a few of the impressive looking cakes on offer.

"Delicioso!" María had said after biting into a slice of Persian love cake.

"So is this one," Oliver mumbled with a mouthful of coffee and walnut cake.

"I'm glad you're enjoying them!" came a nearby voice.

Turning, they found a short woman with wavy, grey hair and twinkly eyes smiling down at them.

"Having eaten one of your own creations last year, that's high praise indeed," she continued. "Your stem ginger cake with cream cheese frosting was wonderful. I'm Maggie. I own the café."

Thrilled to receive a compliment from a fellow cake connoisseur, María gave her husband a gentle kick under the table.

Oliver smiled.

"This is my wife, María," he said, "She bakes all our cakes, and I'm Oliver."

"I have never tried Persian love cake before. Is that rosewater I taste?" María asked.

"It is! I'd be happy to give you the recipe if you like," Maggie offered.

María nodded enthusiastically.

"That is very kind," she replied. "Gracias!"

"I'm rather looking forward to sampling some more of your own creations this afternoon at the county show," Maggie told them.

Oliver sighed.

"Let's just hope we can get the van started again," he said. "We had to miss an event last week."

"That can't be good for business," Maggie sympathised. "Have you ever considered staying put and running a place like this?"

"We have been looking," Oliver admitted. "The travelling can be a bit much sometimes and we'd like a proper kitchen so we can expand our menu.

"We just don't seem to be able to find anywhere."

"You know, I think your van breaking down here might be fate," Maggie said, pulling up a recently vacated seat from a nearby table.

Sitting down, she told them that she was planning on selling the café and adjoining cottage to move in with her soon-to-be husband in the neighbouring village.

"We've booked a three-month cruise as a combined honeymoon and retirement celebration," Maggie explained. "I'm keen for a quick sale and would be thrilled if it was taken on by a couple as passionate about food as you are.

"I can show you round now if you'd like?"

Come September, Oliver and María had found themselves the excited new owners of the Cosy Café.

"I can't wait to see what you've done with the place when I return," Maggie said, handing María a file of her recipes while her new husband waited in the car. "I'd always intended to redecorate but just never seemed to get around to it.

"When will you be re-opening?"

"In a couple of weeks, hopefully," Oliver told her.

"Well, good luck – I'm sure it will go well," Maggie reassured them, climbing into the car. "I'll see you both at Christmas!"

Oliver and María waved goodbye as the happy couple drove off.

They turned to gaze proudly at their new business.

"We'll have to buy some decorations," Oliver mused, placing an arm round his wife. "Christmas will be here before you know it."

"We could put up fairy lights in the windows," María suggested, picturing the café in all its festive glory.

No passers-by would be able to resist popping in for a drink and a bite to eat after peering through the large window at the cosy scene inside.

• • • •

Oliver helped himself to yet another mince pie.

"Do you not think we should leave some for the customers?" María said, raising an eyebrow.

"What customers?" Oliver replied gloomily. "There's no point letting them go to waste."

"But they are going to your waist," his wife chided him.

"I'll have one, and a latte with a generous dusting of cinnamon please!" came a familiar voice.

"Maggie!" María cried, giving her a hug.

"I must say, I like what you've done with the place. It looks nice and fresh," Maggie said, admiring the refurbished café, "and the Christmas decorations are lovely.

"But where is everyone?"

"Take a seat," Oliver said, as he began to prepare Maggie's latte. "We'll tell you all about it.

"This is delicious," the former café owner enthused. "Have you made the mincemeat yourself?"

María nodded.

"I recognise the coffee," Maggie said, taking a sip of her latte. "It's the same blend I used. These cups and plates are new, though.

"They're far more interesting than the boring white lot I had."

"We got them from the new pottery studio down the road," Oliver explained. "The owner was thrilled when we put in such a large order – he's also been struggling to attract customers.

"We were hoping to send some business his way."

"There are lots of tempting new dishes, too," Maggie continued, studying the menu. "I'll enjoy trying those."

"I wish everyone in the village was as enthusiastic about the changes we've made," Oliver said, bringing up the Cosy Café's Facebook page on his phone. "Take a look."

After wiping her hands on a napkin, Maggie began to scroll through the comments people had left.

"'Gone downhill.' 'The food isn't a patch on what it used to be.' 'The new prices are daylight robbery.' What tosh!" Maggie muttered.

"And what's this about smaller cups? They don't look any smaller than mine."

"That is because they are not smaller," María said, indignantly. "We took one of the cups you left behind to the pottery, along with a bottle of water, pouring the contents from one to the other to compare sizes."

"The owner thought we were a bit odd!" Oliver said with a smile.

"We have had to put the prices up a bit though," he conceded. I'd been planning on doing the same, what with the rising cost of everything lately," Maggie reassured him.

"Most of those who have complained have not even visited us," María pointed out.

Maggie shook her head sadly.

"It all seems to have started with Patricia Ambrose," she said, continuing to scroll through the comments. "She chairs the WI and is involved with pretty much everything in the village.

"I'm afraid a lot of people take her word as gospel. You've had some lovely reviews though I see."

"Mostly from tourists who visited shortly after we opened," Oliver explained. "Unfortunately, it's the negative reviews people seem to go by."

"That's true, and you are dependent on the locals during the winter months," Maggie admitted. "Patricia and her flock never did like change.

"You should have heard the outcry when the new vicar opted for glossy paper on the cover of the parish magazine and changed the font."

"It really is hopeless, then," María said, sadly. "We will have to close in the new year."

"Definitely not!" Maggie cried. "We just have to convince the rest of the village that Patricia Ambrose is wrong."

> "I must say, I like what you've done with the place. It looks nice and fresh"

"But how do we do that if nobody will come to the café?" Oliver asked.

Maggie took another bite of her mince pie and pondered the situation.

A wide smile began to cross her face.

"I have an idea," she said. "Would it be possible to place a last-minute order for several of your finest cakes, three dozen mince pies and a selection of savoury goodies?"

"Of course," Oliver said. "When do you need them by?"

"Wednesday night. I'd also like to borrow a couple of those cups of yours, if I may – and you too, María."

"Me?" María asked, puzzled.

"You're coming to the WI Christmas meeting as my guest," Maggie said with a mischievous grin.

● ● ● ●

That Wednesday night, Oliver sat in the kitchen of their cottage, studying the business accounts on his laptop.

They made for grim reading.

"It's beginning to look a lot like Christmas . . ." Bing Crosby crooned from the speaker in the background.

"Alexa, turn off the music," Oliver snapped.

He wasn't feeling very festive. He glanced up at the clock on the wall. It was getting on for half past nine.

He wondered how it was going at the WI meeting at the village hall.

Maggie hadn't filled them in on her plan when she had collected the food, cups and María earlier that evening.

He heard a key turn in the front door and a moment later Maggie and his wife appeared in the kitchen doorway, grinning.

"Oh, Oliver! You will never guess what happened this evening," María cried, as they carried through two stacks of empty plates.

"The giant Christmas tree in the village hall fell on top of Mrs Ambrose while you were all singing 'Jerusalem'?" Oliver suggested, picturing the dishevelled café critic strewn with pine needles and tinsel, while cartoon robins flew around her head.

"Not quite," Maggie laughed, "although she did look rather dazed and confused by the end of the evening."

"Oh, I do hope it has worked!" María grinned.

"I guess we'll find out soon enough," Maggie said.

"Would someone mind filling me in on what happened this evening?" Oliver asked.

"It was magnífico!" María cried, offering Maggie a seat at the kitchen table. "Everyone assumed Maggie had made all of the food we took with us."

"I usually bring along a selection of this and that," Maggie explained.

"Maggie instructed me not to correct them," María continued. "After they had finished – what is the expression you use? – tucking in, Señora Ambrose told everyone that Maggie had outdone herself again and lamented how it was such a shame she had sold the café."

"What, right in front of you?" Oliver asked, aghast.

María nodded.

"I must admit I feared what your wife might do with Miss Teasdale's blancmange at that particular moment," Maggie said, laughing.

"It did cross my mind," María admitted. "Anyway, that was when Maggie told everyone that you and I had made everything!"

"It was all delightfully awkward," Maggie said.

"But that was not all," María continued. "Maggie and I offered to serve the tea and coffee. They were using the old cups from the café . . ."

"I donated a lot of them to the Village Hall after I retired," Maggie explained.

"As she was handing a cup of tea to Señora Ambrose," María continued, "Maggie pretended that she had spotted lipstick on it."

"An Oscar winning performance if I do say so myself!" Maggie joked.

"Do you know what Maggie did next?"

Oliver shook his head, engrossed in his wife's tale.

"She poured the tea from Señora Ambrose's cup into one of our cups – right in front of her and the other ladies, saying how fortunate it was they were the same size."

Oliver smiled.

"I wish I could have seen the looks on their faces," he said. "But do you really think it will work?"

María reached out across the table and took his hands in hers.

"It must work Oliver," she said. "It must."

● ● ● ●

María hurried into the café's kitchen.

"Señorita Teasdale and her gentleman friend would like two sage, butternut squash and Wensleydale fritattas, both with side salads and extra chilli dressing." She beamed, clipping yet another slip on the order board beside Oliver.

It was looking rather full.

"How's our young new employee doing?" Oliver asked.

"Estupendo!" María said, wiping some icing sugar off her husband's nose. "Sadie is a fast learner. She has brought more of her papá's pottery for us to sell, too."

"Do we have any more of the gluten-free mincemeat and marzipan cake?" a freckled redhead asked from the doorway.

"We do, Sadie," María replied, retrieving a large Tupperware box from a cupboard.

"Oh, and do we have any humble pie?" Sally enquired.

Oliver looked up from the cinnamon and orange French toast he was plating up.

"Come again?"

"Humble pie. Mrs Ambrose has just requested a slice to go with her gingerbread latte," Sally explained.

"If not, she'd like one of María's mince pies. She wanted me to tell you that they're delicious."

The bewildered café owners peered through the kitchen doorway.

There, seated at a table by the window, was Mrs Ambrose, studying a menu.

Spotting them, she smiled and waved.

"Do you think she's feeling all right?" Oliver whispered as his phone pinged.

"It is Christmas Eve and the season of goodwill," María suggested, waving back. "Perhaps she is full of the Christmas spirit?"

"I did hear a rumour she was partial to a sherry," Oliver joked, studying his phone.

"What is it?" his wife asked him.

"Another glowing review!" Oliver replied.

He peered though the doorway again.

The café was full of happy customers, excitedly chatting about their Christmas plans, sipping hot drinks and enjoying good food. He smiled.

Mince pie wishes really did come true. ◾

Becoming Mrs Claus

This wasn't how Lucy had planned to spend a busy December morning . . .

BY MARIAN MYERS

"**Y**OU know I wouldn't usually take a Saturday morning off in December," Lucy said to Kimberley, "but Nikki was insistent she needed my help. I didn't feel I could say no."

Lucy ran the café in the village where she lived.

It was still early, but she had already finished all the preparations for the day ahead and was heading out, leaving her deputy, Kimberley, in charge of the café for the morning.

Kimberley was very capable, but Lucy still felt a little anxious.

"Are you absolutely sure you're going to be all right?" she said. "I feel bad walking out on you like this."

Kimberley looked up from counting the change in the café's till.

She smiled reassuringly.

"Honestly, Lucy, I've told you a dozen times, it's totally OK. Stop worrying. Sheryl's with me this morning and she's really good. We'll be fine."

"Well, I'm very grateful," Lucy said, "and I'm only at the school for the morning."

"I know Nikki's in charge of the PTA's Christmas Fair, but I still think it's a bit of a cheek of her to ask you to help," Kimberley said. "It's not as if you've got children at the school."

"I know," Lucy said, "but she couldn't find anyone else to help Santa in his grotto."

"Aren't you much too young to play Mrs Claus?" Kimberley grinned.

"Nikki said I could either be Mrs Claus or an elf. I didn't fancy wearing the elf's short tunic," Lucy said. "She says I'll be able to pull it off because I'm a member of the drama society, although it's hardly the same thing.

"There's no script for this, for one thing!"

"It'll be a tough crowd," Kimberley warned her. "My nephews go to the school and my sister says most of the kids are little horrors.

"They probably want you to be crowd control."

"Don't say that. You're putting me off," Lucy said nervously. "Lots of children come into the café and they always seem lovely."

"I suppose so," Kimberley said doubtfully. "But it'll be very different when they're all hyped-up about Christmas. That's why they need crowd control."

"Stop going on about crowd control," Lucy said. "I'm sure the children are going to be very good when they see Father Christmas, because they'll want to be sure to get their presents."

"That's true," Kimberley agreed. "Who's playing him?"

"I've no idea, but Nikki said it's his first time in the role, so he probably won't know what he's doing any more than I do.

"Gosh, look at the time!" Lucy said, glancing up at the clock on the wall. "I'd better dash. Nikki's a stickler for punctuality."

• • • •

Once at the school, Lucy easily spotted her friend amongst the helpers.

Nikki was wearing a particularly garish Christmas jumper, with a pair of reindeer antlers bobbing about merrily on her head.

"I love the look!" Lucy said, laughing at the vision in front of her.

For a second, Nikki looked affronted.

"I'm just entering into the spirit of things. It's important to the children, you know. You're going to look really Christmassy yourself because we've got you the most perfect Mrs Claus outfit."

She took Lucy into the staffroom, where the Mrs Claus costume was hanging up.

Nikki was quite right – it was an impressive outfit. There was a beautiful red satin dress, a starched white apron and a frilly mob cap.

Lucy was less impressed with the curly grey wig and the round-rimmed glasses.

By the time she had changed into the outfit, she had to admit she looked the part, even if she wasn't feeling confident about her ability to cope with hordes of overexcited children.

She and Nikki headed to the school's chair store, which had been converted into Father Christmas's grotto for the morning.

Inside, there was a red padded chair for Father Christmas to sit on, with cushions on the floor for the children.

Someone had painted a large mural of a mountain view, which was pinned up on one wall, with curtaining covering the other walls.

There were logs and Christmas trees of various sizes all around the room and lots of fake snow on the floor.

In fact, for a room that was usually a school's chair store, it made a very realistic grotto.

"Where's Father Christmas?" Lucy asked. "You never told me who's playing him."

Nikki shuffled awkwardly and adjusted Lucy's wig.

"Didn't I? It's Tim."

Lucy groaned inwardly.

She'd met Nikki's brother Tim on a few occasions when he'd come into the café with Nikki's children.

He'd seemed friendly at first, and she and Kimberley had agreed he was the best-looking customer they had, but as time went on he'd become quite monosyllabic with Lucy.

As he was always polite with everyone else, and was very good with his nephew and niece, Lucy had concluded it was just her he didn't like.

She wasn't exactly delighted at the prospect of spending the morning with him in the grotto.

However, she didn't have long to brood on the situation.

The door opened, and in walked Father Christmas himself.

He didn't seem surprised to see her, so Lucy concluded Nikki must have already told him she'd be there.

He was wearing a red velvet Santa outfit, with a big, padded tummy, large boots, and a thick grey beard, which was held in place by elastic.

He looked rather uncomfortable, and she

actually felt quite sorry for him. She couldn't think of anything to say, though, and Tim seemed equally reticent to talk to her, but Nikki studied them both with an appreciative look on her face.

"You both look magnificent," she said. "You're going to do a brilliant job."

Neither Lucy nor Tim spoke. Nikki looked speculative for a moment, then moved to the door.

"I'm going to check the refreshment stall. There was a mince pie crisis earlier. Alison will bring the presents in a minute – have a great morning.

"You could even try talking to each other!"

Tim waited until Nikki had gone before he spoke.

"We've met before," he mumbled through his beard. "I've been into your café with the kids."

"I remember," Lucy said stiffly. "I got the impression you weren't impressed. With me, anyway."

"Oh, no, I was impressed. I mean, with the café. And you. That is… I didn't mean I wasn't impressed with you –" he faltered.

"Sorry. I like your café. And I like you, too."

He looked relieved to stop talking, and Lucy thought she saw a flush above his beard.

Her own cheeks were warm too.

"It's all right," she said shyly. "I know what you mean."

Fortunately, they were interrupted by Alison, the head of the PTA, dragging large sacks of parcels.

"You both look great," she said. "We were delighted when you volunteered – it made the checks much easier."

"Volunteered?" Tim said. "I wouldn't put it quite like that."

Alison looked surprised.

"Oh. Well, never mind. Nikki said you'd be naturals. Here are the gifts – I'll leave you to it."

"What has my sister got us into?" Tim said.

"Kimberley said the children will be a tough crowd," Lucy replied.

"Maybe she was joking?"

They peeked through the door.

Excited children were being ushered forward.

One of the parents waved.

"It's too late to worry now," Lucy said. "It's time to start."

• • • •

Despite the warnings, the first hour went well.

The children were sweet and delighted with their gifts.

Lucy relaxed and, by their first break, was enjoying herself.

Then the next visitor arrived – Tim's niece, Florence.

"Hello," Lucy said brightly. "What's your name?"

"Don't be silly, Lucy," Florence replied. "I'm Florence."

Lucy shook her head.

"Oh, no, I'm not Lucy, I'm Mrs Claus."

Florence pouted.

"No, you're Mummy's friend Lucy. You sell yummy cakes."

"Shhh," Lucy whispered. "You're not supposed to know that."

Luckily, the departing child didn't seem to hear.

Then Florence pointed.

"And that's not Father Christmas. That's Uncle Tim."

Lucy gave up.

She put her finger to her lips.

"Yes, but we don't want the others to hear, do we? Now, come along – it's your turn to see Santa."

She led Florence over.

"Uncle Tim fancies you," Florence announced. "Mummy told me."

Lucy was taken aback.

Tim looked even more uncomfortable.

"Oh, no, I don't think so," Lucy said quickly. "Anyway, in here he's Father Christmas."

"No, he's Uncle Tim. He does fancy you. Mummy told Daddy Uncle Tim's too shy to tell you."

Tim turned crimson.

Suddenly, Lucy understood – his silence had been shyness, not dislike.

And that realisation made her surprisingly happy.

Tim tried to maintain character, but soon gave up.

"Just take your gift," he sighed. "And tell your mum I'd like a word."

"Daddy said you'd say that," Florence said smugly. "He told Mummy she shouldn't inter… inter something."

"Interfere?" Lucy suggested.

"Maybe," Florence shrugged. "But Mummy said it would be worth it."

"I think you'd better go and find your daddy," Lucy said.

"Before your mummy gets into any more trouble."

"He's not Father Christmas," Florence sang out. "He's Uncle Tim."

She skipped off, leaving Lucy and Tim alone.

Eventually, Lucy broke the silence.

"What do they say? Never work with children or animals?"

"Or my sister!" Tim groaned. "I'm so sorry, Lucy."

He pulled off his beard and Lucy looked quickly behind.

"It's all right," Tim said. "No children to see who I really am."

"Do you think Nikki planned all this to set us up?"

"I'm sure of it," Tim sighed. "But only because – well, like Florence said – I've been too much of a coward to ask you out."

Lucy felt a flutter of butterflies.

All in all, it was turning out to be quite the morning.

"Well," she whispered. "You could ask me now."

"I never thought I'd be wearing a Santa suit when I finally plucked up the courage," Tim said. "But are you saying you might say yes, Mrs Claus?"

Lucy laughed.

"I am, Mr Claus. But shall we agree to wear something different on our first date?" ∎

Illustration: Adobe Stock.

The More The Merrier

Roisin would have to make the most of having two extra guests for the big day . . .

BY EIRIN THOMPSON

ROISIN had reconciled herself to the prospect of a quiet Christmas – a very quiet Christmas.

With her chatterbox mum and energetic dad off spending the season with Roisin's sister, Helen, and her family in Australia, it would be just Roisin and her grown-up daughter, Cara.

Cara's dad, Anthony, had passed away when she was still at primary school.

"If you think things will be a bit flat, we could book into a hotel," Roisin had suggested, when it first became clear that it would be only the two of them.

"Oh, no!" Cara had protested. "I love Christmas in our place, lying on the squashy sofa, with the log-burner lit, and the old snow-globe and the crib on the side-tables and always plenty to nibble."

Roisin had been pleased.

She'd sometimes wondered if Christmas was a disappointment to her daughter, with neither a father nor siblings to bulk things out and create a party atmosphere, but it didn't sound like she had anything to worry about.

Now that they knew they would be at home, Roisin started her preparations in earnest.

She had already posted gifts to Australia – it cost as much to send them as to buy them – leaving her to buy for Cara, primarily, and also a few friends, colleagues and neighbours.

"Are we talking turkey, this year?" she asked her daughter. "Or would you prefer something else for a change? Beef? Or salmon?"

Cara looked aghast.

"Turkey, obviously, Mum!" she exclaimed. "Anything else just wouldn't be Christmas!"

Roisin selected a healthy root-ball tree from the garden centre.

Anthony would be appalled to see her with such a tiny specimen, but Anthony wasn't there to wrestle an eight-footer into a stand in the bay window, as he'd so joyfully done when they'd first been married.

"It's sweet," Cara said, encouragingly. "And it won't take long to decorate."

The red and green streamers went up in the hall, punctuated by hanging golden bells, and when Roisin and Cara stepped back to admire their handiwork, the pair agreed that their home was delightfully festive.

• • • •

Roisin had opened the oven door and was checking the progress of a chicken pie she'd made when Cara came in from a Christmas shopping trip.

"Tea should be ready in ten minutes," she told her daughter.

"Great!" Cara answered. "Let me take my bags upstairs and I'll set the table."

Ten minutes later, as Roisin had promised, the oven timer pinged and the golden pie was placed on the kitchen table.

"Everything OK, love?" Roisin asked.

Cara had already twice looked as though she'd wanted to say something, then decided against.

Roisin suspected it wasn't about their evening meal.

"Yeah!" Cara answered. "Fine!"

But then she seemed to hesitate and Roisin felt a tiny ripple of panic flit across her chest.

"Actually, Mum, I've done something a bit rash."

Roisin suppressed a gulp – what was Cara about to reveal?

"I've invited Ryan for Christmas. I know I should have checked with you first, and I wish I had, but I got carried away," Cara blurted out.

"He's always spent Christmas with his mum and dad. They still ate Christmas dinner together even after they split up.

"But now his mum's got a new partner and she felt the time was right to spend Christmas Day with him and his lot, and Ryan seemed pretty down about it, and . . ."

"And you took pity on him and told him he could come to us," Roisin supplied.

"That's because you have a good heart, Cara, and you'll never find me complaining about that."

"Then you don't mind?"

Cara had only been dating Ryan for a few weeks.

Roisin had met him a couple of times and he seemed nice enough, but he still treated Roisin deferentially, rather than with a familiar hug or a bit of banter.

Perhaps being thrown together for Christmas would bring them all closer together, though, and he could be persuaded to call her "Roisin" instead of "Mrs Duffy".

"Of course I don't mind. The more the merrier," she replied, feeling herself bracing internally for the arrival of an extra, unexpected person.

"I'm so glad you feel that way, Mum," Cara responded, her shoulders relaxing, "because I invited Ryan's dad, too."

· · · ·

For the next few days, Roisin was utterly distracted. Cara had acted kindly, but it would ruin the day for Roisin.

"OK, Roisin," said Karen, her boss, when they met at the photocopier. "Tell me what's bothering you."

"Me? Oh, something and nothing."

"Is it Cara? She all right?"

"Thriving," Roisin replied, but it came out with a sigh.

Karen raised her eyebrows.

"She's invited a couple of people over for Christmas Day," Roisin admitted. "I don't really know them, and I don't think I'm going to enjoy myself."

"Young people? They'll make their own fun. You can kick back with the Prosecco, turkey leg and trifle," Karen said confidently.

"One young person — Cara's boyfriend. The other's his dad."

"Oh. That's different. Is the dad single?"

"Divorced," Roisin said.

"Uh-huh. Now I see why you're stressed."

"It's not a date!" Roisin cried. "That's not what I meant."

"Of course it's not," Karen said, smirking.

"I wish I hadn't told you," Roisin sighed.

Karen softened.

"Sorry, Roisin. I didn't mean to upset you. It might not be the cosy Christmas you planned, but it could be rewarding — more people to appreciate your cooking.

"You might even make a new friend, especially if this relationship gets serious. Don't overthink it — it's just one day."

· · · ·

Roisin decided Karen was right. Her guests were only coming for one meal and maybe a chat.

Christmas Dinner was just an elaborate roast, and with some prep, things would run smoothly.

By Christmas Eve, the festive glow had returned.

Cara made raspberry mojitos while they put together the trifle.

They watched a warm comedy, finished the last kitchen jobs, then switched to the midnight carol service before heading to bed.

As they passed the tree, Roisin recalled how it had once been swamped with presents.

She still stuck to the tradition of not placing gifts underneath until after Cara was in bed.

This year, there were Cara's elegantly wrapped parcels, plus Roisin's gifts for her, Ryan, and Ryan's dad.

Bother! She hadn't asked Cara what Ryan's dad's name was — those tags were still blank.

She must find out first thing in the morning.

· · · ·

After a deep sleep, Roisin woke to festive tunes on the light classical channel.

She felt good — well-rested and ready.

Cara had a lie-in, which Roisin didn't begrudge — it was Christmas.

By the time she came downstairs looking radiant, it was nearly time for Ryan and his dad to arrive.

"I knew I'd forgotten something. I'll just pop up and put my earrings in," Roisin said suddenly.

Upstairs, she remembered she still hadn't asked about Ryan's dad's name, and as the doorbell rang, it was too late.

"I'll get it!" Cara called.

As Roisin descended, she saw two men hanging their coats.

"Hello again, Ryan. Merry Christmas!"

"And this is Ryan's dad," Cara said, as the second man turned. "Hugh."

"Hugo!" Roisin exclaimed.

"Rosie?"

"So you two know each other?" Cara asked. "What are the chances?"

Oh, they knew each other all right.

Hugo hadn't changed much — shorter hair, a few more lines, but still those blue eyes and rugged jaw.

What would he make of her?

"You look wonderful, Rosie... as ever," he said softly.

Cara looked between them, curious.

"We were... friends a long time ago," Roisin offered, to break the silence.

Hugo smiled.

"Just good friends?" he asked, turning to Cara. "Your mum was my first true love."

"Dad," Ryan cut in. "Don't embarrass Mrs Duffy. Bit of a coincidence — let's move on.

"Cara, where should we put our presents?"

They shuffled about, placed gifts under the tree, and were soon settled by the log burner with Bucks Fizz.

Roisin busied herself in the kitchen, her heart racing.

Hugo Lynch was in her front room and about to eat at her table.

It was true — he'd been her first love, and she his.

They'd been inseparable at sixteen, until his father's job moved them away and

both sets of parents had ended the relationship.

Roisin had accepted it, only learning later her mother had intercepted Hugo's letters.

By then, she was with Anthony and content.

Life had gone on. Clearly Hugo's had, too.

"I had no idea," a soft voice said behind her. "This wasn't planned, if that's what you're thinking."

"I wasn't," she said, turning.

"Rosie Reilly. I still can't believe it."

"Rosie Duffy, now."

"I'm sorry for your loss. Cara's lovely — despite everything."

"Ryan's a lovely young man."

"Shy. Like me, I suppose. I feel as vulnerable as a kitten, if you can believe it."

"I always believed you, Hugh. You were the most truthful person I knew."

"And you were the most beautiful. Still are."

Rosie caught her breath and turned away.

"We've done a lot of living since then," she said, stirring the gravy. "We're not the same people."

"Maybe not. But I'd like to find out who you are now, Rosie. I really would."

A silence fell until Cara burst in, dragging Ryan behind.

"Right, Mum — what can we do to get dinner on the table? We're starving."

"Just sit down. I'm ready to serve up," Roisin said.

"After dinner, we thought we'd go for a walk by the river," Cara added.

"You and Hugh can catch up on the last thirty years — if you can remember that far back!"

"I remember," Roisin said, meeting Hugh's eye.

He reached out, and their fingertips touched — just briefly, but enough for electricity.

This wasn't going to be the very quiet Christmas Roisin had imagined.

Not even the awkward one she'd feared. Perhaps she'd been right after all — the more the merrier. ∎

PATHFINDER

Beginning with AGAIN and moving up, down, left or right, one letter at a time, trace a path through 22 words found in the lyrics to *Last Christmas*.

AGAIN | RECOGNISE
AWAY | SENT
BITTEN | SOMEONE
CROWDED | SOUL
DISTANCE | SPECIAL
FIRE | TEARS
FOOL | TIRED
FRIENDS | TWICE
HEART | VERY
KISSED | WRAPPED
LAST | YEAR

T	S	A	N	O	R	A	E	Y	E	C
H	E	L	E	E	K	I	S	S	W	I
R	A	A	G	M	O	S	D	E	T	D
T	B	I	A	A	Y	W	R	A	D	E
T	I	N	A	W	D	E	P	P	W	O
T	E	N	O	G	D	T	A	N	C	R
I	R	F	C	N	I	S	R	I	E	C
E	D	R	E	I	S	E	E	F	E	P
N	E	T	S	R	A	S	E	L	C	S
D	R	I	Y	S	E	T	N	A	I	L
S	V	E	R	O	U	L	T	F	O	O

Square Eyes

Two squares in this scene are identical, though they may not be the same way up or the same colour. See how quickly you can spot them.

Kriss Kross

Fit the words into the grid. Then unscramble the highlighted squares to spell out another word related to winter sports.

Answers on p143

3 letters
HAT
ICE
SKI

4 letters
LIFT
LUGE
RACE
RINK
SLED
SNOW

5 letters
BOOTS
GLIDE
SAUNA
SCARF
SKIER
TRAIL

6 letters
ANORAK
ASCENT
CHALET
ICICLE
JACKET
SLEDGE
STICKS

7 letters
CURLING
DESCENT
GOGGLES
GONDOLA
TERRAIN

8 letters
ALTITUDE
BIATHLON
BLIZZARD
HILLSIDE

Grot Spot

Four local stores have Christmas grottos. From the information given, work out who is working at each grotto.

ELF
My grotto is open seven days a week.

FAIRY
My grotto has the same opening hours every day.

REINDEER
I have three weeks' work exactly.

SNOWMAN
At my £10 per person grotto, it's Father Christmas, not Santa.

GROSS BROS.
CHRISTMAS GROTTO
MEET FATHER CHRISTMAS AND A FEW OF HIS FRIENDS!
OPEN 9-5 (MON-THURS)
9-7 (FRI,SAT)
DEC 3-23

HAMENDEBS DEPT. STORE
SANTA'S GROTTO
NORTH POLE TOY FACTORY
OPEN 8-8
7 DAYS A WEEK
DEC 1-24

LEWIS JOHN
NUTCRACKER GROTTO
GIVE FATHER CHRISTMAS YOUR WISH LIST!
JUST £5!
17 DAYS ONLY
8-6 (CLOSED SUNDAYS)

NICK HARVEYS
SNOWLAND AT CHRISTMAS
RIDE SANTA'S SLEIGH THROUGH SNOWLAND!
ADULTS FREE!
DAILY 9am-5pm
DEC 4-24

Vowel Play

Each clue in this crossword is the answer minus its vowels. Replace the missing vowels to complete the grid. Watch out for red herrings!

ACROSS

1 CHKNG (7)
5 JT (4)
8 NRL (5)
9 CSSDY (7)
11 TWG (4)
12 STRDLS (8)
15 RFR (5)
16 FRSK (5)
19 PSTGS (8)
21 SWP (4)
23 PRPPD (7)
25 CHLD (5)
26 DB (4)
27 TRWLR (7)

DOWN

2 HRSNSS (9)
3 KLN (4)
4 NCTY (6)
5 JS (3)
6 TDL (5)
7 TSTS (5)
10 SCRRY (6)
13 RSTWHL (9)
14 RVMP (6)
17 WDR (6)
18 SPDS (5)
20 PRK (5)
22 SCW (4)
24 PB (3)

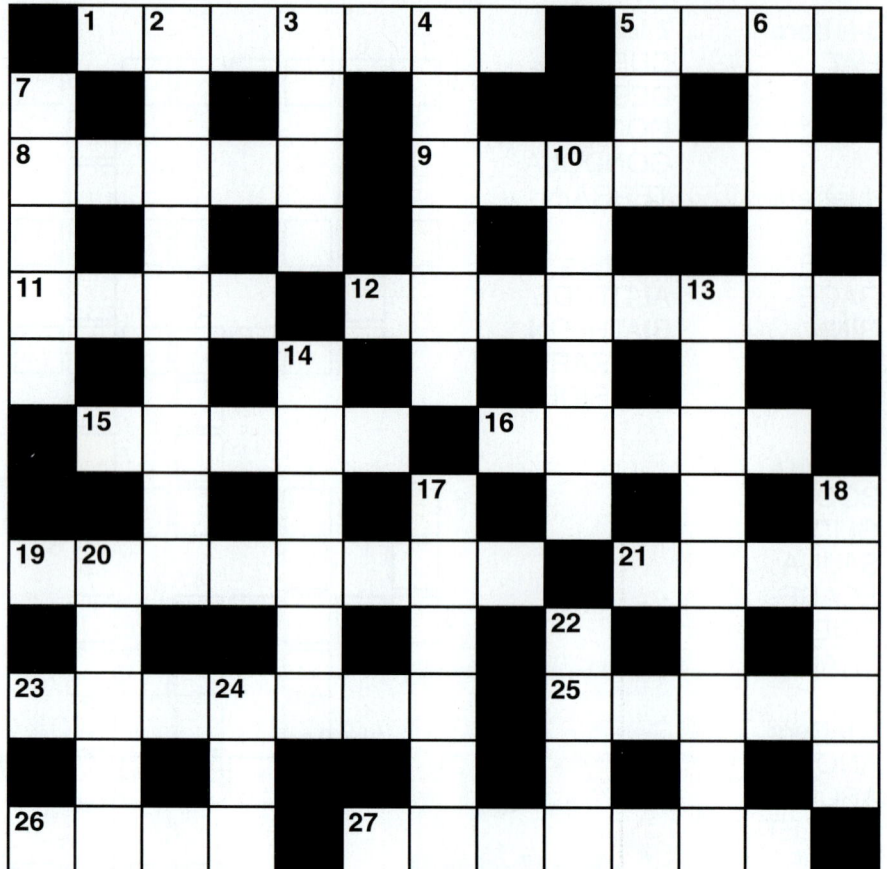

PYRAMID

Each answer contains the letters of the previous answer, plus one extra.

1 15th letter (1)

2 Carry out (2)

3 Bother, hassle (3)

4 Lane (4)

5 Love deeply (5)

6 Tough time (6)

7 Dancer's costume (7)

8 Bespoke (8)

9 News content of a magazine, as opposed to advertising (9)

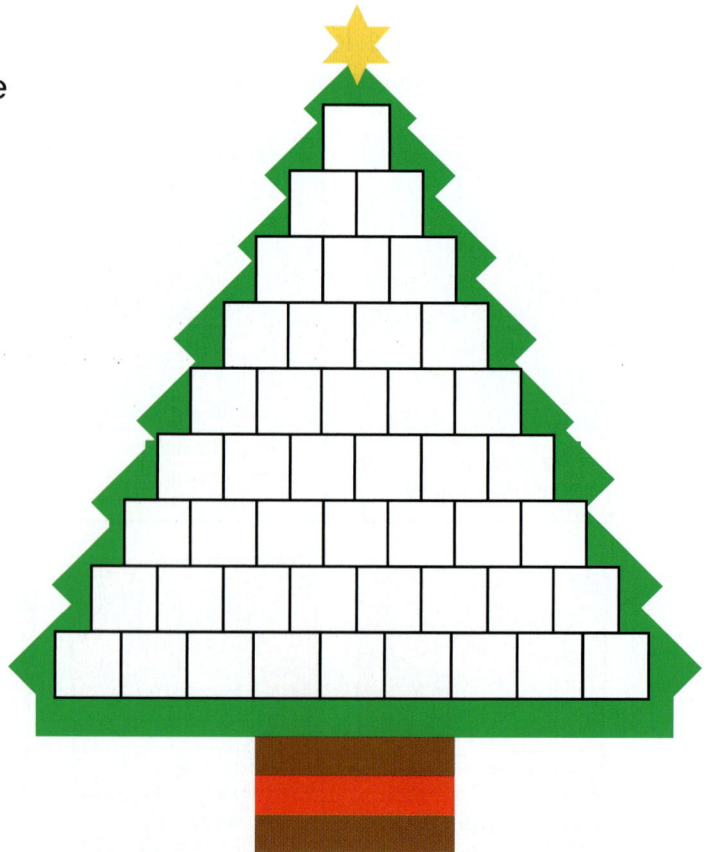

Crossword

Answers on p143

ACROSS

1 Alcohol-free mixed drink (8)
5 Defeat (4)
9 Caterpillar, for example (5)
10 High flat land (7)
11 Cards of the same denomination (4)
12 Cost indicator (5,3)
14 Circus marquee (3,3)
15 Deaden (6)
18 Happening twice a year (8)
20 Real bargain (4)
23 Cooking utensil with a broad flat blade (7)
24 Chocolate-based drink (5)
25 Microscopic (4)
26 Staring in amazement (4-4)

DOWN

1 Units of distance (5)
2 Slicing (meat) (7)
3 Electrically powered public vehicle (4)
4 Bring goods in from abroad (6)
6 Open to view (5)
7 Move into a warm comfortable position (7)
8 Trace mineral found in dairy products (7)
13 Summary (5-2)
14 Look after young children (7)
16 Fastidious, fussy (7)
17 Spicy Italian sausage (6)
19 For the second time (5)
21 Tartan (5)
22 Dull throbbing pain (4)

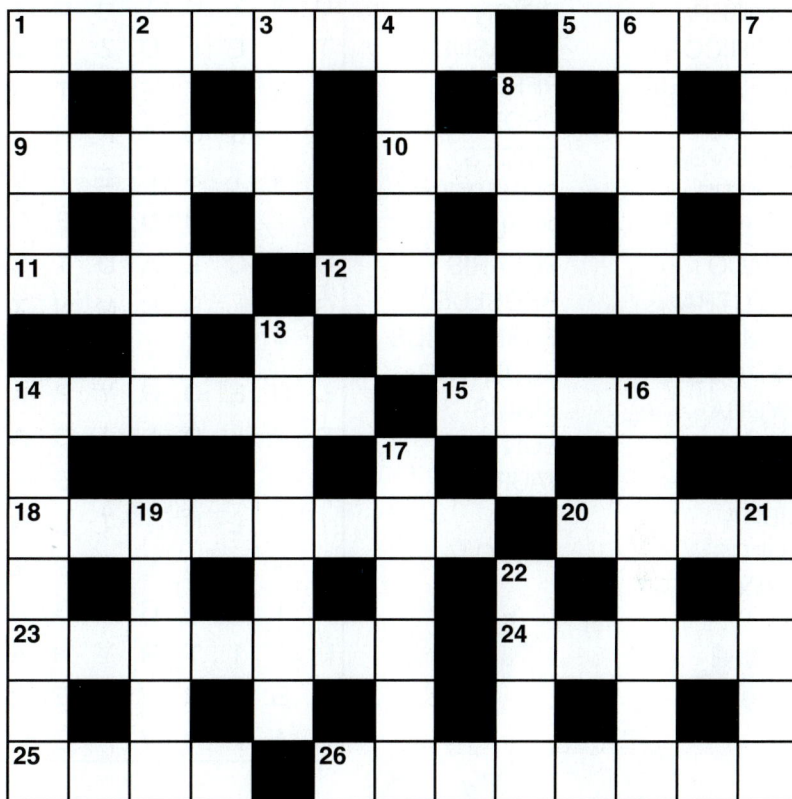

Mini Jigsaw

Fit the pieces into the grid to make six words taken from *The Twelve Days of Christmas*. We've given you two letters to start off.

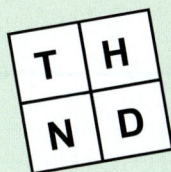

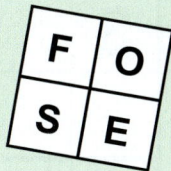

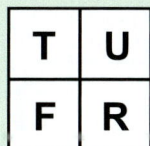

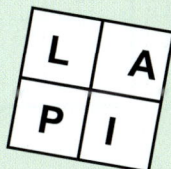

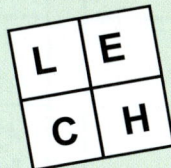

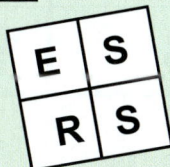

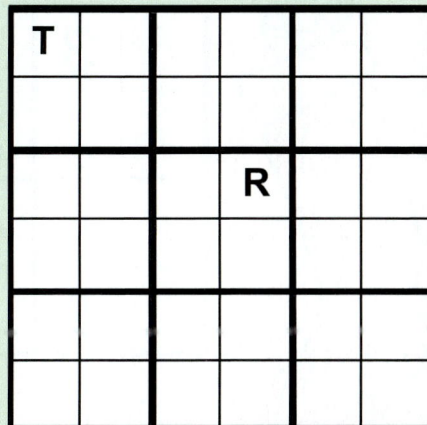

Wordsearch

Find all these star and constellation-related words in the grid. Words can run forwards, backwards or diagonally.

ANDROMEDA
AQUARIUS
ARIES
CANCER
CAPRICORN
CASSIOPEIA
CASTOR
COLUMBA
CRATER
CRUX
DRACO
ELECTRA
GEMINI
HERCULES
HYDRA
INDUS
LEO
LIBRA
LUPUS
LYNX

LYRA
MENSA
NORMA
ORION
PEGASUS
PERSEUS
PHOENIX
PISCES
PLEIADES
PLOUGH
POLARIS
REGULUS
SAGITTARIUS
SCULPTOR
SIRIUS
SUN
TAURUS
VEGA
VIRGO

```
A Q B T T H T B N T H N S S Y D T E N E
T R S U S A G E P E R S E U S M S B C E
D N Y H T H E V R L S L N P I E A U A O
T Y E L D Z E O Z A O L N U C R U X N M
C R A T E R T R G H J U J L B E I O C T
N E B C A P R I C O R N G I L O E S E D
T N I S L E T L O U G M L H V H T E R N
P I Y U U T E O O E L A D E M O R D N A
D O C L A D T S N I E E G B H O E T L I
G S L R N M N X E E D A S V H Y D R A C
O T I A I A N I A D S E C S I P A E A N
L U E O R Y P A I T A I H N Y B E S C D
S X L R L I G A E T M I B S M O T A A E
I T I N A Q S E P A M R E U C O E M Q O
I A L N I T L N O U E D L L R A A R U H
N R V R E E P E I R O O I U P S L O A A
I I T I C O G N S U C E R G N S R N R O
M E I T R Y H A S S B E C E D I N T I L
E S R R H G E P A S A I M R O O N T U E
G A P R V A O O C A R D L N G S I M S E
```

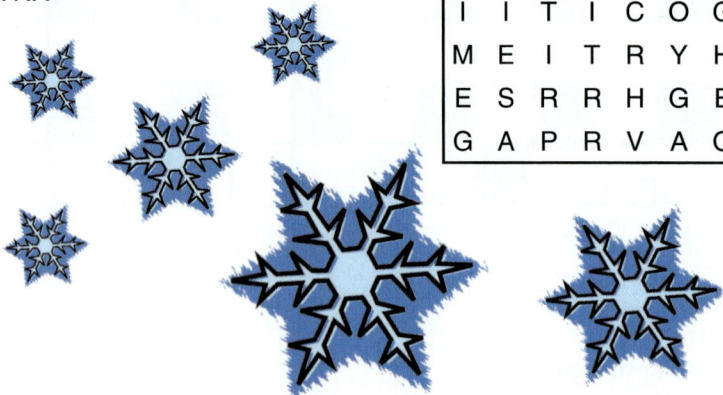

Sudoku

Fill the grids with the numbers 1 to 4 so that each row, column and 2x2 block contains the numbers 1 to 4.

Grid 1: 3 / 2 / 4 / 1
Grid 2: 2 4 / 3 1
Grid 3: 3 / 1 / 4 / 3

Codeword

Complete the codeword as usual and transfer the encoded letters into the bottom grid to discover a Christmas carol.

Answers on p143

A B C D E F G H I J K L M N/ O/ P Q R S/ T U V W X Y Z

1	2 N	3	4	5 S	6	7	8	9	10	11	12	13
14	15	16	17	18	19	20	21	22	23	24	25	26

Bottom grid (carol):

13 26 2 N 23 | 13 5 2 O N 23 | 3 11 16 16 26 8 15

5 O 2 N | 9 26 23 9

Take Two

Each word in a clue can be preceded by the same two letters to make three new words. The three pairs of letters will then spell out a word.

BLED, KING, MINE

GRANT, RAGE, SLAY

CHEE, REBIRD, RICS

Missing Link

Fit ten words into the grid so each one connects up with the words on either side eg - wishing - well - done. Read down the letters in the shaded squares to spell out a festive figure.

SEA					DRUM
ICE					ANIMAL
PEARLY					CRAB
EMERGENCY					POLL
FIRESIDE					ROOM
CABIN					CUT
RUSTY					POLISH
ORAL					BOARD
SUGAR					SUM
SIREN					THRUSH

Ladder

Change one letter at a time (but not the position of any letter) to make a new word – and move from the word at the bottom of the box to the word at the top using the exact number of rungs provided.

T O Y S

T R E E

Plug and Play

Time to plug in the Christmas tree lights! Which one of the twelve sockets will each of the plugs A, B and C fit?

SOLUTIONS

Pathfinder

Again, Away, Wrapped, Distance, Crowded, Twice, Year, Kissed, Someone, Last, Heart, Bitten, Friends, Very, Soul, Tears, Tired, Recognise, Sent, Fool, Special, Fire

Square Eyes

C2 and F9

Kriss Kross

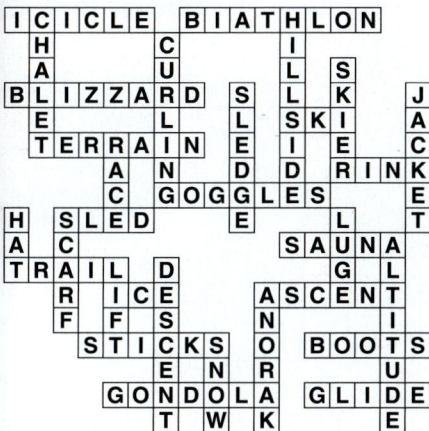

BOBSLEIGH

Grot Spot

Elf – Hamendeb's
Fairy – Lewis John
Reindeer – Nick Harveys
Snowman – Gross Bros

Vowel Play

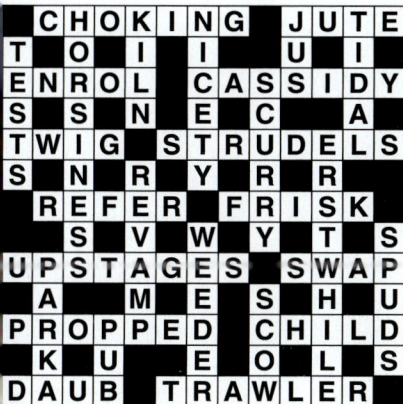

Pyramid

Crossword

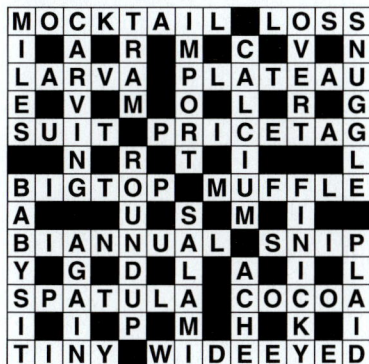

Mini Jigsaw

TURTLE
FRENCH
FOURTH
SECOND
LADIES
PIPERS

Wordsearch

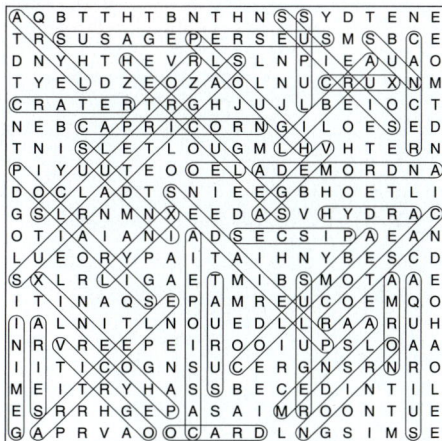

Sudoku

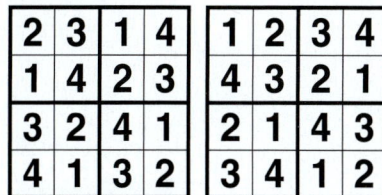

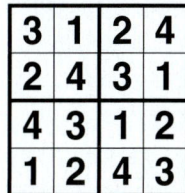

Codeword

DING DONG MERRILY
ON HIGH

Take Two

FA/MI/LY
The added letters spell: FAMILY

Missing Link

The words in the correct order are:
BASS, PACK, KING, EXIT, CHAT, CREW, NAIL, EXAM, LUMP, SONG
Reading down the shaded letters: SANTA CLAUS

Ladder

TOYS, TOES, TEES, TEEM, THEM, THEE, TREE

Plug and Play

A - 5, B – 10, C – 1

STOCKING TIME!

The sky's still dark, it's scarcely dawn,
The house is hushed and still,
Yet in his bed young Theo stirs,
And wakes with sudden thrill.
Today's the day of all the days!
It's Christmas morn at last,
And has kind Santa stopped to call
As always in the past?
Why, yes! Now Theo breathes again,
For though too dark to see,
He feels a weight beside his foot,
It surely has to be . . .?
A stocking, and it's bulging full!
He gently pulls it near.
Oh, let today start right away,
The best day of the year!

Maggie Ingall

A very
**MERRY
CHRISTMAS**
*to all our
readers.*